Prologue

The falcon had laid her eggs in the side of t[he mountain, having disposed] of her mate in order to mate again the follow[ing year. Her previous] attempts had all proven failures as the usua[l two or three eggs failed to] hatch or fallen from the nest when the moun[tain had shaken, but this time] one had hatched her very first. The bird had instinctively returned to the mountain side each year from the warmer climes of the coastal areas where she spent the winter, but the bird population and other food sources were becoming rarer and she often felt hunger.

She had gone hunting again during the morning and managed to catch a small bird which had eased her pangs somewhat though she knew that the food supply was insufficient for a nest full of young this year so only having the one hatched chick was a good thing. Sweeping back along the face of the ledge she finally made it back to the nest to eat her unfortunate prey.

The weeks went by and her offspring grew stronger and eventually made its first flight, the female youngster mimicking its mother, learning as all birds do by instinct and repetition.

Only a few weeks later they left the nest and made the short journey to the south coast where she would migrate to in the winter. High up in the mountains the air was much cooler in the summer and the coast warmer in the winter which suited her purposes. The mother had grown increasingly uneasy as the ground below had shaken and had left the nest finally four weeks before she would have normally done so.

The food was plentiful in the winter months in the south but this would be the last time she made this journey, neither she nor her offspring would ever go back……………………

Part 1

Challenge at the High Elders Table

Chapter 1

The wind howled as it seemed to overwhelm the large stone oval one-roomed house which Carig and his wife Reva dwelt in. This week the weather had turned much colder, more like the season should be. The last few months had been very warm, much hotter than normal and Carig wondered what had angered the Gods so to shift the weather pattern in such a way. The small hearth fire hissed and crackled against the damp and his cattle outside shifted restlessly.

It was nearly time now, Reva would give birth to their first child and Carig knew it would be strong. He yearned for a son but knew this was in the hands of the Gods who were so ruthlessly blowing this northerly bitter wind. The ceremony had been arranged as soon as Reva had gone into labour.

One of the attendant women nodded to him, it was his signal to leave, to let the other women of the village deliver his child. They busied him out of the way, laughing and claiming 'this is no place for a man' to which he was in full agreement. Hoisting his coat up around his ears he made his way from his home to the Elders Hall where traditionally any man who was to become a father was encouraged to drink from the 'Beast of the Codec' horn. This particular horn had been passed down from generation to generation and no man had ever drunk from it without suffering the obvious consequences the next day!

The Elders, all twelve, were waiting and a chorus of greetings welled up from the men within when he entered the door. The title of High Elder belonged to Lendel who also took the name of the village, as his father and grandfather had done before him and had also held that office. The village itself was large, almost a town and boasted a population of well over two thousand heads, and was one of the most Eastern outposts of Codencia Minor, which in its turn was a vassal state to Codencia itself. Codencia Minor had always been protected to the west by the sea and to the east by the mountains and the only access to this insignificant part of the continent was from the South through a narrow gap between the heel of the mountain range and the shores of the Western Sea and the Gulf of Dyn.

Lendel, being the High Elder was the first to speak officially at all occasions, and this more informal gathering was no different.

'Welcome Carig, to our humble meeting place' he shouted amidst the raucous laughter 'since you wife is otherwise engaged are you ready for the horn?'

'Aye I'm ready to see what it shows' muttered Carig, whilst raising his hand to indicate the challenge was on!

The horn would hold thirty two pitches of ale, tradition held the father who drank less than sixteen (in one go) would be the father of a girl, whereas any man who managed more than sixteen would be obviously strong enough to father a son. No one had ever, not in living memory or those recorded by the elder's scribes, had ever drunk the whole thirty two. Ancient folklore claimed the father who drank the thirty two would be the father of a King! Not that anyone believed that nowadays, firstly there hadn't been a King in ages past, not since the last war when Codencia Minor had been forced to accept it had lost its independence to its much larger and more powerful state of Codencia, and secondly no one had every got beyond twenty five. Now Carig was a well built man, not overweight by any means, but could wrestle as well as any in the village and also had, without doubt, the steadiest hand and therefore truest aim when it came to the bow. Of course the under and over sixteen ruling wasn't an absolute given, sometimes the Gods intervened for their own reasons and gave couples girls when boys were expected and obviously the other way around too. Most in the village including those inclined to lay wagers had their money on Carig producing a boy, so it was amidst this general confidence Carig slammed his fist, three times on the table in front of him to indicate he was ready

'Carig son of Gregur, sit upon the chair of fortune, where many before you have taken this challenge' shouted Lendel

'And failed' shouted an anonymous voice from the crowd

Beads of sweat had appeared on his brow as the horn was filled with pitcher after pitcher of the village's strongest ale, he remembered his own uncles tales of the twenty one he had managed, 'the secret is Carig, not to gulp down air at the same time and drink some goats milk before to line your stomach, but most of all don't look at the ale whilst drinking'

Carig had stupidly forgotten the goat's milk and wondered if this really would make a difference, he had of course fasted since the onset of his wife's labour so as not to have his stomach filled with food, and so in all other respects he was ready.

The Elders removed themselves from the Eyrie (the high table at which they all sat) and made their way through the village hall to where Carig now stood, the table in front of Carig was removed and with just as much solemnity as they could manage started to make the circle of hands around Carig. 'Once the circle is completed by the High Elder himself then you must start without delay' said Lendel, 'do you understand?

Carig nodded his agreement and the High Elder (with as much pomp as he could manage in the drunken gathering) completed the circle.

A hush descended as Carig picked up the horn, the ale smelt yeasty, as if it had been stood for too long after been drawn, he closed his eyes and picked up the enormous horn with both hands. Dropping it at this point would involve so many years bad luck that some men employed a helper to ensure the horn was raised without risk!

Not Carig, he was sure of his grip and just as sure he was going to beat the twenty one achieved by his father. Putting the horn to his lips, he raised his eyebrows in expectation as the gathering waited for him to start. The air was still and the men silent as he at last tipped the horn to his mouth, with each gulp the crowd became louder and louder as he shut his eyes and concentrated on the task at hand, half a minute now and he was still drinking, the gathering's expectations were being fulfilled as at least half the contents must have now disappeared. The cheering became louder and louder as Carig continued his quest, men were stamping their feet and clapping to the constant gulping rhythm which Carig had adopted, they knew he must be close to his own fathers effort as a minute passed……but still Carig drank on, ninety seconds and the men of the hall were chanting….'Carig, Carig, Carig'

Finally Carig stopped, the men still chanting crowded round to see how much had been consumed as Carig slumped to the floor in agony, 'I am going to burst' he moaned. Lendel lifted the horn as the men now silent waited for his verdict. Lendel, usually one so loud and full of vigour and full of his own importance simply muttered 'Carig has thirty two' and withdrew to the Eyrie, passing the faces of the astonished men who wondered what this could actually mean. Meanwhile the chant started again and Carig was being lifted on the shoulders of men and being carried towards the Eyrie, as the Elders once again gathered at the high table.

'Men of Lendel' the High Elder announced, 'one amongst us has today done something no man has ever achieved before' …..'Carig, Carig, Carig' the crowd chanted in unison again. Lendel lifted his staff to speak again, the rabble died down… 'We all know of the tales our forefathers have passed from generation to generation. These legends are just that, but it is clear something remarkable has taken place today and whilst few if any of us would actually believe in these more enlightened times that drinking the thirty two would mean a return of a King to our land, there is clearly been a signal from the Gods that times are to change. For now though we must congratulate Carig for it is clear he must now have a son!' ' Carig, Carig' the crowd began chanting again and now the High Elder smiled and too clapped his hands as the full meeting hall descended into the kind of drunken debauchery these occasions so obviously deserved.

No one seemed to notice, or care that Carig's bladder had given way to the pressure of the liquid cursing through his body and he had wet himself….he was too drunk to care, even now, after only 10 minutes or so the effects of the alcohol had permeated his blood cells and made their way to his now befuddled brain.

The party continued as food was brought in, a suckling pig had been slaughtered and roasted as soon as it had been declared Reva was imminent and carved whilst the challenge had been taking place and the men were now in the mood for singing, eating and generally misbehaving as the night wore on.

Hours passed, the men folk as tradition demanded were all drunk to a man. Unnoticed within the carnage the door opened and a small figure entered, a woman stood still, waiting patiently by the door, until she was seen by one of the Elders who whispered into Lendel's ear. He stood and once again raised his staff though no one noticed as the crowd partied on. Above the racket and noise Lendel's voice boomed

'Men of the Hall, a woman waits to speak'.......and all eyes turned to the woman as Lendel raised his staff for the pronouncement.

'Well?' bellowed Lendel

The woman, with just about as much disdain as she could show to the drunken gathering announced.

'It's a girl...........................'

Chapter 2

Carig woke, his head thundering, as he turned to put his arm around his wife, she wasn't there. Pulling himself up from his bed he looked around the house as he struggled to focus his eyes. The wind was still howling, clearly someone had managed to get him home last night, he wondered if it had all been a dream? 'Some dream it must have been to give me this king sized hangover' he thought.

The beads to the entrance rattled as Reva entered, smiling her knowing smile

'How is your head' she laughed,

'Probably as sore as your secret place' laughed Carig in turn. 'Well I have someone here who would like to meet you' she said as she uncovered the bundle she was carrying. 'Meet your daughter Carig my husband, you can see already she has the eyes of her mother!

She placed the child on Carig's chest and he looked at the baby as unrequited love stirred in his proud father's heart. 'She is beautiful, just like you', he said, as he choked down his tears. Reva reached for his hand and looked at him, 'Yes my love, I think she will be beautiful, but something tells me she will be much more than that, she will too have the strength of her father!'

'There is much to do', added Reva, 'she must be welcomed to the village by the Elders and you must put in writing the four tasks you will set for our child as our own parents and their parents did before them. 'It will be so' agreed Carig. 'The Elders will welcome our child to the village at the mid-winter solstice along with the other children who have arrived within this last half year, and that is only ten days away!'

Then you can't lay about your bed ruing your head' laughed Reva, 'Come husband, we have much to do!

Carig peered out of his hut, the wind had abated slightly and the cattle needed tending, he knew the fresh air couldn't cure his head but it certainly wouldn't do him any harm. Reva was nursing their daughter in the corner, 'Won't be long' he said as he headed out into the cold. The cold air was bracing and his stomach was starting to calm down as his friend Naiden shouted to him across their adjacent land.

'Feeling rough my friend?' he asked as he approached the smiling Carig

'Weren't you there?' asked Carig

'No, I had to take the stock to the market in town, it closes for the week at solstice and I need the cash and so do you now' he laughed.

The town in question was Oakenvale, where Carig himself had been born and raised. He spent his formative years within the busy town helping his father with his bow making business, hence his own expertise in that area and his own surname Archer. His mother and father had both died young when the town was attacked by the rebel Vagril and his mercenary band of men who were a curse on the land left over from the Second Codencial Wars. He liked to imagine his father as a hero who had died defending the town and as such died a warrior's death but the truth was he was simply put to death when entrapped by the ruthless gang of mercenaries after their leader had raped his mother. At only nine years old Carig swore upon his father's grave he would one day seek out and kill Vagril and repay him for his deeds.

Fortune has been kind in that he had been at his uncle's hut in Lendel Village when the attack happened, but he was finally orphaned only nine months later when his mother died in child-birth. The child would have been a mercenaries bastard and so Carig felt nothing for the infant who survived, he did not know and did not care what had happened to his infant half-brother but he grieved for his mother who above all else in the world he had loved. His uncle (his father's elder brother) who had not been lucky enough to have children of his own had taken him in at that point and he never once returned to Oakenvale again even though it was not many leagues way. His uncles' house was now his own had been left to him when he had died, and he had dwelt there with Reva for the last three years. He was twenty four years of age, strong willed and stubborn but was ever grateful to Naiden who also took his cattle to town when market day arrived, so Carig didn't have to be reminded of 'that place'

Carig greeted his friend who gave him the six gold pennies he had bartered at the cattle market. 'How about a drink to wet the baby's forehead?' suggested Naiden

On any other occasion Carig would have agreed readily but this time he realised that somehow, his life had changed and his hard-drinking days were probably coming to an end.

'Not today my friend, I have much to do and so little time to do it in' laughed Carig
,
'Well another time then?' suggested Naiden to the already departing Carig who signalled an affirmative over his shoulder.

Carig returned home after the remaining cattle had been fed and watered, the child was sleeping in the home made cot he had erected the week previously. Reva was resting whilst a meal was being prepared by her own mother Revangel, who as any new Grandmother would, was forcefully imparting many words of wisdom to Reva, who just as forcefully ignoring all she said. Reva had been named after her mother but always preferred the shorter version of her name, which was also so much easier for anyone when they were both in the room. Carig liked to tease his mother-in-law by calling her the last part of her name 'Angel' because as he never tired of telling her (and she never tired of hearing it) that she was indeed an angel sent by the Gods.

Carig put his strong arms around the head of his mother in law, covering her eyes....'Guess who?' he questioned

From the smell of that stale alcohol I guess it could only be one person in the village this morning!' laughed Revangel, 'Sit down while I feed you both, you both must be tired indeed'.

'Tired?' exclaimed Reva,' this oaf only fell out of bed not one hour ago, spare him your pity, he doesn't deserve it!

Minutes later the small family settled down to their meal as the world carried on outside and the child slept peacefully. Reva looked at her husband and winked as if a moment had come they had both spoken about previously. Carig grinned back.

'You know we haven't decided on a name', said Reva finally to her mother.

'Well I have my own opinion about that' she declared as Carig and Reva nodded knowingly at each other. 'How about a flower name, since she is so beautiful?' answered Revangel

'I should just call her 'Angel' then I have a Reva, a Revangel and an Angel' joked Carig,

'It is your decision and not my Mothers' insisted Reva, 'men must name girls, women must name boys…you know the tradition!'

Revangel pretended to look hurt but everyone knew it was just a game, a Grandmother would like to impart words of wisdom whether anyone would want to listen or not, whilst Carig had fallen silent has he mused over various names, nothing obvious came to him.

'I am going outside to think' he said, 'but I am taking my daughter with me for inspiration.

Before Reva could object he had scooped the now waking child up, wrapped her up tightly and placed her under his coat, 'Come on little one, we have a difficult decision to make' he said.

The sun was setting as Carig strolled alongside the river on which the village was built, he could still think of no name, nothing which he thought relevant and more than this it had to be original because as he looked down at her beneath his coat he knew in his heart she would be unique, one of a kind.

He walked further past the outlying huts of the village facing east and towards the distant Mountains of Ash, upon which no man, certainly no sensible man would ever venture. The main peak Hellddyn had been silent for some years but everyone in these parts knew how unpredictable this mountain was, it had erupted twice in the memory of men in these parts covering the lands with ash and causing famine and death.

He shuddered inwardly as he again looked down at his young girl, now fully awake but resting peacefully beneath his coat. A fathers urge to protect, welled up within him and he knew this child was going to be very special and a credit to her Mother (and if he cared to admit it, to himself as well). Evening was drawing in and he was still no nearer deciding on a name. Those mountains were not going to give him the inspiration he needed so he turned for home. Up in the sky a shooting star blazed briefly through the heavens and as he gazed upwards Carig's heart was overcome by the beauty of the night sky and this all too rare event he had just witnessed.

He looked down at his daughter resting beneath his coat.

'Celeste' he thought 'Yes Celeste, that shall be your name, and your star too will light up the night sky'.

Satisfied with his decision he turned for home. He quickened his pace now as the wold wolves could be heard howling some leagues distant. At last he approached the lights of the village as behind him the Mountain rumbled.

'The Gods are uneasy tonight' he thought

Chapter 3

The next day the wind continued to blow from the North but the Mountain was at least quiet and the village prepared for the mid-winter fair. This week-long fair was the event all the people in the village and quite a fair proportion of Codencia Minor itself, looked forward to the whole year round. As usual there would be competitions and test of strength and endeavour, the young men would fight for the right to wear the tigers head, a mask which had been hollowed out of a skeleton of an unfortunate stray tiger who had wandered into the village hundreds of years previously and had been brought down (reputedly) by the village elder with only his bare hands! The young men would therefore wrestle for the honour and there could be only one winner. This first competition would mark the passing from child to man for all those who had seen eighteen summers whether they won or lost. The winner would also by right have the privilege of the first dance with the winter Queen a beauty pageant held at the same time amongst the girls who were also approaching womanhood which was their own mark of passing from child to adulthood. This usually threw up some interesting beauty queens who would have otherwise never been considered anything other than plain but most folk would at least admit that even the most unattractive of young woman would look at least acceptable upon this one day of their life! Not that all the girls hereabouts would fall into that category, Codencia Minor generally had some of the most stunningly beautiful women in the land and had for the most part black hair and olive skin. Red-heads were scarce (most men would thank the Gods for that as their temper was supposedly short). Blonde's were just stuff of legend.

The fair was open to anyone within Codencia Minor and the village was swelled as thousands of people descended on Lendel for as much fun and merriment as they could manage in these harsh times. Tents were erected to house the throngs of people and the Elders Meeting hall turned over to the various feasts which took place daily within the week of the fair. The Elders naturally had to attend each one of these feasts, and one year a Codencian reveller had commented that the girth of the Elders of Lendel was such that if there had still had been a King he could have raised a fortune by imposing a tax on the length of an elder's belt!

There were other competitions, an Archery test which Carig had won the last two years running, there were long distance hunting events where the wold wolves were tracked and run down by the men folk to prove their worth, (Revangel had commented the year previously that they would be better suited chasing something edible rather than pursuing the unfortunate wolves who after all were only trying to live themselves). Artists presented their work in the Elders Hall, whilst cooks strove to make the most outlandish dishes which few would ever (want to) taste again! There were market stalls selling everything from trinkets to horses and even jesters held court in a manic half day which had everyone howling with laughter at their antics.

At the end of the fair and once all outsiders had left and the villages of Lendel were once again left to clear up the mess created, then the final act of solstice would take place for those of the village only……..The naming and tasking of the children.

Carig had decided on this second morning since his victorious challenge that he wouldn't defend his archery title this year as he was consumed with the problem of the four tasks and it was time for another to win the event. Something in his heart was telling him that these tasks shouldn't be the normal mundane everyday achievable tasks which everyone gave their children but rather something meaningful which would truly mark the steps of her life's journey. He had a vague idea that the first should be completed as a child, the second as she approached womanhood, the third before she took a husband but the final task he was going to keep to himself, certainly for now as a plan for this final and usually most difficult task formulated in his head. Still as a male member of the village he was duty bound to help with the preparations for the fair which after all started officially at dawn tomorrow at six bells. Sighing to himself that he was still no nearer figuring out what the first three tasks might be, he left the warm family home to join Naiden, who had trained as a carpenters apprentice in his youth and was therefore expected to put up the wooden market stalls, the wood from which would be used for the great bonfire which would be lit for the naming ceremony. Carig's task would be to move all the wood from the sheds at the other end of the village and he knew he had a hard day's toil in front of him.

Kissing his sleeping daughter in her cot, he signalled to his busy wife he was out for the day, no words were spoken, no words were necessary, she knew what was troubling him and she knew only he could solve the problem which was bothering him.

As expected the day was tough but the wood was moved and the stalls erected, the fair was taking shape as the first guests had already started to arrive, the two village Inns would be full tonight and he half wished he could join Naiden in a full nights drinking, tonight though he must bend his mind again to the tasks, the next week there would be too many distractions to think properly.

Later as the cold moon shone brightly he sat on the threshold of his home, Reva had taken pity on his plight and provided him with a decent enough amount to drink and supplied the weed for his clay pipe. He thought of his sleeping baby and her future, the harsh countryside she would grow up in, the sometimes nearer sometimes further threat of war, he recalled his mothers bravery and the way she would never speak of the cruel treatment by the mercenaries and by Vagril himself whilst carrying her unborn child. She dealt with her grief at the loss of her own husband by protecting Carig as he struggled to understand what had happened to their respective life's and why his father had died. Even after all these years Carig could not think of his mother without the thoughts of vengeance welling up inside him, and time in this instance was not such a great healer as so many people had indicated it would be.

He couldn't think, he didn't want to, he was tired and truthfully the efforts of the day and the craziness of the gathering two nights previously had exhausted him. He would sleep, tomorrow would be another day!

He lay upon his bed and was asleep as soon as he closed his eyes; Reva looked at him and thought to herself that he deserved a peaceful night, as she crawled in next to him she couldn't have known he was already dreaming.

He was a Falcon, flying towards the moon, harsh voices he could hear as he swooped down to the castle below. Resting on the battlements he looked around, there in the courtyard was Vagril with another, possibly a child of thirteen summers; he was at Vagril's side. The boy saw the bird on the battlement and quickly loosed an arrow in his direction, Carig lifted off in time to see the arrow skip harmlessly on the steps of the turret. Carig knew at that point he had to kill the child before the child killed him, but what could he do? He was only a bird……only a bird……only a bird.

The dream shifted and he was flying towards the mountains. A voice from the depths, a voice loud and commanding over the tumult of the exploding volcano of Hellddyn as he soared higher and higher over the tormented mountain echoed:

>*Four tasks I give thee*
>*One name you gave me*
>*Three men will love me*
>*One name you gave me*
>*Two lives protect me*
>*One name you gave me*
>*One task define me*
>*One name you gave me*

Chapter 4

One week later and the fair had come to its final conclusion and most folk had gone away satisfied, the locals too had made enough money to see them through the harsh winter. Tonight would be the naming and if Carig had given thought to the tasks he was keeping it to himself, in fact he seemed to be keeping everything to himself now and had hardly joined in the festivities at all the previous week. Reva was worried; her husband had seemed to shrink within himself since the birth of their daughter and he would not speak unless spoken to first. Something was clearly worrying him, but if he couldn't find the courage to discuss it with his wife she didn't know where he might find it.

With the remaining visitors despatched before dusk the pallets and stalls were broken up and piled into a huge bonfire. The villages one by one started to arrive, Lendel and the rest of the elders would be summoned from the hall to perform the solemn task of naming and tasking. Each mother would present her child to Lendel who would record their details in the Book of Names each father would then present the tasks which the child would need to complete during his or her lifetime. Many failed either through over ambitious parents or some simply didn't take them seriously enough to try, but Carig and Reva would have been described as traditionalists and would be expected to present something of worth. One by one the parents of the children were presented and tasked, most tasks this year were not very challengeable and the villages were becoming rather restless and bored with events. Finally it was Carig and Reva's turn, Lendel had insisted because of his challenge some nights previously that Carig had earned the right to be last. Reva approached first and Lendel went through the speech again for the twenty third time that night.

'Who presents the child' he asked

'Reva wife of Carig' she stated with some pride

'What is to be the name of your child' he continued

'Celeste Archer' declared Reva

The name was quickly added to the list of other children written in the book, they would be added to the village family tree in the Elders Hall by a scribe within one day. Lendel indicated to Carig to come forward.

'Name the tasks' said Lendel

Carig turned to the crowd and for a moment was silent, staring ahead he said

'Four tasks I have prepared for my child and she will prove her worth to me, to my wife and to our families and ancestors'

The crowd murmured their approval at his words

The formality of the initial words dispensed with he stood silently. The crowd started to become slightly restless as they waited expectantly. Carig looked at the crowd once again then back at his wife holding their child tightly.

'She will tame the untameable!'

Silence prevailed......... 'What could that mean?'

'She will prove herself a man!'

Ridiculous!!.... surely Carig had suffered a breakdown or worse was drunk on this solemn occasion, the crowd now all started talking at once but Lendel smashed his staff on the table.

'People, people.... let our deluded friend finish, I fear though he will regret this foolish statement in the morn, nevertheless it must be recorded, continue!!'

Carig, still staring unmoved at the crowd declared

'She will follow her father's path'

'To drunkenness' someone shouted from the crowd as they all laughed at the now ridiculous spectacle.

Unmoved Carig spoke one last time.

'She will free the land from its occupation!'

The crowd was bored with events now, Carig having shown himself to be a drunk or worse still losing his grip on reality, was no longer an amusing spectacle. They fell silent and looked to their Elder

Lendel spoke finally 'So the names and tasks have been spoken, so they have been recorded, does anyone here challenge the rights of the parents to name and task?'

This was a formality, no one ever did.

'It is done!'

Lendel turned away, Carig had made a mockery of tonight's events and he would deal with the consequences tomorrow morning.

'Tonight's festivities are over' he ordered to the very dissatisfied crowd.

They dispersed quickly leaving Carig, who was still unmoving and his wife Reva, who now came to him. Without a glance she took him by the hand back to their hut.

Carig slept and once again he dreamed………there was a battle and death, fleets of sailing ships, the scene shifted, once more the castle he had dreamt about previously, he was still a Falcon, the sneering youth who had shot at him before had grown, but still he shot his arrows

Chapter 5

Carig received the summons to the Elders Hall at first light; he was still saying nothing to his wife who was as confused as anyone about what had transpired the night before. Not wanting the silence to continue Reva asked

'Shall I come with you?'

'No' he replied 'the Elders Hall is no place for a woman and harsh words are likely to be spoken this morning'

'I am not afraid of a few profanities and insults' declared Reva

'It's my problem and my problem alone, please don't push me, everything will become clear in time'

It was pointless arguing, she knew that very well, once her husband made up his mind about something his decision was final. She just hoped that Carig, who had always been thoroughly respected, would not become a laughing stock in the village.

He made his way to the Elders Hall expecting a tough morning ahead with Lendel his judge and the other eleven Elders his jury, but when he pushed the door open he was surprised to find only Lendel present, sat at the Eyrie, with the naming book unopened in front of him.

Carig strode to the table and awaited Lendel's reaction. When it came it was not how he expected it to be. Lendel indicated to Carig to join him, to actually sit in one of the other Elders seats. Who could gainsay the High Elder? So Carig dutifully walked around the edge of the long table and sat next to Lendel without a word.

Lendel opened the book,

'You can read for yourself the tasks you set', he declared 'I am duty bound to instruct the scribes to record exactly what you said, do you confirm this is an honest representation of last nights events?'

Carig nodded still not able to bring himself to talk

Lendel shut the book and looked at Carig

'There is more to this than meets the eye, which is why I summoned you here alone, why the rest of the Elders are not present and why no one is scribing our conversation'

Carig nodded once more

Lendel put his hand on Carig's shoulder

'Come my friend, tell me what ails you?

Carig stirred, his face pale like one returning from a nightmare

'Lendel, I have been having troubled dreams, for some time, in fact the entire time my wife has been with child, the dreams themselves are contradictory and confusing but I believe they have given me a degree of foresight. I truly believe my young baby girl is going to be remarkable in ways you or I couldn't possibly imagine, and I could not let the naming and taking be as mundane as everyone else's were and besides'……he hesitated now before continuing…….'the tasks were, are in some ways connected to my dreams, I can't expect you or any man to understand, all I can do is beg for your understanding and forgiveness for causing the uproar last night'

Lendel was thoughtful, 'It's not my place to change any scriven tasks' he said ' The Gods found it in their heart to bless you with this baby girl and to allow you to drink the thirty two. In my mind, this act alone gives you some measure of flexibility. My worry is for you Carig, you have held yourself up for ridicule amongst the village and word is bound to spread. You may find those who you could always count as friends have suddenly found your company hard to bear. For now my friend you may go!'

Carig bowed to the High Elder and made his way to the exit of the hall. He hesitated momentarily before pushing the door open. The people of the village were going about their daily business. Carig noticed no-one spoke to him but many stared, some shaking their heads others stopping to point whilst whispering to each other. Regardless he strode on, he had hoped to see Naiden, at least he wouldn't predisposed to judge him, but Naiden wasn't around (or he was making himself scarce) so Carig had little choice but to make his way back to his home.

Reva was inside and looked up as Carig entered; her face looked weary and troubled.

Carig sat beside her and taking her by the hand said, 'My love, it seems only you may be prepared to support me now I have made an apparent fool of myself to the village people and the elders'

Reva looked at him with concern but smiled.

'No doubt mother too will find a plausible excuse for your action last night, but I am your wife and no explanation is necessary'

Carig looked again at his wife and smiled in turn

'To you I can explain as only you would understand'

Reva sighed 'Well it will give the villages something to talk about for the next six months until the next naming and tasking ceremony'.

Part 2

Celestial Child

Chapter 1

The talk didn't die down for six months though the initial hostility towards Carig dissipated as village life carried on just as it always had. Reva however was pained to see how much Carig's standing seemed to have gone down within the village and how little respect he seemed to command. It was true Naiden had remained a true friend but Carig's regular circle of friends seemed reduced on a yearly basis until there was only a handful left.

Carig was besotted with his girl however and nothing seemed to shake his belief that she was in some way special. Celeste went everywhere with Carig and the bond between them was unbreakable. Six years had passed since the naming of the child and the village remained virtually unchanged. Carig and Reva had tried for more children but they had not been blessed further by the Gods and so a small unlooked-for barrier had grown between them. To all intents and purposes married life carried on as with any married couple but more than one villager commented that Carig seemed to have replaced his wife's company with his daughters. In truth however Reva was not sad; her girl was growing quickly and showed strength of character even at this early stage of her life. She was taller than other children her age and fiercely intelligent. She had her own time with her daughter, the days were for Carig when she joined him tending the cattle or hunting on the plains but the evenings were given to her and her daughter, where Celeste could act like a normal girl and help her mother cooking or washing.

On a warm early autumn night Carig and his friend Naiden were in the Gate Inn with Cirard the village apothecary.

Cirard had a son Bracen the same age as Celeste and they had become friends playing together in what had been the warmest and driest summer in living memory (now a distant memory as the northerly wind had broken some weeks before). Bracen too was tall for his age though not as well built as Celeste. But they played, wrestled and fought like two boys. It had in fact brought Carig and Reva a lot closer to Cirard and his wife Leadel since they at least had their children's fondness of each other in common. Leadel was with Reva this night as their husbands were drinking in the Inn with Naiden.

Carig downed another tankard of ale and signalled to the Innkeeper for three refills.

'Strange things you hear if you listen to the news from the sea' declared Cirard

Since Codencia Minor was separated from the rest of the continent by the mountain range and could only be entered from the South the people relied somewhat on the sea-merchants for goods and for news (good and bad). Cirard had recently been in Southaven the only port in Codencia Minor to pick up supplies of herbs for his business.

'Rumour has it that the frozen wastes to the north might be traversable by ship since the warm summer had melted most of the pack ice and that might open the way for more trade' he continued.

'Good for your pocket no doubt' laughed Naiden

'Well it is true that being on the arse-end of the continent and having only one way in to our little land does somewhat narrow opportunities for a business man like me' agreed Cirard

'I don't mind a bit of increased trade' said Carig 'so long as they (meaning the rest of the world) leave us to ourselves'

'I don't perceive any danger' said Cirard, 'who would be interested in this little rat-hole?'

'I'm not so sure' observed Carig, 'we have had war before remember?'

'Oh but that was many generations ago and things are not as they used to be, if it comes down to it Codencia is a big old country and anyone wanting to get to us would have to go through them first......and what for, what could be of interest here?' asked Cirard

Naiden rejoined the discussion 'maybe increased trade from the north might bring some good people in and some better opportunities for those of us without?'

'Without what? asked Cirard

Carig let out a belly laugh, 'honestly Cirard, are you so naive sometimes, our friend Naiden here is talking about the blonde Nordencian women of legend, that's his only interest in the north'

'I have never seen a blonde' explained Naiden

'None of us have' said Cirard and Carig together and both burst into laughter at their friends expense.

You might as well forget it anyway my friend, said Cirard ' the news from Southaven was that Nodencia was having enough trouble with border disputes with both Midencia and Westendcia, not that that should worry us overmuch both being at least a thousand leagues away!'

Carig nodded in agreement, and wondered if the other two had any real idea of how far away a thousand leagues actually was, distances of this kind were quite out of their reckoning.

'They can fight all they want' muttered Carig, 'to my mind you replace one ruler with another, nothing changes except tax increases, life goes on regardless'

'Aren't you just a bundle of fun tonight' laughed Naiden in turn, 'have you no pride in your country?'

'Codencia isn't my county Naiden, Codencia Minor is!' declared Carig

What's Codencia got to do with anything? They haven't been at war for many years and their borders are quiet' said Naiden

'Maybe too quiet' thought Carig to himself.

The overdue ale was brought to the table and the conversation moved on to other topics, the usual stuff of Inn-houses, the weather, the local politics of the Elders, the prices of everything (including ale) and Carig contented himself to listen to all that was said without contributing too much to proceedings. Half an hour afterwards he excused himself to his two friends who were discussing the legality of the new whore-house at the other end of the village (it was pretty obvious Naiden, given his lack of sexual opportunities would be on the side of the fledgling business).

Carig walked to the exit just as another was entering, the stranger looked like a weary traveller, one who had endured too much sun and ridden too far and for too long. He was cloaked and wore a brimmed hat which covered his blue eyes. Carig had half a mind to return to his seat and listen to any news this traveller might bring (since visitors were rare from outside Codencia Minor), but then he had probably had enough to drink tonight and he knew he had promised Celeste a trip to the hot springs the next day since she had never actually seen The Geyser of Dyn which was less than half a days ride away.

Carig's mind, now made up strode home through the village to his welcoming hut. Leadel looked up and saw Carig entered, rather too quickly she said 'I had better go now Reva……. and thank you for an entertaining night'

Carig wondered idly what could have been so entertaining but turned his mind to his daughter who was sat up in her bed in the corner.

'Have those two old washer-women kept you awake Celeste?' laughed Carig, 'we have a long ride tomorrow, so you need to rest, we have an early start in the morning'

'I helped mother prepare our food for the day' answered Celeste,' I am really excited'

'Sleep then child' said Carig as he pulled the curtains to her corner.

Reva looked at Carig and remembered when he seemed to want to spend all his time with her, how he used to be so loving and how he never went anywhere without kissing and hugging her. Now it was all Celeste, not that she really minded, she had lost her sexual drive after the birth and never really regained it. Carig was too much of a man to complain to her and she wondered if the lack of sex was a topic of conversation at the Inn as it had been for her with Leadel. Bringing herself out of her musings she said to Carig

'I don't know why you want to go dragging her off for twenty leagues, to see exploding water and those stinking mud pools'

Carig simply replied, 'Reva, what can I do? She is so inquisitive and she listens to what people tell her. If she thinks going to the mud pools and seeing a geyser is an adventure then it must be so for her'

Reva sighed, it was pointless, the connection between father and daughter was so strong that she knew she couldn't come between them, why should she anyway, they were both happy, or seemed to be anyway.

'I will go see mother then whilst you are out for the day' declared Reva, 'I am worried about her health, she seems to have almost withered away in the recent hot weather, even though its now turned and is more seasonal'

This made Carig feel guilty and torn. He loved his mother-in-law and their relationship had always been a good one. He knew he didn't visit enough, but there again she did live a little too near to Oakenvale for his liking, you could certainly see the town on a clear day from her place and he didn't like the memories that place brought back even now. He looked at Reva, she was in fact becoming very much like her mother, certainly like her mother when she had been first introduced to Carig many years before. He still loved her, he knew this in his heart, he just felt things had changed after Celeste's birth, almost as if, as a man he had only so much love he could give at one time. He had loved his wife and indeed her mother, but now there was a child too, and she had quite rightly taken away the majority of his love, well, at least that's how he felt about it.

Carig sat beside his wife and held her hand in-between both of his.

'You know, we ought to consider moving to a larger stone built house, something bigger for Celeste, she will want her privacy in not many years hence, and maybe we could consider moving your mother in too?'

Reva studied his face, he had said something similar after Celeste had been born but she had not been in agreement then, selfishly wanting the new family unit to herself (and not sharing it with her own mother). He seemed very genuine again, no doubt her mother was just an after-thought and it was for Celeste's sake that he had made this suggestion, but it would certainly make things easier. 'You really want this' she asked

Carig nodded, 'It would make a lot of sense' he said

Chapter 2

At sunrise, Carig roused Celeste, 'come on little one, it's time to go'

'But it's so early' complained Celeste

'Don't make me tickle you' he laughed as he threw back her bed clothes.

'Father!' she complained, 'you aren't allowed to see me like this'

'Have you heard our six year old duagther?' he asked his wife as he flung her over his shoulder

Soon enough they were packed and ready, Carig on his horse with Celeste riding confidently in front on the specially made double saddle he had purchased the month before.

'Now don't wear your father out' shouted Reva to Celeste as they rode off......'and don't let him eat all the food!'

Carig and Celeste turned out of the village gate and headed east. The day was cold again, but fortunately thunder storms and heavy rains were rare (they tended to build on the other side of the mountains and head west with the usual prevailing wind). Snow had never been seen in Codencia Minor. Carig hoped to make good progress and expected little to slow them down on the way, and so it proved apart from the constant questioning from Celeste:

'How far have we gone?'
'How far is it to the geyser?'
'How long will it take?'
'How far does it explode upwards?'
'Why does it happen?'
'Can you bathe in the mud pools?'

Other than the child constant questioning it was a relaxing ride, he wasn't pushing too hard, they had the whole day and it was pointless wearing out the horse unnecessarily.

The mountains were looming much closer now and for a few minutes Celeste had been quiet staring in wonder at the approaching volcano.

'Has anyone ever been up there' she whispered

'No one but a mad man would venture that journey Celeste it is far too dangerous' he replied

'What's that smell?' she asked

'That would be the sulphur' explained Carig

'It smells like rotten eggs' she complained

Reining the horse in, he slowed to a trot.

'Why are we stopping' asked Celeste

'Because we are here' replied Carig

This smelly pool is it! she exclaimed rather disappointingly

'Just wait and be patient' Carig insisted

Celeste helped unload the horse and she lay a blanket on the ground, the pale sunshine was at least giving off sufficient heat to make the day comfortable, as she was sitting down she heard a bubbling sound then suddenly a massive explosion of water came from the surface. They both turned laughed at the spectacle Celeste's finger tracing the column of water as it shot into the air, but her finger remained pointing as the water collapsed back on itself

'What's that' she said as she pointed up to a large bird flying overhead

'It's a bird' came back the slightly sarcastic response

'No father, I meant what kind of bird. I have never seen one like it before' she said

Carig shielded his eyes from the sun and studied the hovering bird as it glided on the warm air created from the hot pool below.

'It looks like a Mountain Falcon' he said 'I hope it's not looking for little girls to eat' he added mischievously.

'Father I am six you know, I'm not stupid'

'More like sixteen' he thought to himself before adding, 'look Celeste how high she is now, look how she glides, she must be looking for prey'

'What will she eat' asked Celeste 'and how do you know it's a girl?'

Falcons eat other smaller birds, sometimes mice and rats, when they can't get hold of a tasty six year old' he said laughing. 'I can tell it's a she by her colouring, if you saw her closer you would tell her from a male falcon because she would be bigger'

'So the girl is bigger than the boy?' asked Celeste

'She is' answered Carig

'That's like me and Bracen' she said confidently

'There's no answer to that' thought Carig as he looked at his daughter. It was truly amazing how much she had grown; she was already taller than some nine year old girls in the village.

'Look Celeste, see how it dives and swoops' said Carig

The falcon which had been circling and hovering had gone into a long dive, the speed was startling and the unsuspecting starling didn't stand a chance as the claw hit it at speed, the falcon then dived further catching the stunned bird before it hit the ground, at which point it turned and finally headed back to the mountain.

'I would like a Falcon of my own' she declared

Carig laughed 'they are wild my love and not pets, better for you to have a cat'

'Which would live longest?' asked Celeste

'I'm not really sure, probably both around fifteen years' her father replied

'In that case it's the falcon' she declared

Celeste didn't listen further as she lay on her back looking in the air at the falcon heading away to its cliff side nest. Behind her the geyser bubbled and exploded into action once again, but Celeste barely noticed, she had her eyes fixed on the departing falcon.

The day wore on without much further adventure; they both bathed in the hot (but smelly) mud pools by the geyser and managed to clean themselves off between eruptions. They played games, and talked, he pretended to wrestle (and let her win, though in truth he thought her uncommonly strong). As the afternoon wore and turned colder, Carig could tell his daughter was tired, though too proud to admit it. He told her eventually it was time to go and her objection wasn't too vociferous which in itself was proof of her tiredness. He hoisted her up onto the saddle and mounted the horse behind her. It was late afternoon and it had been a long day for her. Her head was nodding as he held firmly onto her with one arm as he skilfully guided the horse across the rugged plains. The journey back was uneventful; Celeste slept occasionally waking to ask the age old question 'Are we there yet?'

They were approaching the village gate again and Carig roused Celeste as he slowed the horse down, passing through he turned right passed Naiden's small-holding and down the path to his own hut. He expected Reva to be inside, probably having prepared something warm, so he was slightly surprised when he entered to find her not there.

He was a little annoyed, not that he expected his wife to always be there when he returned from journeys but more so because he knew Celeste would have been excited to tell her of their day. Still, there was time, it was past sunset it was true, and he wouldn't have advised Reva to make the journey from her mothers in the dark, so maybe she had called in to see Leadel on the way back. Carig prepared some food for Celeste and himself, but in truth he wasn't really that hungry, he had planned to go down to the Inn again tonight, but clearly he couldn't leave Celeste on her own, which was probably bothering him most about Reva's absence.

He played the doting father for the evening, insisting Celeste bathed, and dutifully turning away when she asked. He sat in his chair and intended to let Celeste fall asleep on him; he knew he would be in trouble for not putting her to bed, but it was quite nice to have this closeness together.

He sang a lullaby which she always liked him to sing, one he had made up when Celeste had been a baby.

You are the keeper of my heart,
I care for you so much.
I even love your tearful eyes
Your tender little touch.

And so my little princess
Before you go to sleep,
Remember I am your daddy
And I am yours to keep.

The night wore on as Celeste slept on his lap, Carig felt his own head nodding, he worried that Reva still hadn't returned, but there was little he could do tonight. His last thought was that he would ride to his mother-in-laws in the morning with Celeste to see what was wrong.

He woke with a start, a candle was burning, Reva was sitting at the table, head in her hands. He lifted Celeste up and placed her in bed; she turned over and carried on sleeping. He walked to the table as Reva looked up at him; her eyes were swollen and red from too much crying. Before Carig could ask she said

'We don't need a bigger house now……. my mother is dead' she sobbed

What can a man do in a situation like this than be there for his wife? He listened as she explained that Revangel was still in bed when she had made her way to her house, that she was very weak, and that she barely spoke. Reva explained how she had sat alone and watch her mother die in front of her and how she felt so guilty for not being there to nurse her in her final days.

Carig said nothing, he let his wife talk and cry and talk again, she got angry with the world, angry with herself, even angry at Carig, and she sobbed again uncontrollably for a time as Carig held her to him, stroking the back of her head unable to find the words of comfort he imagined she wanted to hear. The night wore on and eventually an exhausted Reva eventually indicated she needed to sleep.

In bed together Carig still stroked his wife's long straight black hair until she finally slept

'Tomorrow is going to be a long day' thought Carig as his eyes shut.

Carig was once again flying, this time his dream was over the ocean, he could see the ship moving slowly, men driving their huge oars into the water against the calm sea. He swooped further down towards one of the masts where he rested and looked around.

A bare-chested, yellow haired man stood on the deck silent like a ghost, needing no instruction to his men who were manfully driving the ship on.

The man looked up at the Falcon with his fierce blue eyes which unnerved the bird, who then spread his wings and left the mast heading back to its nest in the distant mountains.

Chapter 3

Carig was up early the next morning to tend to the cattle, preferring to allow Reva to sleep in since she had such a tough night, besides the beasts needed feeding before they departed to Ravangel's own hut later in the morning. Carig walked away from his hut alongside the path towards the gate of his small-holding. He saw Naiden in the distance.

He whistled to his friend, who came over shortly afterwards, rubbing his hands together to ward off the cold northerly wind which had strengthened somewhat overnight.

Carig told his friend about Revangel who sadly shook his head and declared

'Way, way too young, my heart grieves for your wife'

Carig nodded in agreement and looked on solemnly; a short silence ensued until Naiden suddenly declared

'You should have stayed in the Inn the other night; the traveller who came in asked a lot of questions'

Carig remembered the travellers keen piercing blue eyes beneath his hood and asked

'What kind of questions Naiden?'

He replied that the traveller had asked all sorts of questions about the men of the village, Codencia Minor in general, whether the small earthquakes they had been suffering on a regular basis were a recent phenomenon, what kind of businesses the people had, the types of animals they kept. Naiden further added 'It was the general consensus that the traveller was a tax inspector from Codencia, and we should all start hiding some of our cattle as there is now bound to be some kind of census as a result'

Carig frowned and asked

'Did he take off his hat at all?

Naiden thought for a moment and said

'You know, I don't think he did..... why?

'No reason' answered the now thoughtful Carig

Naiden looked at him and laughed

'Well it's clear you have your own thoughts about this which you prefer to keep to yourself; however I am giving you due warning....... hide your cattle my friend!'

They left after further friendly words and Naiden agreed to tend his cattle whilst the family were away for a few days sorting out Revangel's affairs and her funeral arrangements. She would of course be laid to rest and burned along with her own clothes as tradition demanded; her belongings would of course go to Reva unless a declaration of transfer was found. Carig was sure there wouldn't be one.

There would be the difficult task of explaining her grandmother's death to Celeste, under normal circumstances he would leave such matter to Reva, but after last nights breakdown he wasn't sure she would cope. Reva was going to need his support and he would have to be as understanding as she had been at the naming and tasking ceremony.

Hunching his shoulders slightly against the northerly wind he made his way down the path towards the village, he thought it would be best to let one of the Elders know the family would be gone for a few days.

A horse being hard ridden approached from the direction of the centre of the village, Carig could see, even from a distance that it was the traveller who had been responsible for so much discussion in the Inn and the rest of the village. The rider slowed the horse down to a walk as he approached and Carig again felt the keen gaze of the heavily cloaked rider as he studied him intently.

Carig decided at that point he would speak to the man, but before he got the chance, as if by acting to some unseen signal the rider stirred in his saddle and urged his horse again to a gallop.

Carig looked round to see the black horse disappear over the brow of the hill towards the village gate in a cloud of dust. Carig felt distinctly uneasy about this encounter but shrugging his shoulders made his way to the Elders Hut. He had other things to worry about this day.

Chapter 4

Two more years passed and village life carried on as normal. Celeste being such a young child had quickly accepted the death of her grand-mother; the same could not have been said of Reva however. Much as he tried, Carig didn't seem to be able to give his wife the words of encouragement she needed and the barrier between them grew wider. They had moved however, just a few months after Revangel's death. The cost of the stone built house hadn't been prohibitive and had been partly financed by selling Ravangel's land to her immediate neighbour who wanted the land for his own increasing herd and the hut for his eldest soon-to-be-married son.

The house was much warmer than their previous home, though truth be told the weather again had been uncommonly hot, even in the winter months. They had even managed with the sale of their own herd and small-holding (complete with house) to purchase a very small summer-house residence in an inlet called Salint Bay, on the coast, right on the furthest southern tip of the land, which was actually part of Codencia. This had been at Reva's insistence as she seemed to want to occasionally put as much distance as she could between herself and the place of her mother's death.

Since the sale of the small-holding Carig, now without cattle earned an effective living as an out-rider for one of the Elders named Pallos. Each Elder had such a rider who always rode alongside during frequent business elsewhere in the small country and some time to Codencia itself (which was how Carig had stumbled across the summer house, during one of these trips away). Pallos himself was unofficially the second highest Elder, though of course would not ever assume the position of High Elder unless that post was not duly inherited by Lendel's own son.

Carig's regular trips away from home had started to affect his close relationship with Celeste who had grown still further in the previous two years. Still it had certainly given his daughter more time to bond with her mother and she had certainly been the main source of comfort to Reva following the death of her mother. In truth, Carig felt decidedly uneasy about family life, Reva had withdrawn almost totally and wanted little to do with him, Celeste too was becoming much more independent and Carig felt almost like a redundant husband and father when he returned from his journeys. It was to be expected, he knew Celeste was growing up so quickly and besides spending time with her mother, spent every other available opportunity at Cirard's playing with Bracen. Carig too enjoyed his independence just a little too much and since his wife's withdrawal had found no difficulty in maintaining a number of female acquaintances on his travels. Only Naiden remained unshakeable in his friendship with Carig and would occasionally accompany him, with permission from Pallos, on trips abroad, certainly those which might involve the pleasure of the opposite sex. Naiden had still not found a woman to finally settle down with and showed no inclination to do so.

It was a mild spring evening and Carig had spent nearly a month at home whilst Pallos had been otherwise engaged with the birth of his second son (and third child) and he would no doubt be thinking about the naming and tasking ceremony after the fair and subsequent mid-summer solstice. Celeste was again at Bracen's and it was nearly time for her return, he had made his mind up to give her a little while longer and settled back into his chair. Reva was washing in the stream which ran outside the house which fed the local wells and dams and was a tributary of the river Oaken upon which the village had been built and created plenty of fresh water for the area around Lendel.

Suddenly and without any kind of warning the room started to shake and ornaments fell from the shelves and pictures detached themselves from the wall. The shaking lasted around thirty seconds and then stopped as abruptly as it had started.

The minor tremors had been an ongoing nuisance for a number of years but they had seemed to be growing in intensity, everyone knew there was little that could be done about this and everyone feared the possible consequences. Carig listened; sometimes the birds would give another indication of possible after-shocks, they sensed trouble long before the average man could. As he listened, he could hear the sound of distant thunder which he thought unusual as the day had been relatively clear. The sound was becoming louder and louder and Carig decided to step outside to warn Reva. Just as he stood up Celeste came running through the door and shouted

'Father, it's the volcano, you know, the one where we went to the pools'

'What about it?' asked Carig fearing the inevitable response,

'It's exploded, there is a big cloud growing from it and I'm frightened' she added

Carig took his daughter's hand and led her outside, Celeste clearly shaken by events kept hold of him, not wanting to let him go. Reva too was looking away to the East where the column of ash was rising further. She looked round as her husband and daughter approached

'Carig, I am scared' she said as she looked out again at the mountain. Carig held her with one arm whilst his other encompassed Celeste.

'I think we should make haste and pack' said Carig staring at the ever increasing black cloud which was rising into the sky. 'We can travel light and make our way to Salint, I know it's a lot of travelling for you both but its is out of reach of the volcano's influence'

'Do you think we really are in danger here this far away' asked Celeste, mirroring the thoughts of her mother

'I'm not sure' replied Carig, 'it's better to be safe than sorry'

Looking up at the clouds overhead he could see the prevailing wind had turned westerly so maybe the people of Northern Codencia and South Western Midencia would feel the full force of the Gods' apparent anger. His mind was made up however; he would ride with his family to Salint before returning himself to Lendel. As a fairly prominent man of the village he didn't want to add to the population's obvious discomfort by leaving and not returning. Of course he would need to seek permission from Pallos first, but he would no doubt grant it as he too would be mindful of his own family's safety at this time.

'Go now and pack' he said to Reva 'and take Celeste with you, we need to travel through the night and we need to travel light. We have sufficient supplies in Salint'.

He ran down the main street of the village to the Elder Hall. He wasn't sure if any of the Elders would be there tonight. There was general confusion with women screaming and men shouting, frightened villages heading too to the hall. Lendel had already arrived and had sent out instruction for the other Elders to attend, clearly a quick decision needed to be made.

More people were pouring in, probably the whole male population of the village (and a few females too) all clamouring to be heard. Small disagreements and fights broke out as frightened people tried to get the best position to hear the High Elder. Carig stood still and saw Pallos approach; he looked weary but nodded at Carig as he saw him in the crowd. Eventually Lendel at the door of the Elder Hut made a sign to the people that he wanted to speak. The clamouring died down and people listened intently to his words.

'We and our forefathers have long dreaded this day and being so near to the mountain have made some provision against this eventuality. What is needed firstly is to get the women and children out of the village, if any of you have relatives further away then I suggest you depart there, if not the advice is to go to Oakenvale where we have already despatched our fastest riders to warn them of the impending danger and likely fugitive situation. Some of you may prefer to go further to the coast at Southaven. The instruction is however that once the women and children have been made safe we must return to protect our village against whatever might befall, whether man-made or otherwise. I need every able bodied man from the age of eighteen back in the village by the beginning of next month. We will register their return; those men who disobey and fail to act on this instruction will feel the full weight of my jurisdiction as I invoke emergency laws from midnight tonight, to last until the year end at winter-solstice. There will be no discussion at this time; the Elders will alight to Oakenvale where further decisions will be made. Go now, make haste and be prepared for the unexpected, the next few months will prove challenging'

The crowd were all pushing to get away first made as much haste as the hundreds of men (and women) could. Needing no further permission from Pallos (as Lendel's own instruction would override everyone else's) Carig quickly made his way back to his own home where he found Reva and Celeste waiting.

Reva was crying, her whole world had been turned up-side down this last few years and this event just added to her frustration. Celeste was looking at the mountain which was glowing red against the darkness of the night and wondered if she would ever return

'Father' she cried 'I must go see Bracen before we go!'

'No time Celeste', insisted Carig, 'Cirard is going to have his hands full moving his full apothecary business to Oakenvale'

'Then we must go there too' declared Celeste

'I will never go to that accursed town Celeste, do you not know your family history?' he asked

Celeste was unperturbed and with far too much disrespect for an eight year old replied to her father under her breath

'Just because his stupid mother got killed there we all have to suffer'

But Carig heard what she said and before Reva could stop him, struck Celeste across the face with the back of his hand. Celeste was not going to show anyone she was hurt and simply wiped her face grimly whilst staring at her father. Reva put her arms around Celeste and loved her, she was angry herself; no man should ever hit her daughter, not even her own husband.

Carig threw the double saddle towards Reva and Celeste and mounted his horse without a word. Reva saddled her horse and put Celeste in front of her as they followed Carig into the night. Celeste kept her eyes on her father in front rather than on the spectacle of the volcano.

Carig rode on ahead, far enough away from the two women in his life, they couldn't be allowed to see the pain he bore or the tears he now wept.

They rode on further through the night and all the next day making infrequent stops to water the horses and eat such supplies which had been hastily put together. Throughout the whole journey Carig had neither spoken nor even acknowledged their existence.

At dusk on the third day Carig had left the camp fire to see if he could snare some rabbits to eat. Reva took the opportunity to talk to her daughter

'He didn't mean to hurt you' she said

Celeste looked around to ensure Carig wasn't there and said to her mother

'I don't care…..I hate him' she declared

Reva shook her head, 'please don't say what you don't mean my dear, at some point in the future a day may come when you rue those words'

'At least my mother loves me' said Celeste

'And so does your father' answered Reva

On the afternoon of the fourth day they approached their house in Salint. They could smell the sea breeze and had heard the gulls from some distance away during that morning. Carig still riding ahead had at least tried to be a little more communicative when he returned the previous evening, though it was clear there was definite tension between him and Celeste.

The house was sheltered from the worst of the wind from the sea it was situated in a dell which faced north-south and the house was at the bottom of a steep embankment which protected the place from the often fresh westerlies. Of course a northerly wind would be funnelled straight down the dell but they were far enough south here for it to make little difference to the overall temperature.

The further south they had ridden they had lost all contact with the still venting volcano since the prevailing winds were westerly and not in their direction and the warmth of the spring sunshine this far south was very welcoming. Unpacking their few belongings they had all gone to bed early, Reva and Celeste exhausted from the long journey.

They broke their fast the next morning and Carig again made to depart.

Kissing his wife on the brow he could find little to say other than 'look after Celeste'.

Carig looked at his daughter stood there next to his wife, he held out his arms to her in apparent reconciliation. Celeste hesitated but was pushed gently by Reva. She broke into a run and Carig scooped her up and swung her around just like he used to do. He kissed her too on the brow and studied her face.' You have grown Celeste' he said with a smile 'I need you to watch over your mother, she needs you right now, I will be back by mid summer, hopefully with good news'

Celeste, emotions finally getting the better of her cried

'Please Daddy don't go!'

Carig couldn't look at her, he lifted her up and gave her back to Reva and walked back to his horse without looking back

Reva never saw her cry again………..no one did save one person!

Chapter 5

But Carig did not return as planned in the summer, there were many hastily made promises broken by the men to their spouses during this time, some of which could have been avoided, some could not.

The mountain had erupted for just over five-weeks and though the prevailing wind had been westerly as Carig had foreseen the huge amount of ash had been blown so far into the sky that it had sat above the prevailing winds, raining down ash on the already drought affected plains. In places like Lendel as much as half an arms length of ash had fallen and to a lesser extent also in Oakenvale, and many house roofs had given way under the sheer weight on top. The huts in the region were totally devastated by the ash and never again would the traditional hut type home of Codencia Minor be built. Southaven had been spared the worst of the fall out and had only a thin scattering of ash for its coastal population to worry about.

The news from Southaven however suggested the peoples of the continent to the north and to the east of the volcano had suffered greatly from the out-falling of ash and fugitives had flooded into the north-eastern part of Codencia furthest away from the problem. Many had said that the open lands of Codencia should be made open to the peoples further north and if land was available they might be forced to take it for themselves. None of this concerned the men of Lendel over much since they had problems of their own. Many roofs had to be replaced and the wells and dams drained and restocked since the water had been polluted by the falling ash. The mountain remained a threat however and the tremors continued throughout the whole time the men were at work during the summer.

Though Carig had not managed to get back to Salint as promised he had sent word of the progress being made. His own house had been one of the least affected having taller structures at either side, so for a while he had been housing other men of the village whilst their own places were being cleaned up or in some cases totally re-constructed. The men had already started to grumble about the lack of contact with their families but the High Elder was insistent that no one should come back until the village was made totally safe. Mid-summer came and went and for the first time in living history the mid-summer solstice happened without the usual celebrations though the men in the village had at least had a day off on the day itself since they had managed to restore the Bridge Inn (one of the first buildings to be restored back to its former glory predictably)!

Money was short, but Lendel himself had devised a method of paying for goods within the village with vouchers which could be redeemed once village life eventually got back to normal. The only person who really prospered during this time was the Innkeeper as there was little to do on an evening once the days toil had been completed. Even supplies of ale were low and men had been forced into drinking other beverages to ease their days (and nights). Red wine from the vineyards of Southern Codencia was brought in when the ale started running low the last thing Lendel needed was disgruntled men, it was hard enough them not having their women around and indeed their children and though Lendel was of the opinion his men drank far too much it was a forgivable sin in the circumstances.

So it was one late summer evening when the men were once again at the Inn spending their hard-earned vouchers that a rider came hurrying up from the Southgate, making his way to the Elders Hut he found no-one there, but noticing the lights of the Inn were on made his way there. Once he had settled his horse in the already crowded stable adjacent to the Inn he made his way inside. Few men bothered to notice him; they were far too busy with their own amusements to worry too much about the newcomer.

The rider made his way to the bar and asked for the Innkeeper who eventually same over to speak to him.

'A stranger in town!' he declared, 'what can I get you?'

'I need to see the person in charge' he answered

'That would be me' said the Innkeeper laughing

'No I mean of this village' came back the answer

'Ah, in that case, that would be Lendel you would need to speak to' declared the Innkeeper

'Then where is he?' asked the stranger.

'Come with me' the Innkeeper motioned

Stepping behind the bar the rider followed the Innkeeper along the length of the bar and into a door at the back of the bar. The door was pushed open and the stranger could see five men sat around a table obviously in full discussion of something important since Lendel looked up and said 'What is the meaning of this?' The question which had been asked so many times by many people of the world, not really asking for an answer but rather questioning the reason they had been disturbed.

'Sire' he started.' I come with tidings from Southaven, and I was bidden to ride with haste throughout the land, there are twenty more like me given this task. I am instructed to summon the leader of each community I reach to a grand council meeting in Southaven to take place next month. I was asked to hand you this scroll.

Lendel took the scroll and read it to himself. Looking up he said

'Fellow Elders, those of you who are present tonight, I must impart grievous news. For the first time in many generations there is war on the continent once again'

Lendel turned to the rider and indicated he should sit whilst a meal was prepared and drink brought to his table. 'Tomorrow, we will house you with more hospitality'

'Nay' said the rider 'it is sufficient I eat, drink and sleep if I can for tonight only for tomorrow I still have far to ride and many more villages and towns to reach!'

'What more can you tell me' asked Lendel

'Not overmuch but sufficient to quell rumour I hope', answered the rider

He told Lendel how the government in Codencia itself had been approached by an embassy from Midencia. This embassy had pleaded for a long established alliance to be agreed as it borders were being threatened by men from the north. These men were wild and took few prisoners, only ones who were experts in their field. Women were raped and children put to death for the sport of their dogs. It seemed that a once dominant clan of the north-men had been usurped and the new clan had for years been spoiling for pillage and gain at the expense of anyone they came into contact with. They had already overrun much of the north of Midencia; they were quick to exploit the weaknesses and general disarray caused by the eruption. Furthermore the ice-sheet to the north of the continent had broken and the Northmen had for the first time in living memory sailed vessels from the normally ice-bound north further down the coast burning and looting as they went. Fearing a possible invasion themselves the Westendcian's had thrown in their lot with the north-men eager to gain whatever lands they could at the expense of their nearest neighbours. The Valdencian's had suffered heavily from the west. The whole continent it seemed was in uproar and so far only Codencia had managed to avoid any conflict itself. There were no guarantees this could be maintained.

Lendel listened to all that was said, as other the elders questioned the man further. Eventually, once he had told his entire tale and answered as many questions as he could, he was allowed to his bed. The other Elders, obviously concerned, looked to their leader.

'I shall go to the grand council and will take Carig who as you know is Pallos's outrider with me. He is a capable rider and the countries best archer so I will feel most secure with him by my side. I will clear this with Pallos in the morning' he added.

Turning to a waiter who had been serving food and drinks he motioned him to the table.

They say the walls have ears, but so do bartenders. If you want to keep your tongue within your mouth you will not speak a word of what has been said tonight until I address my people myself, do you understand?' he asked

The bartender nodded silently

'Then go fetch me Carig, if he isn't too drunk, I must speak with him now'

Chapter 6

Southaven wasn't only the largest and therefore most important port in Codencia Minor; it was also the unofficial capital of the land. In past generations it was where the royal seat had been before the First Codencian wars which has taken place hundreds of years previously. The small coastal state then had a form of government by the people until the second Codencian Wars less than twenty years previously when it became a vassal of Codencia itself. By the charter agreed with the conquering Codencian's the minor state was allowed to gather its government together only in a state of emergency, otherwise the land would be ruled by edict from Codencia itself. Obviously the outbreak of war throughout the continent was such an excuse and Codencia would have its hand full enough with its warring neighbours to worry too much about its vassal state showing growing seeds of independence.

The first council was due to meet the next day. Carig and Lendel had arrived without adventure some three days previously and Carig it had to be said was bored with proceedings pretty quickly as Lendel arranged lots of pre-meetings, gauging the mood of the other delegates. He had been allowed to bring Naiden along with him for company and also because Lendel liked to play the person of importance by bringing two colleagues instead of the invited one!

Naiden as usual had wanted to spend the evening pursuing the women folk of the town, even if it meant paying. Carig had a first resisted, the whores of Southaven had a reputation for only having the most basic requirements of hygiene, which could only mean one thing in Carig's eyes. But he was weak-willed in this matter, especially since Reva had turned her back on him in the bedroom, so was quite easily persuaded. As it happened they had stumbled across a couple of young girls who to Carig's naive view of the world couldn't have *that much* experience. They had met them in one of the many Inn's near the harbour which also served the sailors who frequented these parts, and Carig had to admit they didn't look like the average whore who he had seen in that establishment in Lendel which Naiden was obliged to visit to relieve his frustrations. In fact they looked clean, well dressed and with hair which had obviously taken some time to arrange, to all intents and purposes they looked like a couple of well educated young ladies. Fortunately for Naiden and himself they also benefited by having the most fabulous bodies and a sexual appetite which even Naiden found difficult to match.

Lendel in the meantime, further towards the centre of town was through with his business of the day and knew that the council would convene the next morning, so had made up his mind to go to bed early, read the agenda for the next day before partaking of some well-earned rest. Running a village, even a large one of four thousand residents as his own came as second nature to him. To meet like-minded even more self-opinionated Elders from villages and towns much bigger than his own had made him realise his own limitations. He was too old for that kind of ambitious posturing. Lendel knew instinctively who the real power-brokers of the council were and had allied himself to the largest and most influential group of these. This group were pacifists by nature but equally pragmatic when it came to suggesting how many men ought to be spared for Codencia's cause, especially when it meant less of their own and more of someone else's.

Still the day was over and it was well past midnight and he could reflect on a day well spent, these were his last thoughts as he drifted into a peaceful sleep.

The peacefulness of his slumber didn't last for more than a couple of hours. He woke with a start; dazed and confused he could hear some kind of disturbance outside, and people running up and down the stairs of the establishment he was housed in. He made his way slowly to the window whilst rubbing his tired eyes, there seemed to be a fire, as he peered outside he realised there was more than one fire, in fact much of the town seemed to be ablaze. Lendel quickly dressed and was about to open the door, when it simply disintegrated in front of him under the blows of at least three axes. Lendel had no time to think, his one thought was for self preservation as he tried to get to the window, his last thought before the axe blow clove his head in two was how far the drop would be if he jumped. He needn't have worried.

The Northmen had lain off the coast during the day, a blanket of fog had masked their approach, and they had known that the bay often threw up this kind of dense fog especially in the summer months when the air was hot and the wind calm. The fleet of two hundred ships had escaped sight by ensuring any unfortunate vessel either approaching or leaving Southaven was quickly sunk and the men on board slain without question. Just before dawn still under cover of the night, the invaders had taken to rowing boats and silently made their way to shore. Few people were about at this late hour, even the hardiest reveller had long since been thrown out of the Inns by the quayside. Stealthily this first group of men positioned themselves around the town, disguised as Codencian's, some acting drunk, some pretending to sleep on the floor, in the gutter or in the stables as most vagrants did.

When the second wave of armed men reached the shore, the cry went up and they stormed the town. At this point the first wave lit incendiaries and basically flushed all men and women out of their homes and other accommodation. The plan worked perfectly, men were slaughtered in the street before they even had chance to arm themselves, the women were all rounded up and had their belongings including whatever jewellery they had ripped from around their persons as they were made to stand and watch the utter destruction of the town. Later, every one of them would suffer a much crueller fate as they were made to dig the graves of the butchered men before being unmercifully raped by the conquerors, some lucky ones managed to escape during the confusion but not many and most of these were hunted down and suffered even worse from the Northmen when they were recaptured.

Carig had also heard the commotion at the same time as Lendel, but since the house he was in was some way up a back street in the port the invaders hadn't yet reached him. He and Naiden of course had no idea what was going on, but heard the noise and tumult and could smell the burning in the air. They rushed outside only to be confronted by a group of armed northerners rushing up the street burning as they went.

'More Condencian scum' one of them cried as they charged at Carig and Naiden. Carig being strongest and the best armed too put up the fiercest resistance, Naiden on the other hand had almost immediately thrown his own sword to the ground and knelt surrendering himself with the thought that he might be spared. He was beheaded as soon as his sword hit the ground. His assailant walked over at his lifeless body as he turned to burn the house they had just emerged from.

Carig was over-powered but had fought bravely killing two and wounding another, he had no doubt he would be cruelly put to death, his last thought was for the two girls they had just left, still inside the burning house.

He saw the club too late as it swung towards him…everything went black

Chapter 7

Though the slaughter at Southaven was terrible for those who suffered at the hands of the Northmen, it was only a small piece of the puzzle as all lands were now in chaos. During the next weeks more ships had arrived and if people thought that the attack on Southaven was just a skirmish or to simply carry off supplies they were soon mistaken. Those men not slaughtered and who were deemed most useful (or had put up the best fight) were imprisoned and taken away on the first fleet of boats no doubt to the north.

The second arrivals though less cruel certainly knew all about the land as they went from town to town, village to village, dealing with any resistance they found. Not that there was much, most of the leaders of Codencia Minor had been in Southaven during the attack and those left behind had no appetite for fighting. New town councils were set up, each headed by one of the Northmen as the army which had steadily grown stronger and stronger with more men arriving daily by boat moved further South East towards the gap in the mountains which led to Codencia itself. Clearly this had been long in the planning and the attack on Codencia Minor was no doubt to create a second front in a possible war against Codencia further inland at the other side of the mountain range.

Chapter 8

Reva sighed as she sat on her own one late autumn afternoon. Carig had been away for some months now and though she had missed him for his company on the long evenings especially, Celeste had more than made up for his absence with her help around their small home. Nothing seemed to much trouble for this girl and even when Reva herself slipped into more depressive moods she would be naturally be brought out of it simply by Celeste's innocent yet enthusiastic view of the world. Only the night before she had declared

'It's my guess that the mountain has stopped exploding now and father and the rest of the men will have cleaned all the village up, in fact, I bet that the place is even nicer now than it was before'

No word had come from Carig for a few weeks and though old tales would imply *'no news is good news'* she didn't believe it for a minute. In her mind, *'no news meant bad news'* that had always been her own experience.

'Mother' she continued, 'when we go back can I have my own animal to care for?'

'When we go back………' Reva had thought, 'when would that be?'

She hadn't answered Celeste she now realised as she thought to the events of the night before, 'well she hadn't pushed it so it couldn't be a major issue', she thought, in truth she didn't want any animal in the house, as she already had one, and she smiled grimly as she thought of her husband, probably up to his neck in ash. She wondered idly where Celeste was, as she had been out for a few hours, not that she could come to much harm here so long as she kept away from the cliffs. She had spoken to her dozens of times about the danger of the cliff-side and what would happen if she fell onto the rocks below. Celeste would smile politely in apparent agreement, but deep down Reva knew where her child probably was. At eight years old she was fiercely independent, with an inquisitive mind, the problem was she had no friends around here; they were quite secluded with no other family for a half a league along the coastal path. So then danger became her best friend in the absence of Bracen and she seemed to have this fascination with wild-life, birds especially, and more worryingly the ones specifically which lived on the cliff-side.

Of course not much later Celeste came back perfectly safe and just a little hungry and Reva forgot all about her concerns whilst they both busied themselves with the evening meal

'Tomorrow we must go to Lifey to the market, supplies are getting low' said Reva to her daughter

In truth, they still had a reasonable amount of food in the house but Reva needed company and some adult communication. Money wasn't too tight, she still had some left from her mother's property sale, but she knew it wouldn't last forever and she ought to give some thought to selling trinkets on the market. There were plenty of stones and shells at the bottom of the cliffs and she could make bracelets and necklaces for market. She couldn't support them both on what she would make but it would certainly add to the dwindling money pot. Reva had decided too that the market gave her an opportunity to look at any competition and to sea what kinds of prices they were charging. Clearly she would have to be more competitive having no reputation or experience to fall back upon.

The next morning dawned clear and sunny and they made their way to the market early it was only an hour's ride. Celeste was certainly of a mind to find other children to play with and she wasn't disappointed as there were many there. She waved nonchalantly at her mother who had told her to meet at the stalls selling fruit at midday.

Reva walked around the market, comparing prices, making an occasional necessary purchase. She sensed some tension in the air but couldn't put her finger on why that should be. She listened too; this was a good way of gathering news since they were so secluded. However on this morning she wasn't prepared for what she heard.

Many women were at a meat seller's stall who was auctioning his stock. It was a good place to gather, even for those not intending to spend. Reva's curiosity was piqued when she heard the name Southaven; here at last was some news from home.

A woman was explaining events at Southaven to her astonished friend, who could find nothing to say just than the predictable 'you don't say' or 'nooooooo' in apparent defiance of what she was hearing.

Grabbing the woman's arm just a little too roughly she demanded

'What is it you have heard?'

The woman informed Reva that she had ridden south from the borders to get away from the trouble in Codencia Minor; apparently the port of Southaven had been ransacked by men from the north, some kind of invasion. People were fleeing to Codencia in the hope they could find sanctuary there.

'Did you hear anything about my village Lendel?' asked Reva with obvious concern

'Lendel?' asked the woman shaking her head, 'no I have not heard of that place'

'What else has happened?' Reva asked

The woman told her that the invasion had carried on for some weeks; many people in Southaven had been killed. The invaders had spread throughout Condencia Minor but had not carried on their slaughter. Now they were taking over established villages and towns, establishing their own control. The woman also added that she had heard much of the continent was at war, that Midencia had nearly been completely overrun and the only apparent safe place for now was Codencia itself.

Reva was now really worried about her hot-headed and strong-willed husband.

'Do you think they will come here' she asked the other woman

'No that's the strange thing' she answered. 'The Northmen seem to have overrun both Midencia and Codencia Minor but when they got to the river at the Gap of Dyn, they seem to have stopped.

Without thanking the woman Reva turned and left looking for Celeste, she wasn't hard to find being one of the loudest of children. She found her pinning an unfortunate ten year old boy to the ground who had the audacity to claim boys were tougher than girls. Calling to Reva who looked up somewhat disappointedly at her mother released the boy at her mother's insistence

'Why are we going early?' asked Celeste

'We are not yet' answered Reva, 'I must find a way of getting a letter to Lendel'

Celeste frowned and asked 'Has something happened to Father?'

'No silly, I just want to find out how things are going there' she lied

She found the market office and the officer in charge regretted that there would be no post outriders going into Codencia Minor this week, probably not even this month considering the trouble reported there. Reva quickly scribbled on a piece of parchment available for such purposes and addressed it to Lendel, the High Elder of the village with her own address on the rear of the letter for its response

She looked at the officer seriously, 'this is important, please make sure it goes at the first opportunity!'

Chapter 9

Reva didn't expect a letter for a couple of weeks at least, but when nothing arrived inside a month she started to worry. Another month went by with no news then one early winter morning about four weeks before the winter solstice there was a knock on her door and a letter was pushed under the frame.

Reva, walked to the door and looked at the letter on the mat, reaching down she picked it up, she could hardly bring herself to open it, her hands were shaking as she realised her heart was racing and she had broken out into a cold sweat.

She opened the letter; someone's fair hand had news to report.

She took the letter over to her chair and sat down, and read

For the attention of Reva Archer
Salint Bay
Salint
Codencia

Dear Reva

I have sad news to impart. The clean up operation went as planned for some weeks after all the men had returned. One evening the Elders received a letter, summoning them to a council in Southaven. The scroll had told us that there was trouble throughout much of the continent, old hostilities had been rejoined and that Midencia had begged Codencia to honour their traditional alliance. The council was to discuss our response; the emergency government was invoked to make important decisions since clearly Codencia would expect us to provide whatever men we could for the cause. Lendel took Carig and Naiden with him to council.

One night, as you may have heard, the port was attacked and conquered by men from the north who then spread throughout the land. One of their kind is now the High Elder here and none of the other Elders dare breathe a word of opposition. I am risking much sending you this letter and I had to secretly have it scribed and sent by someone who still remains loyal to me.

News is confusing and sometimes contradictory but it is clear these Northmen had been spying out our land for a long time and knew exactly when to attack the port when all the government was there. Clearly someone within our country was a betrayer and whoever that might have been should be cursed for eternity.

However, clearly you will want news of your husband. I am afraid to report I have only a little and I cannot be absolutely certain that what I have heard is the actual truth. We know Lendel was killed in the attack as were all the Elders of every town and village, the Northmen knew exactly who they were and where to look for them, Carig it would appear from some reports I have been given was taken prisoner but nothing has been heard of Naiden. They have both been scribed as missing in the Elders book. All we do know is that some people were carried off back north if they were thought to be useful, my hope is that both Naiden and Carig are still alive, though I have no way of knowing.

Reva, don't come back here, it isn't safe yet, though the villages and towns seem quiet we heard reports of mass raping of women in Southaven when the attack occurred.

I am fortunate, as in my position I do get to hear what is going on, and obviously the new Elder needs people around him whom the villages still trust. From what I can gather the Northmen's lines of communication and supplies are stretched and they will go no further this year, preferring to consolidate their gains. This only leaves Codencia and the most southern part of Midencia still free.

Stay safe Reva, if I hear anything further about Carig's whereabouts I will try and get word to you

Yours in haste

Pallos (2nd Elder)

Reva was stunned, her worst fears confirmed, taking the letter she threw it on the fire, Celeste was too young to understand and she didn't want Celeste reading the contents. What to actually tell Celeste was going to prove difficult but she must tell her something as even children playing will talk of the outside world and that kind of information was open to exaggeration with the worst possible scenarios. Everything in her life had gone wrong, first her mother, then the volcano, now the news of Carig. She didn't feel like she could carry on with this life.

Though carry on she must but she couldn't find the courage to talk to Celeste that day or even the next, in fact a number of days went by as Reva decided it was best to stay secluded and not go to market. Deep down however she knew what she must do no matter how much it hurt, better to hear it from her mother than from some random stranger. It was better not to have the child's hopes dashed at some later stage so what she told her now must be final. That night, by the fire side, Reva indicated to Celeste that she wanted to talk.

Holding both her hands and looking at her beautiful daughter she said

'Celeste, I have something to say that is going to upset you, I want to tell you its ok to cry, because not all tears are a bad thing'

Celeste looked at her mother with her big brown eyes shining in the firelight and asked 'What is it, are you ill?'

Squeezing her hands tightly Reva explained, 'no it's not me I want to talk about, it's your father'

'Is he coming back?' asked Celeste excitedly ignoring the warning from her mother that it was bad news.

'No he isn't, he won't ever be coming back' cried Reva as she broke down in front of her eight year old daughter, 'Celeste my darling, the news I have to tell you is that you father is dead, killed in Southaven in the summer'

Celeste gave no reaction; she stood up and went to the door as if half expecting to see her father walking down the path. She opened the door and looked out and then back at her mother who was crying, her body hunched over and shaking with her head sobbing into her hands. Celeste walked over to her mother and put her small arms around her, hugging her tightly.

The next morning they both rose later than normal, the emotion having made Reva over-tired, Celeste because she had spent much of the night comforting her mother. Over a small breakfast, Reva told Celeste a little of what she knew, sufficient to keep her informed but not enough to scare her.

'This war….. Does that mean it will spread even to us?' she asked

Reva wasn't expecting this, she had thought Celeste's first questions would be about what had happened to her father, but no……..it was for the two of them she appeared concerned

Let's hope not' said Reva trying to smile at her worried daughter, 'maybe we are far enough south not to concern those fighting!'

They talked for a while, Celeste asking why men fought each other, who the Northmen were, what invasion meant? A whole topic of conversation, not once did she mention her father.

Time went on, mid-winter passed and still Celeste would ask nothing of her father who she had loved so dearly and had been such an important part of her life. Reva guessed she was just blocking the pain out and it would surface eventually. Life carried on; there was no further word from Pallos so obviously he had heard nothing further.

On New Years night Reva told Celeste that Salint was going to be their permanent home and they wouldn't ever be returning to Lendel. Celeste hadn't even looked up from her food and gave no answer, there were still no tears, no tantrums, in fact nothing, no kind of reaction at all. Inside though the now nine year old girl was hurting...…hurting for her father…..hurting for her bereaved mother…..hurting for her friend Bracen who she now believed she would never see again.

She wouldn't cry though, she had sworn it to herself on the day her father had left.

Part 3

......the forgotten tasks

Chapter 1

Celeste was fourteen, nearly fifteen years old and already as tall as most men. Her figure had blossomed but her strength clearly evident. She was a good head taller than her mother, who had accepted the advancing of the years gracefully, even though it meant not hiding the inevitable specks of grey in her hair. She believed she had brought Celeste up well and though her schooling had been basic, Reva had tried her best and her daughter could read and write and had enough skills to calculate money matters, which in truth was about much as most ordinary people hereabouts attained.

Celeste had carried on with her love of the wild, she had turned bird watching into a hobby and this revealed a more gentle side to her nature. Just below the surface though was Celeste, Carig's daughter and her temper could be violent and mood swings unexplainable, certainly more than could be explained by the onset of puberty two years previously

She had taken to carrying a sword which had belonged to Carig, the Gods only knew why, since there was little immediate danger around here, it was almost as if she had nominated herself her mother's protector, and wherever Celeste went, the sword went with her.

Elsewhere in the world the initial onslaught by the Northmen had abated and all of Midencia was now free again and acting as a buffer to the North from the occasional skirmishes. Only in Codencia Minor had they really maintained their occupation, and apparently life went on there much as it had in the past. Apparently it was a different clan of the Northmen who had settled after the initial invasion and they were less aggressive and war-like though no one would want to test their fortitude in battle. Reva had received the occasional letter from Pallos but the last one had been more than twelve months previously. She had long stopped expecting to hear anything about Carig and now half believed her own tale to Celeste that he had been killed during the invasion. She shivered inwardly as she reminded herself that Codencia Minor was only three days hard riding away and the ever present threat of Northmen was still there. Most of Codencia had stayed in a state of semi-military preparedness however though little of this reached Reva's ears on the coast and what she did hear she truthfully did not want to know. She wanted nothing to spoil her increasingly idyllic life with the teenage Celeste.

At the same time Celeste was striding confidently on the cliff top some distance from her home, she had been watching the gulls on the cliff-side and had been amused to observe seals playing in the sea. Only the previous year she had seen dolphins but when she had told her mother she was dismissive as if it didn't matter. 'She could be such a bore when she wanted' Celeste had mused

She had made up her mind to go no further that day, certainly the wind was in a southerly direction and she could see on the horizon that a possible storm might be approaching. It looked some distance away and she could vaguely make out the noise of an occasional rumble of thunder far in the distance.

Then she heard something else, the squawking of a bird she thought. She strode towards the cliff edge and peered over, she could see nothing but the ever present gulls but she could still hear the other distinctive sound. Quickly looking around the fern at the side of the path she saw movement. Kneeling down she saw the bird, it appeared to be a young falcon, probably in its first year, but it was clearly injured and Celeste wondered what kind of bird could possible hurt a falcon. She picked up the bird gently and spoke to the poor hurt creature

'Now then little one, where is your mother and who has hurt you so?'

Celeste wouldn't have known that the youngster would have been old enough to have flown the nest some weeks previously or that it had fallen prey to an attack from another older mating falcon. Clearly one of its claws looked damaged and one wing was bloodied and the bird seemed unable to move it.

Celeste emptied the contents of her bag onto the floor, the shells and stones she had been collecting for her mother could be taken back another time. Gently placing it in her open bag she strode of in the direction of her home, constantly checking the bird was still breathing. Celeste knew from its dark blue head and wings with it speckled chest it must be a female, she had of course seen many such falcons over the years on the cliff side and smiled at the memory of the falcon she had seen with her father when they had gone to visit the Geyser of Dyn. A small tinge of regret welled up inside her chest, she had not given enough thought to her father recently, her mother had always maintained he was dead, but how could she had known for sure? Still one thing was obvious; he had never some back so something awful must have happened to him. Shuddering at the thought of her father dead somewhere in an un-marked grave or worse still a rotten carcass being eaten by vultures without any kind of honour, she again turned her attention away from the memory of her long lost father to that of the bird.

Reva was less impressed when Celeste showed her the contents of her bag.

'What in all the gods names are you going to do with that' she had asked

'She is going to be my pet' answered Celeste

'But you don't know anything about keeping a wild bird' she replied

It was only that night, alone in bed, that Reva had realised the significance of the find, Carig's first task at the naming and tasking ceremony all those years ago had been to tame the untameable! How could he have known? She knew that he had claimed some degree of foresight as a result of the various and confusing dreams he suffered whilst she had been pregnant with Celeste, but she had put the named tasks down to Carig's exhaustion at the time. She had certainly never spoken to him about it after that particular evening.

She tried to remember back to the events of that night, what had the second task been? She thought for a minute then remembered...... *to prove herself a man*, she laughed to herself at the reaction of the villages at the time who believed Carig to be drunk or worse still taken leave of his senses, still she had to admit to herself that she had absolutely no idea what the second task might actually mean. She smiled inwardly at the memories of a time when their love had been secure and life all seemed so promising. Her expression changed and her heart sank as she remembered the third task *'to follow her father's path'* but if Carig was indeed dead as she suspected that could only mean one thing! Why would a father say such things or wish it on his only child?

As much as she might try Reva could not remember the fourth task, not that it mattered, as far as she was concerned they were never going back to Lendel or Codencia Minor so Celeste would never see the Elders book or read the words. Celeste knew nothing about the tasks and Reva wanted it to remain that way.

Some months went by, little changed outwardly in their little house, Celeste had just passed her fifteenth birthday, and though she had no experience of falconry she had managed to feed her small friend and tend to her to such an extent that when she was clearly alright to fly away again to the cliff-side she had chosen to stay where she was. Some unexplainable connection had been made between them and the bird had even nested in the eaves of the small barn by the house they lived in which was unusual for a hunting bird to act so tamely. Celeste had for some reason named her Keri and she would fly to Celeste's arm with only a whistle or call of her name. She wouldn't move at all for Reva or anyone else for that matter, in fact Keri took a very dim view of any visitors calling to the house and would fly and screech overhead until Celeste called her off. It was a peculiar sight, a tall and imposing fifteen year old girl striding through the market with sword at her side and strange bird on her shoulder, but folks eventually got used to the spectacle and Celeste became a popular diversion on market day in Lifey, especially for the young men! All of whom wished to talk to her, but none dared!

Chapter 2

Vagril strolled along the ramparts to the castle, the Northmen, once such a threat, had predictably descended into clan warfare amongst themselves so much so that the threat of invasion had all but disappeared. It was true, this particular castle had held out longest against the Northmen, but in reality they had simply ignored it, pillaging the villages and towns of Midencia and preferring not to lay siege to any of its castles on the northern border. If rumours were correct Codencia Minor was still occupied, but that was far away, not as the bird fly's obviously, but the journey by foot or horse would take much longer, around the mountain to the Gap of Dyn and then up into the coastal state.

He knew in the past, he had been a scourge on that small land, but he put that down to the singular aggressive nature of most men in their twenty's. He had however earned a good living as a mercenary and fortune had always smiled upon him in battle. His only son was the result of a rather distasteful rape of an unsuspecting woman in some forsaken place whose name he couldn't remember. He was surprised as anyone when he was presented with a young child a year later when he had ridden back through the town. His mercenary friends thought he had gone mad when he accepted the charge of the child, but something within him had stirred a fathers pride no doubt. As he remembered his past he subconsciously fingered the pendant he wore round his neck. He had been told it was called Obsidian, not that he cared what its name was, he just adored its smooth texture against his skin. He polished this trinket daily until it shone like a diamond.

His son was now a man in his own right and didn't know the details of his mother only that she had died during child-birth. Vagril himself had abandoned his mercenary ways and became a more than respectable community leader in Castletown in the north of Midencia. Ultimately he had married into money and titles and now the imposing castle overlooking the town was his after his wife's father had passed away.

Vagril and son had lived within the castle for many years, firstly as an advisor and counsellor to the incumbent lord and then as a lord in his own right through marriage. This marriage had produced no further children and Vagril was justifiably sure it was his wife who was in fact barren.

He had much to think about this day. His son was going to reach his thirtieth birthday whilst Vagril would celebrate his fifty third. They shared birthdays since Vagril hadn't the faintest notion of when his son's birthday actually was.

His son was out on the plains hunting, he had a keen eye and good aim and though not as good with a sword as Vagril it was said he could shoot the eye from a deer at one hundred paces. It was a gift to be sure, nothing you could teach someone, but it brought him some fame by his own right and also out of the shadow of his father Vagril. He was popular with the ladies and had yet taken no wife, though he seemed secure in his own manhood since he had no end of opportunities with the fairer sex

Vagril made his way down to the keep and confidently strolled out of the castle towards the local town. He had business to take care of and celebrations to plan. He relished in the fact that he was still a man's man, and could drink freely with the men in town. Though he was a lord he didn't necessarily have to act the part. The truth was he was more at home in the Inns than in the castle with all that falseness and finery. The walk to town was only five minutes and Vagril liked to walk briskly, he had put on far too much weight in the comfort of the castle and this was one of his few opportunities for exercise.

A shadow moved from behind a tree as Vagril passed, stealthily it moved, quietly tracking the steps of the unsuspecting man still beneath the eaves of the tree but almost parallel, just a few steps back from where Vagril was striding. As he approached the bridge over the river which flowed through the town from north to south, two men stepped out from behind a cart which was blocking the way over. Vagril frowned, still not suspecting the very worst which could happen nevertheless was sensible enough to at least unsheathe his sword. His soon-to-be assailants did likewise, but unless they were both very good Vagril was confident, he had taken on two people in sword fights before and come out on top and age hadn't slowed him down just yet. Gripping the hilt of his sword he pointed it straight at the approaching men. Both had their swords out, their stance and defence looked weak and their reach and their swords were not as long as his.

'Come on then bastards' he growled 'give me your best'

Vagril stumbled forward as he felt a keen pain in his back, too late he realised he had been assailed from the rear as well, the knife was deep, the pain excruciating as it had crashed through his ribs and into his lungs. Three men stood over him as he lay prone on the ground blood seeping from beneath his cloak

One of them put a sword to his face as he laboured to breath through the pain.

'Revenge is sweetest for those who have long tasted the bitterness of regret' said one of the men as he ran his sword against Vagril's cheek

'What is it you want', gasped Vagril. 'Whatever it is I have the power to deliver'

'Death' replied the man, he pulled the pendant from the neck of Vagril and pierced him through the heart with his sword.

There was no further sound and no one approaching the bridge from either side. The men pushed the cart down into the river and then quickly and expertly beheaded the stricken Vagril and placed his head on a stake at the side of the road before disappearing quietly into the night.

It was some minutes later those in the castle and those in the town heard a woman scream.

Chapter 3

When the next letter came from Pallos, Reva was extremely surprised to hear from him. Nothing had been heard from Lendel for a few years and even Celeste had stopped talking about the place.

She had returned home in the afternoon to find the note under her door. She recognised the style of script immediately. Surely after all these years Pallos couldn't be writing about news of Carig. She got up and looked outside to see if Celeste was about, even now she felt protective towards her daughter though in reality she knew just who was protecting whom. Celeste was eighteen after all and quite formidable too.

'I'm forty two and couldn't possibly still have the feelings of a twenty four year old' she thought, if that was true however, why was she shaking and so nervous about opening the letter?

Again as before, she sat down in the chair by the fire and read.

Reva Archer
Salint Bay
Salint
Codencia

Dear Reva

I feel so guilty about not writing to you sooner, if there had been anything to report then of course I would have done. The truth is I am still no wiser about what happened to your husband all those years ago.

I can almost imagine you thinking 'then why is he writing now?'

No man could ever consider writing to you a waste of time Reva but on this occasion it is village business which concerns me and the High Elder, (yes it's still the same northman, actually little has changed and our new overlords are not much different to the old one's, historians might point that out as inevitable).

However I digress, the reason for writing is legal and must be dealt with by you with as much speed as possible.

It is nearly ten years since you left Lendel and throughout all that time your house has remained empty. I have personally seen to it that the place should not be disturbed, but legally now, under the present law, any house which remains unoccupied for ten years and a day becomes vacant and the property with all its belongings made ready for auction.

The law is clear and there is little I can do about this matter. I would imagine the place has some worth and though I do not know, and furthermore have no wish to know your financial status I am sure the funds from the sale of this property might see you through to old age.

I have to, by law give you six-weeks notice of the impending sale, presuming this letter takes the usual length of time to get to you then I guess at most you have a month to make up your mind and to return to claim you own if you so wish.

From a personal point of view it would be nice to see you and little Celeste, this month is the mid-summer fair once again so the village will be busy. I will of course allocate you as much time as you need if you decided to return and afford you the necessary legal representation

Yours sincerely

Pallos (2nd Elder)

Again Reva burned the letter, but she knew she was going to have to tell Celeste the truth sooner or later. Pallos had been right, money was indeed tight and the sale of the house in Lendel was necessary. There was nothing for it other than to do exactly what Pallos had suggested; she would have to go with Celeste to Lendel and soon at that. She decided she would tell Celeste some of the story when she came in but not the parts mentioning her father. She wasn't ready for that conversation just yet. She made up her mind, they would go to Lendel on the week of the mid-summer fair, with all the additional people there for the celebrations her arrival shouldn't cause that much of a stir after all these years.

Not long afterwards Celeste came into the house and took off her scabbard and placed it by the fire. No doubt she had been out with Keri again along the cliff tops, where one went inevitably so did the other. Satisfied the bird must by now be in the barn Reva said to Celeste.

'I have some news from Lendel'

'Father?' questioned Celeste

'No' replied Reva, 'it's from Pallos and concerns our old house. It seems by the new law of the land any unoccupied house will be sold by auction if not reclaimed after ten years'

'Let me see the letter' demanded Celeste

'Oh I'm sorry' her mother replied, 'I have thrown it on the fire, I never thought'

Celeste looked at her mother suspiciously, never once had she ever seen any of the letters which had periodically come from Pallos over the years, her mother always destroying them before she got chance to read.

'What are you hiding mother?' she asked

Hiding…..hiding, what do you mean girl?' answered Reva without much conviction

'Always you burn those letters, I am eighteen now, not a little girl!' declared Celeste

Reva looked at her daughter and thought to herself that she found it hard to remember now when Celeste was indeed a little girl; she had been taller than her for about five years and certainly took her physical strength and strength of character from her father's side.

'Celeste, don't be angry' she pleaded, 'all I ever wanted to do was protect you and I thought that hearing news from home whilst you were growing up might unsettle you and cause you unnecessary pain'

Celeste relaxed a little at this and Reva took the opportunity to explain her version of events in the letter.

'We must go back to Lendel for a short time; Pallos has agreed to look after us whilst we are there and will give me the necessary advice about how to proceed legally. It will be a break for you Celeste, you have been secluded here for long enough, its time you met with people you own age'

Celeste nodded, maybe it would be an adventure, and she wondered what had happened to her friend Bracen after all these years and whether he still lived in the village. She wondered too about his parents Cirard and Leadel who had always been so kind to her.

'Right' she announced. 'It is agreed then, but I will be taking my sword and my bird with me,'

Reva sighed loudly 'Do you think that is really necessary?'

'Always' replied Celeste,....... 'always!'

Celeste took leave of her mother and went to the barn, opening the door she didn't need to call or whistle Keri flew straight down onto her arm.

'Well my friend, we are to make a journey, to where I was born, I am hoping you will come too, but I cannot demand it of you!' exclaimed Celeste

Keri of course could not answer, but hopped further up her arm onto her shoulder which Celeste took as an indication she had indeed understood.

Celeste continued 'we are going to somewhere where they don't understand birds like I do and people may be frightened of you, so I think it is best for you to follow, you keep your distance, and beware of archers, you would be a trophy to some youngster if he could shoot you down. Stay in sight Keri for my heart tells me I am going to need you before the end'

The next day Reva went alone to Lifey to obtain a travel permit, even now there was distrust of the Northmen occupying Codencia Minor though there had been no incursions from there since the initial invasion. Both sides had border guards and both sides had more men posted by each side of the river than was really necessary. Still an uneasy balance was maintained.

Reva sat across from the Superintendent, who had no doubt been give her application to travel some minutes previously. Typical for an official he had kept her waiting past the appointed hour and motioned for her to sit down without saying a word. Ten minutes of uncomfortable silence ensued as the officer scribed on official scrolls, taking another from the stack on his left hand side he proceeded to make a spelling alteration, a marginal notation then placed the scroll on the right before pick up another. Reva had decided that due reverence had been satisfied and it was now time to speak, but as the thought occurred to her the officer looked up and said.

'I have you application to travel' he hesitated as he looked down again to check he had her name right, 'Mistress Archer. You will take with you one Celeste Archer, you wish to travel to Codencia Minor, is this correct?'

'Yes' she replied, not seeing any reason to further expand on the conversation

'May I ask why you wish to travel' asked the officer

'You may, but I reserve the right not to tell you' said Reva

The officer, who no doubt had many similar conversations in the past, put the application down and looked directly at her.

'Mistress Archer, that indeed is you right, but it is also my right to ask questions and decide who gains travel permits and who doesn't, now if you prefer to waste my time, then I must ask you to leave for I have work to attend to.'

Reva had no choice but to apologise

'Your pardon Superintendant, sometimes people take seriously that which was only meant in jest, I have been told I have a peculiar sense of humour. The truth is I make the visit because I have property there which has to be claimed by that country's law, and also it is the birthplace of my daughter and she is keen to revisit the land of her father'

'So' said the Superintendant, 'when the sale of your property goes through you will have to pay tax to their government?'

Reva frowned, she hadn't thought of this.

'I suppose that will be the case,' she said wondering where this line of questioning was taking her, 'and no doubt be forced to pay for the legal representation too' she added as she shook her head sadly.

The Superintendant looked on without emotion and then replied

'That is not the end of your woes I am afraid Mistress Archer, the money you make from your purchase will be taxed here too and you will be asked to provide a statement of all your dealings there'

Reva nodded in agreement, she was now eager to end this ordeal and get back to Salint with the permits. Why had she mentioned the sale of the house, why hadn't she just said it was to visit friends? She reproached herself for her apparent stupidity.

'It is done' the officer handed Reva the document without looking up.

Celeste though was beside herself in anger when Reva told her what had transpired in Lifey.

'You should have taken me with you' she said 'I wouldn't have let him talk to you like that; he would have tasted the sheen of my blade'

'This is precisely why you didn't go Celeste. You may think you are adamant and strong willed, you may believe quite rightly that you are a match for any man, however the one thing you lack is tact. You must learn to be more politic.

'Being diplomatic has cost you much mother, maybe you are not as shrewd as you think you are!' observed Celeste

Chapter 4

It was a dull morning, raining and most un-summer like, when they set off for Codencia Minor, the border was only three days gentle riding away then another half day to Lendel. They would as a result of this arrive at the village when the fair was in full swing and so Reva hoped they would be able to remain anonymous for a time.

She looked at Celeste riding alongside her. She had her father's sword of course but there was no sign of the bird, though she had no doubt it would be tracking Celeste's every movement.

She could hunt as well as any man and was very skilful with the bow so Reva had no worries about being hungry on the journey. Her main concern was at being seen as two women riding alone and thus vulnerable, she had no doubts Celeste was very capable but her hot-headed nature was likely to invite trouble rather than avoid it.

Reva smiled at her daughter who hadn't noticed her mothers gaze. She was so powerful in her gait but she also displayed assets which most men would find irresistible. Her breasts were large but firm and she always showed far too much cleavage to Reva's mind. She always wore her leather skirt, way too short. Celeste even from being a little girl had maintained that this was because of the warm temperature but Reva suspected it was more than that nowadays. The thought occurred to her that Celeste might find a man whilst in Lendel but then reproached herself with almost immediately that she would frighten half the men with her strength and the other half would be intimidated by her obvious sexuality. It was going to take on special kind of person to tame her girl!

The journey proved uneventful and the days cleared to leave a more familiar dry and arid feeling, Reva now noticed Keri high up in the sky as she followed their movements. Eventually they came to the top of a small hill; there laid out before them was the Gap of Dyn. They had seen the spur of the mountain range from some distance off of course, but the whole river valley was a welcome sight after so long.

Within minutes they had reached the Codencian side of the bridge which crossed the river to the north. Reva showed the official documentation to one of the guards who let her thought without question. Riding onto the bridge Reva said to Celeste,

'Nothing silly Celeste, keep your sword where it is and let's please try and get through without incident

On the other side of the river five Northmen guards were stationed at the bridge end, it was a hot day and this posting was tedious. Checking people in and out of the land wasn't their idea of soldiery.

Heglin had been in Codencia Minor since the week after the invasion and had now settled well as most people had. He had taken no wife, the black haired olive skinned residents here were not his taste, and he much preferred the pale blondes of his homeland. Still there occasional opportunities for fun and he was still fairly young after all. These were his thoughts as he saw the two women approaching from the other side of the bridge. One was clearly middle-aged but the other was a sight to behold as she rode confidently towards him. The other men too had noticed the women especially the tall and extremely attractive young one who now was only a few paces away.

Reining her horse in Reva handed over the scroll to be checked, it all looked official and correct to their obviously disappointment, still Heglin was in the mood for some sport he had bored soldiers to deal with and planned to play these mice before he let them go.

'Get down from your horses' he commanded

Without a word both slipped out of their saddles to the floor below

'Is there a problem' asked Reva as she gripped her daughters arm with some reassurance.

'That remains to be seen' answered Heglin

He stood in front of Celeste who was taller even than he was, then moved to her horse, he had a stick, some kind of cane and he put the tip of the cane under the scabbard and lifted it to see more.

'Interesting toy for a young lady' he observed 'I wonder if she wants to play' he said to amuse his friends

Reva's grip tightened on Celeste's arm

Heglin ran the tip of his cane up and down the front of Celeste as she stood without a word; he paused as it reached her cleavage with was now glistening with sweat

'Well silent one, you look very impressive, but have no tongue to match your stature' he sneered

'Since you don't have a tongue, maybe you would like to experience mine' he said as he leered at her body. He traced the cane down the front of her body and let it rest on her inner thigh. The other men laughed loudly and one of them said,

'Heglin, give her to me, I can give her more than she could possibly take'

Still Celeste said nothing and stared straight ahead.

'Is that right' he laughed in Celeste's face, 'you think you could accommodate Sela or a few other Northmen today?'

Celeste was motionless whilst the insults and sexual taunts continued. All were aimed at her whilst Reva clung on to her daughter arm.

Eventually the men became bored since neither wanted to engage in what was after all just harmless fun. They wouldn't dare pursue that kind of activity whilst on duty. Satisfied he had shaken the two women sufficiently, the smaller and eldest one had looked terrified throughout, he gave the scroll back and said

'You can go'

Without a word they mounted their horses, after around a furlong out Keri flew down from where she had observed proceeding unnoticed and landed on Celeste's shoulder. They galloped off without a word.

Later they made camp for the night and Reva worried that her daughter hadn't spoken at all since the crossing said,

'Celeste, I was really proud of you back there, you showed your true strength'

'That may be true', answered Celeste, 'but taking that man's insolence was the hardest thing I have ever had to do in my life'

It was early afternoon the next day when they finally came into view of Lendel, to Reva's eyes it didn't appear to have changed much at all, to Celeste, it was only a place of dim memory, she could remember some faces of girls and boys of her age group and people like Cirard, Leadel and Naiden their neighbour of course. Her memories other than that were quite lost in time and the bustling fair below promised some excitement.

Celeste spoke quietly to Keri

'Fly my friend; I am safe here, but not too far where you cannot hear my call'

The Falcon immediately flew up in the sky and almost out of sight. Eventually Celeste couldn't see her bird but had no doubt that Keri had far better vision and would have no problems identifying Celeste even from high up in the sky.

They rode into town, unannounced and for the most part unseen, though some did stop to wonder who the impressive young lady was who had the confidence and bearing of a man.

Chapter 5

They were housed in Pallos's rather too grand accommodation, he had obviously fared well under the new over-lords and Celeste and Reva had both been placed in separate guest rooms.

Celeste had never experienced anything so lavish and it made her feel a little uneasy

Pallos had greeted them again the morning after their arrival and broke his fast with them. It was agreed he would spend a few hours sorting out the legal formalities with Reva before organising an auction on her behalf for some time after the mid-summer fair. He apologised he couldn't dedicate more time to them but this was an important time of the year for the village.

Celeste decided the legal formalities of a house sale were not for her and decided to have a look around the fair. Memories started to come back as she saw familiar stalls, familiar sights and familiar smells. She overheard a conversation, apparently the wrestling competition was today and she was eager to go and watch, not only for the obvious attraction of semi-naked men rolling about in the mud but more because it had been a place where she and Bracen would often play fight when they were younger, pretending to be in the competition. She decided too after the event she would go and see if Cirard's business was still there. She had quite forgotten to ask Pallos about her friend amidst all the comfort and splendour of his home. She would have to ask however because she had no clear recollection of where it was.

Pushing her way through the crowded fair she eventually came to the small arena where the young men would wrestle. The competition had already started and the first couple of rounds were obviously sorting out the real contenders from those who had been told to fight simply because it was their duty to do so.

She didn't notice the muddied defeated young man make his way from the arena after round one directly to where she was standing. Moving through the crowd he approached Celeste from the rear.

'I don't believe it' a voice said behind her

She looked around to find a tall but wiry youth stood grinning at her.

'Celeste!' he declared, 'unless my eyes are deceiving me'

Celeste smiled, 'You have me at a disadvantage sir' she said as she pretended not to know who he was.

When his shoulders dropped ever so slightly she put out her arms and pulled him towards her. Gripping him way too tightly she said

'Nice to see you again, my old sparring partner'

Bracen laughed, 'alright alright, if you would prefer it to breaking my ribs, you could accompany me back home, so I can report my predictable defeat to my father, seeing you might assuage his disappointment in me, Mother too will be delighted after all this time!'

'Later' agreed Celeste, 'let us watch the competition first, I am enjoying the spectacle!'

She linked arms with his and smiled, Bracen too was grinning, and if his friend could see him now arm in arm with this rather impressive beauty they would be insanely jealous!

The competition wore on as the men fought bravely in most cases. Bracen and Celeste shared tales of their childhood each recalling long forgotten episodes the other had not remembered, the morning turned into afternoon as the warm sun beat down on the excited crowd. Eventually in the early afternoon it finally came to the final, it looked to be a foregone conclusion as one of the largest young men, apparently from Oakenvale, had easily beaten all before him, his finalist opponent had a much tougher journey through the competition and already looked hurt and bloodied. Predictably the bout only lasted minutes as the exhausted man conceded.

The victors arm was raised and he was presented with the tigers head

'Who would deny the right of this young man to be crowned champion?' asked referee

No one spoke, until Celeste stepped forward and said,

'He hasn't beaten every eighteen year old in the village'

People looked around and some gasped as the impressive young woman confidently stepped into the ring

Bracen tried to pull her back but she let go of his arm dismissively.

'I would fight you', she declared, 'if you don't mind losing to a girl'

The referee interjected, 'regulations dictate women are not allowed'

Celeste looked at him angrily and said,

'Rules are made to be challenged, and I reserve the right to challenge you now' she said to the mildly amused champion.

The referee had the sense to shut up without a further word

'Well' she said to the smiling man in front of her, 'can you take the challenge?'

'Sure, another few seconds out of my day won't be much difference' he laughed confidently.

Facing each other now they circled, he thought she certainly looked impressive, but still only a girl after all. He extended his arm to grasp at hers. Celeste quickly grabbed the arm and pulled him forward, over- balanced he stumbled forward onto his knees. Celeste retreated and said grimly 'Not a good start!'

The man looked up at her frowned and said to her (but more to the crowd),

'I simply lost my balance'

'Then lose it again' she declared as she quickly swept her left leg under his right tripping him to the ground,

This time she pounced on top of him, pinning him with her not inconsiderable weight, one arm was crushed beneath him so he was temporarily disadvantaged, but he was not crowned a champion for no reason and summoning his strength used his body weight to tip Celeste over, but she was far too quick. He had meant to roll back over on top, that way too pinning her in turn to the ground, but she had moved like a cat and was now stood above him whilst he grovelled vainly in the dust. This was ridiculous and he was now getting angry, which was precisely what Celeste wanted.

She taunted him, with hand on her hip asked

'My mother could defeat you!'

This enraged him still further and he lunged and tried to grab at her waist to ensure she couldn't slip away this time. Celeste expertly stepped to one side and delivered a well aimed blow to his back with her elbow as the man again over-balanced and fell forward. He got up from the ground quickly and roared as he charged.

Fortune might have turned against Celeste, as this time he managed to prevent her stepping away as he held on tightly to her belt, pulling her towards him he managed to get both arms around Celeste as he grappled with her, but the man clearly injured himself further in the ensuing fall and groaned in pain as they both hit the ground together

Celeste quickly to her feet asked if he conceded

The now bloodied champion was not going to be cowed so easily declared,' I can beat you with one arm'

Celeste again used the move she had used previously; taking his right leg from under him, as he fell to the floor she kicked his thigh and asked 'You going to fight me with one leg too?'

The man got back to his feet with a limp, he was being shown up by a woman and this could not be borne.

'Trial of strength' he declared

'As you wish' replied Celeste

They gripped hands each trying to bend the others wrist back to force them to their knees. She was strong, he had to admit, but he had never been beaten at this game and he was sure of the outcome. As their fingers intertwined to get a grip he increased the pressure in an attempt to break one or more of her fingers. He looked at the woman in front of him; she showed no reaction at all the more pressure he put on.

Then in a moment of horror he realised that she, a mere woman was bending his wrists back down, he would need to go down too to avoid his wrists been broken, in agony he looked up at the triumphant girl who was bearing down on him, further, further, further, until he could stand it no more. He dropped to his knees.

Celeste put her boot to his chest and he keeled over.

She spat with disdain as he lay on the floor and then told him

'I am more a man than you will ever be'

Bracen burst through the ring of spectators and came to her side; he desperately wanted to avoid any further confrontations. This man had been shown up in front of his peers and he knew what a wounded animal was capable of so pulling Celeste by the arm he insisted she follow him. Not fully understanding his urgency she allowed him to lead as he pulled her through the disbelieving crowd out towards the market, hurriedly following his footsteps through the stalls and circling the circumference of the fair, until at last they came to a familiar shop.

Surely this was Cirard's Apothecary? She paused in front of the shop breathing hard after the fight and flight.

Bracen sensed her question without it being asked

Yes it's still here' he said, 'and I am apprenticed to my father'.

Chapter 6

Celeste spent the afternoon with Cirard, Leadel and Bracen but eventually bid them goodnight, promising Bracen he could call for her the next day, she made her way through the streets towards the Pallos residence. The crowd had thinned somewhat after the market stall holders had put away the wares for the day. Most would be eating or drinking and the Inns would be full again. Celeste realised through the excitement she hadn't eaten since the morning breakfast and she would welcome some hot food from Pallos's well stocked larder.

When she reached her destination she found Reva waiting for her, she didn't look amused.

Celeste realised she had been out all of the day and her mother would have no doubt be worried so in an attempt to ease her mothers obvious anger started to tell her about her afternoon at Cirard's. Reva's expression didn't change as Celeste finished explaining her absence.

Finally she spoke

'Do you understand the word anonymous?' she demanded

Before Celeste could answer she continued

'I wanted to slip in and out of here unnoticed by as many people as possible and I wanted peace and quiet during my stay here, but now I will have neither. What were you thinking? The whole village and probably half of Codencia Minor now know about your antics today, how you wrestled a champion to the ground and made a laughing stock of the whole competition. People will be asking questions, wondering who you are, even your long-lost friends today will no doubt glory in your triumph and see no reason not to admit to knowing who you are, where you are from and who your father was'

'And why shouldn't they know?' asked Celeste, growing angry in her turn.

'Because I wished it' said Reva, 'have you no respect for your mothers wishes?'

'I would respect your wishes if they made any sense, why the secrecy, what is it about us that you wish to keep so quiet, and what has my long dead father got to do with anything?' shouted Celeste

'Enough' shouted back Reva, 'I will not allow such disrespectful behaviour, especially as we are guests here'

A dawning of realisation hit Celeste and she looked quizzically at her mother.

My father?...you know something of my father? What is it you are not telling me? she asked forcefully

Reva, turned around and walked back to her room

'Come with me Celeste' she said

Celeste stood motionless like a statue as she watched her mother enter her bedroom, her childhood with her father, memories now resurfacing. Finally she strode forward and entered the room. Reva was sat on the bed, she looked crestfallen, but Celeste was in no mood yet for reconciliation that could come later, for now she needed to know what her mother so obviously knew.

'Celeste, the day has arrived that I have dreaded for the last ten years, a day that I knew I would have to admit my secret and a day that I might possibly lose my daughter' Reva shook her head sadly.

'Go on' said Celeste

'Ten years ago, when we first moved to Salint, you remember? When the Helldyn erupted? Well your father went back to clean up the village with all the other men to make it habitable once more'

'I know all this' said Celeste

'Wait, I haven't finished,' interrupted Reva, 'your father went with Lendel to Southaven with Lendel to a council meeting and whilst he was there, an invasion occurred and the whole of Condencia Minor was overrun by the Northmen'

Celeste made as if to speak again but Reva carried on.

'Some months after this happened I received a letter from Pallos, the letter since destroyed, told that there was a possibility your father had been taken prisoner by the men from the north. The rumour was they took prisoners back to their homeland if they thought they might be useful. Your father was an expert archer, hence our name, so all these years I have lived a lie, pretending he was dead, to protect you my love. I thought that accepting his death would be easier than the uncertainty of not knowing where he was or indeed whether he was dead or alive. What else could I do?' wept Reva

'You might have told me sooner' glowered Celeste, 'this is unforgivable and I am too angry for words, in the morning we will speak of this again'

With that Celeste, turned and walked out of the room leaving her mother crushed and devastated on the bed

Celeste didn't sleep well that night, too much was whirling around in her head, half forgotten memories came and went but try as she might she couldn't get a clear picture of her fathers face, time had all but erased his image, but she recalled the love they had for each other, she recalled the time spent together, she even recalled the argument before leaving finally for Salint and the farewell a few days after. The next morning she stayed in her room, Bracen came and went without an explanation by Reva of Celeste's mood. Eventually Reva came to her, with food and a warm drink.

'I am still angry mother' she declared

'I know child, and you deserve to be' observed Reva

'I have made a decision, said Celeste,' when the mid summer fair is over and it is time to return to Salint; I won't be coming with you'

Reva's sad eyes looked at her daughter

'Is that it then, you punish me with revenge?'

'No I do not' argued Celeste,' I am not coming with you because I am going north, I need to find my father'

'Celeste, please think' pleaded her mother, 'he could be two thousand leagues away, across countries you have no experience of, over mountains and deserts, and he could be anywhere, if he is still alive at all.

'He is alive, I feel it in here' said Celeste as she tapped her chest 'and I will find him'.

'You will need to get permission from the High Elder to leave', said Reva with some resignation.

'I need nothing from anyone' replied Celeste,' now go, leave me alone, my decision is made!'

Reva did as instructed, this was hard, she was frightened, she didn't want to lose her daughter, but what could she do?

Celeste waited for a few minutes before quickly dressing; she stole out of the house without anyone knowing. She had to find Bracen, maybe he would understand, she needed someone to talk to, and she felt her whole world had just collapsed about her. She made her way to the scene of the competition the day before, fewer people were about and she quickly retraced her steps with Bracen back to the apothecary.

Leadel was apologetic, her son wasn't about, he had asked for the day off, maybe he was in the Bridge Inn. Thanking her for her kindness, Celeste made her way through the village to the Inn.

Pushing open the door she entered the smoke filled room, if she felt uncomfortable about being the only woman in there she didn't show it. Striding confidently up to the bar simply enquired 'Bracen?'

The Innkeeper motioned towards the corner where Bracen sat with a group of other young men who had abandoned their card game and were now glancing admirably across the crowded bar at her. They were then taken slightly aback when she strode over to where they were sat.

'Chair?' stammered one of them, 'Drink?'

'No I need Bracen' she said, motioning to Bracen with her first finger.

Bracen duly obliged to the obvious envy of his friends, men moved from their seats in the crowded bar in order to let her through as they made there way through the Inn towards the door outside.

'Bracen, we need somewhere to talk privately' she said as they left the Inn and into the street in front.

'What about the old dam just outside the village, remember, the one you always pretended to throw me in?

'I remember,' laughed Celeste

Few observing them could have known that amidst the laughter and genuine affection a decision was about to be made which would affect both their lives. They walked quickly arm in arm through the market and past all the stall-holders, villagers and visitors many of whom were pointing out Celeste as the young woman who had caused all the furore the day before, then out to the southern gate of the village. Turning left at the gate the followed the path of the river, up to the dam some six furlongs outside the gate

They arrived and both sat down. The place was peaceful, just a couple of children were playing at the north-side of the water so they would have their privacy. They sat for a moment in silence before Bracen ventured,

'Celeste, I called for you this morning but your mother indicated you couldn't be seen, and I went away confused. I had thought I had maybe said something or done something to upset you'

Celeste looked at her worrying friend and smiled.

'No Bracen, please do not concern yourself, our friendship has survived ten years separation, I will not abandon you without a word again!'

Bracen wondered if there was another hidden meaning in this reply, something she didn't want to admit to herself.

'What is it then?' he asked moving closer to her

Celeste relayed the story of what had happened the night previously and the conversation she had with her mother that morning.

Bracen listened intently to all that she said

'I must go' she said eventually, 'I must find him'

Sensing a degree of vulnerability within Celeste, and imagining he knew what she actually wanted him to say he declared,

'Yes you must, and I shall go with you too!'

Bracen put his hand to her mouth to stop her objection; she brushed it away with amusement, her eyes sparkling.

'You like adventure?' she asked

'I think every day in your company would be such an adventure' replied Bracen with obvious love in his voice.

Celeste, missing this overwhelming hint simply replied,

'Bracen, you need to think carefully about this, it could be very dangerous'

'Someone needs to look after you' explained Bracen, 'you being a poor defenceless woman in such a cruel cruel world'

Celeste laughed 'you are going to protect me?'

Bracen made no answer as he stared across the calm waters of the dam towards the mountains in the East

'Yes I will' promised Bracen to himself.

Celeste shuddered, not because of the cold, but more so because of what Bracen had promised, the fact she was pulling him away from his family and the enormity of the task ahead of them.

'What will you say to your father and mother?' she asked

Bracen frowned and looked back at Celeste.

'I think I will have to take the coward's way out and just leave a note' he said. 'Mother will be upset, father will simply think it's reckless and will not understand why it is important to me,'

Celeste nodded and said, 'For my part, my own mother knows why I must leave but I am not going to tell her the manner of my departure or indeed who I am going with or when I am going to go,'

Bracen stood up and looked thoughtfully at Celeste.

'We will need maps, we will need supplies, we will need horses and we will need the cover of the night, if we are going to slip out unnoticed' he said.

Celeste stood up in turn and brushed the dust from her clothes.

'One horse only, I have my own, we must travel light, for we do not know how long a journey this could be there is plenty we can hunt so we will not starve. Pallos has a map of Codencia and Midencia on the wall in the corridor outside my room. I will take this, though my heart tells me that the path laid out before us is going to be neither straight nor readable by any form of map. My first thought is that we should try and cross the bridge of Dyn at night when it might be least guarded, then follow the river Dyn north as it goes through Codencia and Eastern Midencia'.

'Will it take us far enough North if we follow the river?' questioned Bracen.

'I am not sure' replied Celeste, 'I don't think we can look too far forward, I imagine each day will present its challenges some predictable some unforeseen. However I believe time is pressing and though I know we must take a little time to prepare for this undertaking I believe we should take the opportunity and make our move during the night tomorrow.'

'At least it will be a new moon, so we should be able to slip out unnoticed hopefully?' suggested Bracen

'It is decided then,' replied Celeste. We will meet at this spot, at midnight tomorrow. To avoid any suspicion I feel it might be best not to see each other during the day tomorrow and for you especially to go about your business as you always would, is it agreed?'

'Very good,' answered Bracen, 'it shall be so.' For now, I will return to the Inn, and will make up some innocent story about why you wanted to see me so urgently.

He grinned widely at the thought.

Celeste, noticing this look on his face, and knowing absolutely the conversation and explanation they were likely to have wouldn't be so innocent, simply added,

'I hope you are not going to bring my reputation into question?'

Bracen, still smiling replied 'Ah Celeste, you have to let me live out this fantasy in front of my friends, they will be most envious.'

With that he turned away to go.

Celeste pulled on his arm and he turned around. She looked at Bracen and smiled, he looked at those big brown eyes and melted under their gaze, they moved closer, his arm encircled her waist. He pulled her body gently towards his and she did not resist. Slowly Celeste moved her face closer. She shut her eyes in expectation as their lips met, but only for a few seconds, before she pulled away.

'There she said, that is a starter for your rampant imagination' and she laughed as Bracen visibly blushed.

He couldn't have known or even suspected that this was the first time she had ever kissed a man with anything approaching passion. She had to admit though, it was a pleasant sensation.

Part 4

The Journey North

Chapter 1

The night was warm and calm with hardly any breeze as Celeste stole out of the house unnoticed. Making her way to where the horse was stabled, she untied him and put her hand on his nose as he neighed gently

'Shh quiet Bren' she said, as she saddled her black horse. She quickly untied him and led him out through the stable door. Looking up at Pallos house there was no sign of life so everyone must be sleeping. She closed the stable door behind her. She walked through the courtyard as quietly as she could leading her horse until they came to the open entrance of Pallos' residence. She looked back one final time up at the window where she knew her mother was sleeping and mounted the horse, encouraging him into a trot. She rode through the village square, past the scene of her recent wrestling challenge and out towards the Southgate. No one was on the gate at this time of night and she followed the river up to the dam where she and Bracen had made their plans previously.

Bracen was waiting, sat upon his own horse, he looked tired and worried.

'Are you sure you want to go through with this?' asked Celeste

'I am certain,' replied Bracen, ' just didn't sleep too well last night, I don't know if it was the thought of adventure, the guilt of my departure or the kiss which caused it' he added sheepishly.

Celeste didn't answer; she was looking towards the mountains in the east. She sighed then without a word she pushed her horse on and Bracen dutifully followed, a few more furlongs out she pushed the horse into a steady gallop, riding skilfully she looked behind to see Bracen in full pursuit. They had some leagues to go tonight if they were to reach the bridge over the river Dyn and the border crossing before the end of the night.

They paused only briefly in the dead of the night by a stream which ran down from the mountains in the east. Though time was precious Celeste knew she couldn't drive the horses too hard if they were going to be any use on the journey, Bracen chewed on an apple whilst the horses both drank from the stream.

'Have you given any thought as to how we are going to get across the river without being seen?' he asked

'Yes' she replied, 'we will go straight over the bridge, I doubt anyone would expect two travellers to cause any kind of trouble in the depths of the night'

First Edit – July 2011

'I hope it doesn't come down to trouble' replied Bracen as he threw his half eaten apple into the stream.

'One thing is certain Bracen, we are not going to get through this adventure without drawing swords at some point' she insisted

'Who said anything about drawing swords?' he said with some alarm

It was about an hour before dawn as they reached the brim of the hill which overlooked the bridge crossing the river. They dismounted their horses and led them down a steep shale incline.

Only about twelve furlongs away, there seemed little sign of any activity on the bridge. Celeste peered through the stillness and gloom of the night, the first rays of the impending day were starting to appear in the west, in another hour it would be dawn.

'Follow me, but whatever happens stay on your horse,' she ordered Bracen, 'leave the talking to me and if I shout out 'go', make sure you go as if your life depended on it!'

'What about the other side?' asked Bracen

'I doubt we will have much trouble on the Codencian side' she answered

They were only a furlong out now and as the two horses and riders approached the bridge a man, came out of an out-building and held out his hand to stop them.

Sela was tired of this posting and tomorrow would be his last day. Together with Heglin who was currently dozing inside, they would see out the last watch before being replaced mid morning allowing them some leisure time before they had to report back to Southaven. The last thing he expected to see was two riders this early in the morning. As they approached, he recognised the girl, the tall impressive but silent one they had taunted a few days previously. She would have certainly recognised him. He felt a little uneasy now; Heglin probably wouldn't hear if he shouted and if he left his post they might both just ride through without producing the necessary documents.

'Identification' he demanded

Without a word Celeste slipped from her horse, she rummaged about within the pouch on her saddle as if she was looking for something, sighing as if she hadn't found what she was looking for she went to the other side of her horse, where she unsheathed her sword from her scabbard and walked towards the plainly shocked guard.

Edging backwards the Sela attempted to get back to the door of the outbuilding; maybe he could wake the slumbering Heglin.

Before Sela could shout she was on him

'So you wanted to see what I could take?' she spat, 'how much of this can you take!' at which she rammed the sword into the guards throat, he made a gurgling sound only as he hit the floor.

Celeste wiped her brow, and pulled the sword from the mans throat, imagining the deed was done as there was plainly no one else around she walked back grimly to her horse, however from the shadows of the outbuilding a knife flashed and sailed through the air striking Celeste and embedding itself in her left shoulder.

She cried out in pain 'Go Bracen!'

Bracen, unaware of what had just happened pushed his horse into a gallop and jumped the barrier crossing the threshold of the bridge.

Celeste grimaced as she pulled the knife out of her arm and held it with the same hand, in her right was her sword as she advanced again towards the building where Heglin stood, with his own sword drawn.

'So you have a tongue after all' he snarled

Celeste did not answer this time; instead she circled Heglin parleying with her sword.

He lunged but she expertly parried, he lunged again, this time she stepped to the side.

'Impressive' said Heglin, putting two fingers to his mouth he whistled loudly

Another man came from the confines of the outbuilding, sword drawn, but Celeste whistled too and in that moment hurtling from the sky swooped Keri, faster than an arrow with extended claws, she dropped from the sky in the blink of an eye and raked at the unsuspecting newcomer to the fray. Howling in pain he dropped his sword to protect his eyes as Keri again attacked at speed again aiming for his face.

At the same time Celeste made her move as Heglin was momentarily distracted by the bird. She lunged forward, knife in hand and as Heglin tried to ward of the impending sword stroke, Celeste stabbed him deep in the stomach with the knife in her left hand. Holding still to the knife she forced him in agony back into the outbuilding. Panic was etched all over his face as she turned the knife within his body and as she made an upward movement to make the kill.

'Accommodate this you bastard' she said as the knife ripped through his innards towards his heart.

Stepping over the prostate body she exited the door, the third man clearly dazed was on his knees searching for his sword, his face covered in blood.

'You I shall spare' said Celeste, 'maybe you can send word to those in charge that there is one maiden in this land who would stand up to a Northman'

With that she turned and left, quickly mounting her horse she urged the gelding towards the barrier and he jumped without hesitation, they galloped over the bridge, the strong turbulent waters of the River Dyn churned underneath and Celeste saw in front the barrier on the border crossing into Codencia itself was indeed unguarded at this hour and Bracen was waiting expectantly having dismounted his horse.

Celeste slowed down, the pain in her shoulder was excruciating, as she reached the other side she slipped from her horse onto the ground, having passed out with the pain.

Bracen ran over to where she lay and saw the blooded stain on her tunic and the gaping wound beneath. They couldn't stay here, the Codencian's would too no doubt have their own guards on this side of the river and as dawn approached he thought he could hear voices of men approaching. Celeste was coming round, her head swimming no doubt because of the blood loss.

'Celeste' urged Bracen, 'we must ride a few furlongs, out of sight of the bridge and then I can tend your wound'

Celeste nodded but said nothing as he helped her into her saddle and quickly mounted his own.

'Quickly to that Copse over there, we will have some shelter and you can tell me what happened,' said Bracen

They galloped over to the trees he had seen, they were not too sparse and would afford them some shelter from prying eyes.

Bracen made sure they were deep enough within the trees, having helped Celeste to the ground; he looked within his supplies taken from his father's apothecary the day before.

He had some alcohol which he could use to wash the wound as the risk of infection was great. He helped Celeste take off her tunic, under normal circumstances he would have been delighted to see her upper body without clothes but on this occasion he was too concerned to notice her obvious sexuality.

'This is going to sting Celeste' he said as he dabbed opened the bottle with the pure distilled alcohol inside.

She grimaced as he bathed the shoulder; he then made a poultice and told her to put as much pressure on as she could. This would mean lying on the ground or against a tree, with the poultice attached using her body weight to ensure maximum pressure.

'I need to leave you for a while' he said, 'I know of a plant which has healing attributes, I must staunch the flow of blood if you are going to remain strong enough to ride.

He took his coat and put it over Celeste's body more to keep her warm more than to protect her modesty.
'I won't be long' he said, 'rest and try not to move too much'

Bracen disappeared from view as he went in search of the plant he wanted, Celeste still laid on her back whistled and Keri flew down and perched on a log at her side. She put her head to one side and looked at her.

'You probably saved my life' she said to the falcon, 'I guess that puts us even'.

Keri unconcerned preened herself whilst sat on the log

'You know I am going to have to introduce you to Bracen, I cannot keep you a secret from him' said Celeste

So it was some time later Bracen crept stealthily through the bush to where she was still laying, he didn't notice the falcon in the tree above her as he was only concerned with Celeste's welfare.

She looked at him and smiled through her pain

'Did you find what you looked for?' she asked

'Yes' he replied, at the other side of the Copse I found this'

Celeste looked quizzically at him

'It's called Aloe Vera' he said, 'it grows where it is dry so I was lucky to find some so near the water, and it is good for healing. I came back by the river side and collected water too

Bracen helped her sit up, she kept the coat hugged to her front whilst he bathed her shoulder in water then applied the leaves of the plant.

'I will pack the leaves onto the shoulder' he said, 'it might feel a bit strange at first and might cause some irritation on your skin, but I imagine you would prefer that to the pain?

He bandaged her with fresh cloth ensuring the leaves were pressed up tightly against the wound. Celeste felt some warmth return to her shoulder and looked at Bracen

'Thank you' she said

'What happened back there?' he asked

Celeste told him the full story, how these men had taunted and threatened her and her mother the week before, how they had been explicit in what they wanted to do to her and how she had kept silent for the sake of her mother.

'When I saw him again, and the other, I could not help myself, I was enraged and only had revenge in my mind' she declared

Bracen shook his head and looked sadly at his friend

'Celeste, you cannot go through life thinking you are invincible' he said, 'taking on three men in that fashion is nothing short of reckless!

'I had help' she replied and whistled

Keri swooped down and sat on Celeste's unharmed shoulder.

Bracen was amazed and asked 'You tamed this bird yourself, they are meant to be untameable so the legends say! Surely this is a Mountain Falcon?'

Celeste explained the events four years previously, how she had found the injured bird and nursed her back to health, from that point on she said, Keri had never let Celeste out of her sight. She hadn't in all that time mated which was strange and she had shown a peculiar understanding of what Celeste said to her.

'You are telling me this bird can understand our language?' Bracen asked.

Celeste was thoughtful for a moment then replied

I don't think she understands it word for word like you and I, I think she just gets an overall picture of what I want her to do. I cannot explain it any better than that'

Bracen looked at the bird and declared

'I would rather have her on our side than against us, do you suppose she will accept me?'

'Only if I tell her to' said Celeste with a grin, then winced in pain again as she made too much of a sudden movement

'We ought to rest here for the day' said Bracen, 'the plant is very effective and you will find that apart from some soreness you will be able to use your shoulder a little tomorrow after some rest. I know it is still only mid-morning but I don't want you to risk moving today and reopening the wound'

Celeste sighed, they had only gone one nights riding and already she had been injured, it could have been much worse if the knife throwers aim had been more accurate.

She reluctantly agreed to Bracen's view point.

'Since we have so much time to spare today, come tell me about your life since we were eight and played together in Lendel' she said

The next morning dawned; they had fallen asleep together under the warmth of Bracen's coat. Celeste felt at her shoulder, it already felt a little better, leaning up and looking at Bracen laid at her side snoring quietly, she shook him gently

'Come on my hero' she declared,' it's time to move on'

Bracen looked at her almost hurt and replied,

'Don't patronise me Celeste, I did my best for you'

'If my shoulder would only allow it I would wrestle you to the floor for your impertinence' she laughed

'Then I have you at a disadvantage' he replied as he got to his feet and offered his hand to help Celeste up, 'how is your shoulder this morning?'

'Better' she replied, 'Still sore to the touch but I feel ready to move on now'

'First we should bathe it again, I need to restrict any possible infection, then I will need to stitch it somehow' he declared

'Are you sure you just don't want to see me out of my tunic once more?' she asked

'Well there is that too' he admitted with a laugh

Some time later the wound finally stitched and dressed they made ready to depart, Bracen saddled the horses and led them to the outside of the copse with Celeste following with Keri sat on her arm.

'Any idea where we go now?' he asked

'North' she replied, 'We will follow the course of the river as long as we can, it will give us fresh drinking water daily for us and our horses, though we may be open to prying eyes as the traffic on the river will be busy, that can't be helped. Let us hope everyone who sees us considers us to be just two weary travellers going about our business!'

Chapter 2

Mid-morning in Lendel was different in two aspects, in Pallos' house there were feelings of resignation and loss for Reva, in Cirard's there was frustration and anger.

Reva had decided to let Celeste sleep and not disturb her. She knew her daughter was still very angry with her and she didn't want any excuse for another argument. Mid-morning came and went and there was still no sign. Reva decided she would take up some fruit and cheese for Celeste and then she might feel more inclined to talk to her. She listened at the door but could hear no movement inside, pushing the door open she stepped inside but the bed was empty and her clothes gone. Reva noticed a piece of parchment on the pillow of the bed; she felt she already knew just what was recorded in Celeste's hand. Nevertheless she read:

Mother

It is not like me to run, and in truth I am not running from you. I feel I am running towards my destiny. It would have been too painful to say goodbye and I could not bear to think I had caused you pain and to see you in tears.

I ask forgiveness of you, I reacted badly to your news about my father and I realise you were only doing what any mother would do to protect their child.

My advice to you would be not to sell the house in Lendel, it's where you belong, in and amongst friends and not secluded by the coast.

You may find initially my leaving might cause you some unpleasantness within the village but that will soon abate.

Farewell my mother and best friend, one day I promise, I will return.

Celeste

Across the village just an hour before, the scene had been different in Cirard's apothecary. Cirard was exasperated with his son; once again no doubt he had too much ale in the Inn the evening before and as a result had slept in. Two nights in a row he had spent the entire evening there. Only the Gods knew what possessed him to drink as much as he did. One day no doubt he would grow up; maybe with Celeste's appearance he might show some degree of maturity; however it had not been evident these last two days.

'Leadel' he shouted back to his wife who was busying herself in the house, 'wake that sluggard up and send him in here without breakfast, I will teach him to drink like he does!'

Cirard had to make some deliveries that morning, people expected their herbal remedies delivered in a timely fashion and though he was the only apothecary in the village he still valued their custom.

Some minutes elapsed until Leadel came in the store and he looked around, she was holding a piece of parchment.

'He's gone' she sobbed,' gone and taken off with Celeste to who knows where!'

She handed Cirard the parchment

Mother/Father

There is no easy way to break this news to you but break it I must. I have left with Celeste; we are going on a quest to the north. It is not my place to say what this quest is but I feel I need to be at my friend's side as she makes her attempt. I am sorry Father that I leave you during a busy time for the business, there is bound to be some other young man you could apprentice. I thank you for your knowledge and your wisdom; it should prepare me for the tasks ahead.

Mother, for you I can only leave words of love, parting would have been too painful and I would not have been able face that confrontation.

This quest will make me a better man (one way or another)

Bracen

Cirard was beside himself with anger. This could not be borne; he had so much to do and now this! Well his customers would have to wait for their deliveries; he was going to sort this out with Reva. Snatching the parchment from his wife's hands he barged out of the shop.

When he arrived at Pallos' residence some minutes later his mood had not changed and he was incessant with rage.

'Reva, get me Reva' he barked at the first person he came across

Shortly afterwards Reva came out to the courtyard, she too was carrying a piece of parchment. Her eyes were red and swollen and she looked up at Cirard painfully.

'Under any other circumstances I would have been pleased to meet you again' said Cirard, 'but in truth, I have no love for you nor your family, not since one of yours is responsible for taking away my son'

Reva could find nothing to say, she handed Cirard her own parchment which he in turn read. He handed it back to Reva and looked at her ageing face, worn with care and the inevitable advancement of the years.

Reva shook her head,

'You know Cirard, first it was my mother, then the volcano, then Carig left and never came back and now this! I too feel my life is cursed and would no doubt feel your pain more acutely if mine hadn't been so prevalent for all these years!'

Something softened within him as he looked with some pity at the broken woman stood in front of him.

'Do you know where they have gone?' he asked

'To look for my husband, her father'

'He could be anywhere, if he is alive at all' said Cirard about his former friend

'Indeed' said Reva, 'I pointed that out to Celeste two nights ago, but she grew angry with me but then made her decision and would not be gainsaid'

'We could follow them?' suggested Cirard

'It is hopeless, 'replied Reva, 'they have a days start on us and have taken horses, well one horse certainly and we don't even know where they are actually going. I wonder if they do?'

To this Cirard had no answer and his rounded shoulders sagged in resignation

'So it shall be then, 'for today I must lose my son and you your daughter and both our hopes and desires lessen with the waning of the years'

At this he turned around and strode back to his shop, speaking to no one on the way, but walking briskly and with purpose. He still had a business to run.

Reva watched him go and then a moment of realisation hit her. It hit her so hard she laboured to breathe her chest tightening as the thoughts entered her head. First it was the bird, that Falcon, she didn't have to guess, and she knew it would be with Celeste too

Second it was the competition, she had uttered the words, 'I am more a man than you will ever be' or something along those lines, that was also in the tasking!

And now thirdly she had followed her father, just as he had predicted eighteen years ago. Again she strove to remember the fourth task but it would not come to light, no matter how she tried she could not place what Carig had said that night.

She stumbled back to the house, all this was too much, and she would take her leave of Pallos in the morning and return to Salint, away from the memories and away from the future. The house could go, she didn't care, and she didn't need it. Reva felt the years were drawing in and she had little left to offer the world, Pallos could have the house, she would sign it over to him in fact. Then finally she would be alone.

Chapter 3

They followed the swift river northwards for six days and nights; the land was reasonably flat and at the riverside trees marched along the bank on either side. They saw no one, as they walked along a path which had obviously been trodden by someone's feet. On the seventh day the trees thinned out then failed altogether, they could only just discern the mountains now in the west, sixty leagues from whence they had come.

The ground now had become increasingly wet and boggy and it was clear the river hereabouts fed the swamped land. The journey became increasingly hazardous as they tried to pick their way across the fen leading their horses. They were bitten unmercifully by midges and other insects, especially on the first night. The one positive thing of the journey was the speed at which Celeste's wound had healed. She could move the shoulder freely now and the strength had all but fully returned.

On the second day into the fen they had traversed what had easily been the most difficult part of the swamp; twice they had struggled to pull the horses out of the stinking mire. Both were covered from head to toe in mud and were both fast becoming increasingly frustrated by the slow progress they were making.

'If this goes on', muttered Bracen, 'we might be marooned in sludge forever'

Celeste ignored him, he had been increasingly sullen the last couple of days and she wondered if he was beginning to regret his decision to follow her on the quest to find her father. They sat on a hillock, just above the reeking mud; the horses tethered some way off on the one piece of hard ground they had found. Since leaving the shelter of the trees the food supply had been low and they have survived lately on berries and fruit picked along the way. Hunger was going to be a factor if they didn't find meat soon. The last of the bread had gone too. They did not need to fill their bottles with this unclean water. The river could still be heard some way to their left so they knew in an emergency they could at least find the fresh water they needed.

Keri had fared better, there were plenty or rodents for her in the area, and Celeste wondered if she would understand the need for them to have food. With nothing to lose she whistled to her friend who dropped out of the sky in an instance and settled on her arm.

'Since you can't talk to me to let me know how far this damned fen goes on for, maybe you would be kind enough to catch us a rabbit, or something else edible,' she ventured.

Keri flew up into the air and gracefully glided on the updrafts from the river; she circled for a time then flew off into the distance.

'Seems your bird has abandoned you' said Bracen somewhat sullenly

'Bracen', replied Celeste, 'I do not know what is troubling you, or why you are so negative these last two days but I do not need this, I am troubled enough without you acting like a child'

'It's just these bites' he complained, 'I wonder what they eat when they don't have a man to feed off?'

'Don't you have anything in your supplies which treats bites?' asked Celeste

'Stupid' said Bracen at once, 'not you' he added, 'but me, all this time I have been carrying herbs within my bag to use for cooking, and these too will relieve the itchiness. I know I have Basil and Rosemary in my supplies and Lemon Balm too, that one should leave a bitter taste in a gnat's mouth'

Bracen quickly applied the lemon balm to his legs and arms and did the same for Celeste, he was concerned the mud or insect might have infected the wound but he needn't have worried as it had totally scabbed over and was healing fast.

Unnoticed Keri had returned and she sat observing them, at her feet lay a rabbit. Bracen laughed and pointed to the bird

'Look she does understand what you say' he said, 'the major problem is going to be starting a fire in this fen, I doubt if there is anything dry enough to burn'

He tried his best but even the few twigs lying around were soaked, they couldn't eat the rabbit raw. Bracen threw the rabbit back to Keri who gratefully attacked it with relish. Bracen turned and looked at Celeste with some frustration.

The next morning they rose again and plodded through the marshes, the land began to rise slightly and the ground became firmer, some half a furlong to the left they could now hear the river gurgling which meant it must be running and not stagnating as in the marshes. This gave them renewed hope. All the time they had been travelling at this side of the river bank they had not seen a single person. All that was soon to change, but for now at least they were clear of the mire and the stench. Celeste told Bracen she needed to go down to the river to bathe and politely suggested he did the same afterwards. Before she went Bracen strolled over to the much happier tethered horses and pulled from his bag two more leafs which he had used to staunch her wound.

'Wait Celeste' he said, 'if I can push the sap out of these leafs it will assist your bathing. The sap is good for your hair too apparently.'

He ground the leaves together and she cupped her hands to receive the oily liquid, she then quickly applied it to her hair.

'No peeping Bracen' she warned.

Bracen said nothing, but wondered if that was actually an invitation and not a warning. He couldn't possibly even second guess what went on in her head. He waited a few minutes and crept stealthily through the brush and positioned himself behind a small boulder. Celeste was naked, totally naked, and she was washing the mud from her body. Bracen could not take his eyes from her, she was absolutely stunning. Her long black hair just covering her breasts, her flat stomach, her long bronzed legs. He couldn't help himself, the arousal was too much, almost subconsciously his hand went to his manhood which was totally erect as he stared at her pubic area whilst she rinsed the mud from her body.

'What are you thinking' he reproached himself.

He crept back away from the river and back to the horses. No doubt the bird would have seen him watching but the bird couldn't talk, so he was safe. Not long afterwards and covered with only a blanket Celeste returned and said demurely

'Your turn'

Something in her voice suggested she knew he had been watching but it was hardly something he could admit to her. Grabbing a second blanket he set off for the river, but to his astonishment Celeste followed him.

'What are you doing?' he asked

Celeste smiled, 'you are a boy, and people tell me boys sometimes need help when it comes to cleanliness. I thought I might wash your back for you'

'But, but, but' stammered Bracen, 'I will be naked'

'Seems only fair' replied Celeste, 'since you clearly enjoyed watching me!'

He set of at a run and she quickly followed. He reached the river side and quickly removed his clothing, keeping his back towards Celeste to hide his manhood and his embarrassment. He dived in, when he came to the surface he looked for Celeste but he couldn't see her, he looked behind him, still nothing, then from under the water she emerged. They splashed water at each other; she cleaned his back, and then finally dared to face her. They were both now only waist deep in the water and Bracen could see her breasts clearly and the promise of something far better below her stomach, the darkness of the area keeping him hypnotised. Celeste for her part wasn't afraid, no man had ever seen her naked, or touched her body before, but she felt she could trust Bracen. She didn't know what love was to be sure, but she definitely felt more than just friendship for this youth stood naked in the water before her.

'Isn't that uncomfortable when you are riding?' she laughed as she pointed to his erection

He moved towards her, he took her hand, she didn't resist as he pulled it towards his throbbing manhood. She held him like that and he groaned in pleasure. He moved her hand backwards and forwards which was just as well since she really didn't have a clue what was expected of her. He reached to touch her between her legs.

'No' she said adamantly,' not yet, I have never slept with a man before, in fact up to the last fortnight, I hadn't actually kissed one!'

Bracen was astonished, he had his share of dalliances back home whist growing up as teenagers often do, he had actually made love twice in the past, once at fifteen with an older woman from the village who reputedly enjoyed younger men and once with a girl, about his own age, who had come into her fathers apothecary wanting advise on sex, herbs and potions! He had made love to her on his father's shop floor! No one, however in his experience had a figure or the sexual appeal of Celeste and he was in truth pleased that no one had experienced her before he got his chance.

'Kiss me again Bracen' she ordered

This time, the kiss was longer their tongues exploring their mouths, he was even allowed to feel her breasts and she moaned with pleasure as he kissed each nipple. He could wait for the ultimate prize; for he was sure now it was just a matter of time.

When the bathing (and kissing) was over and Bracen's manhood had disappeared to a rather disappointing size, she led him back to the horses where they dried each other. They needed to eat still so she asked if he could try and catch a couple of fish from the river whilst she prepared a fire. The wood around here was much drier and there was plenty of fern to get it started. Bracen duly obliged and they ate with relish and between mouthfuls said to Celeste

'I am worried about the horses, we have hardly anything left for them to eat and if they are to be any use at all to us then we need to find some way of feeding them.'

Celeste nodded in agreement.

'According to the map' she said, 'not far after the wetlands (which I presume are what we have just traversed), we should come to a town. You might be able to sell some of the herbs you have been collecting on the way. There is bound to be an apothecary in town or a market place to exchange and barter'

'How far?' enquired Bracen,'

'Not really sure' she replied, ' there is no scale to the map, but if I look at the distance from Lendel to Salint where I used to live that would be three and a half days riding. Since we have travelled just over a week, sometimes slowly as we picked our way through those stinking pools, I would guess if I traced the river on the map, say twice the distance from Lendel to Salint but in a straight line by the river, I should be able to roughly calculate where we are in relation to the town'.

A moment later she looked up hopefully at Bracen.

'It looks like half a days ride from here, we might even find somewhere comfortable to rest tonight, did you think to bring any money?

'I have twenty silver pennies' he replied,' it should last us a few days, come on, it must be only about five leagues away, if we make haste we might even get chance to eat and drink before bed'

Celeste's calculations were almost exact and it was approaching dinner time in the evening when they approached the white walled town. Keri left them as they approached the white walled building, no doubt to hunt, she would pick up their trail when they set off again.

Bracen enquired what it was called; Celeste looked again at the map.

'It is Kaisley' she said

'I have heard of that place, there is a red wine we import into Codencia Minor called Kaisley Rose, they have fields upon fields of vineyards apparently, or so my father has told me. Father was something of an expert, or at least he liked to think he was, he told me the chalky soil around here was good for the roots of the vine and it made a wine of a slightly bitter after taste'

'I would prefer a comfortable bed and soft pillow,' she said.

They rode to the entrance of the town; there was no gate as such, just an archway under the chalk walls. They saw people for the first time, no one seemed to notice or care about the two youngsters who were riding confidently through the town, but more than one man glanced in admiration at the tall and olived skin beauty who rode in with the equally tall but gangly youth.

Eventually they found an Inn, it had stables so they would be able to feed and water the horses. Bracen stabled the horses whilst Celeste made her way inside the Inn to barter a price for accommodation with the Innkeeper. It was a noisy and crowded place with men gambling, drinking and chatting amidst raucous laughter. As Celeste entered the bar, the men became quieter, nudging each other as they leered appreciatively at the woman striding towards the bar.

The Innkeeper came over with a smile

'We don't often get young ladies in here on their own, so please pardon the stupid expressions of the men-folk; they mean no harm at all'

'Come and sit on my knee' shouted one old timer as he gulped down his beer

'Are you sure your heart could stand it?' shouted back Celeste with a grin

'There Erik' another laughed, 'One more besides your wife and four girls who can put you in your place'.

The whole place descended into laughter and hoots of derision aimed at the unfortunate Erik.

'I need food and rooms for two', she declared to the Innkeeper. 'I have stabled two horses as well'.

'The price should be three silver pennies for that' he said

'Three' questioned Celeste, 'are you sure you are not taking advantage of me?

'Looking at you dear, I don't think there are many men here, or even in this town who would try to take advantage of you, only maybe in their dreams!' Oh alright then, I will throw in breakfast for good measure, is it just the one room?' he asked

'Two if possible' replied Celeste

They shook hands as Bracen walked in.

'Three pennies for stabling and food tonight and tomorrow morning' she said

'That is good, in fact it's a bargain, did you put your sword to his throat?' he laughed

Celeste frowned she had in fact quite forgotten to take it from the horse and had come into the Inn unarmed.

'Two rooms Bracen' she said

He looked ever so slightly crestfallen! Though his demeanour changed more favourably when the Innkeeper told him, that guests who stayed for the night had their first drink on the house!

They ate well; the food was hearty and warm and was followed with plenty of fruit. Bracen had the sense to put this to one side as it would help the following days. Celeste refused the offer of drinking in the Inn. Tonight she would relax and for the first time since their journey began, sleep without any sense of danger. Bracen on the other hand had no such qualms; the promise of a good beverage was too much of a temptation.

Chapter 4

The next morning over breakfast they decided to stay another night, the Inn was comfortable and a welcome change from the dirt and stench of the fen. Bracen decided he would go into the town and find the local apothecary, he had picked up a few plants on his way which grew wild and he had no doubts he could earn a couple of silver pennies at least. Celeste too wanted to look around town, she had never seen a place this size before and she liked the people she had met so far.

Bracen had already eaten and gone in search of the apothecary so Celeste went down into the Inn where she found the Innkeeper busily tidying up the room from the night before and preparing for what he hoped would be another busy and therefore profitable day.

Celeste approached him and held out three more silver pennies. He looked up and smiled, wiping his brow he enquired.

'Are you staying another night?'

'Yes indeed, 'she replied, 'we have ridden for nearly two weeks and though we have far to go, I feel an extra day is of little concern'

He took the silver pennies from her and weighed them in his hand as if considering a proposition.

'You know, I am really busy at this time of the year and I could do with some help occasionally, you saw last night how crowded the Inn became and I have only one pair of hands and very demanding customers, though I shouldn't complain', he added.

'I wondered, I mean if it doesn't appear too forward, what I mean to say is' he was stumbling over his words.

'Are you offering me work' asked Celeste with a smile

'Well you couldn't blame me, you saw the reaction of the men in here when they saw you, and I reckon a pretty face around here could do wonders for business.'

'You are very kind', said Celeste looking around at the Inn as if considering, 'you might be right about a pretty face, I would imagine there are plenty of girls much prettier than me in this town who would like to take you up on your offer'

'But none with a figure like yours' he thought to himself.

'Well it was just a thought, maybe one day eh?'

'Maybe' agreed Celeste, 'for now I came to ask you for advice, for it has been told to me that the most trustworthy people in each town would be the Innkeeper and furthermore that all news tends to channel through them'

'Now it is you turn to flatter me' laughed the Innkeeper, 'please call me Daal incidentally, what is it you need news of dear?'

'Not so much news but more like directions', she explained, ' I am Celeste by the way, I travel north but the map I have only shows blank spaces once I get to Midencia and then nothing further north than that'

'There is nothing further north than that except the impassable Cynric Mountain range'

'What about the Northmen' asked Celeste 'surely there must be land on the other side of the mountains?

'None would want to venture there' he replied, 'I have heard there is a pass far to the east, through Westendcia, but that land is full of barbarians and not a place to venture they say. Of course you could go to the North West hundreds and hundred of leagues, past the Bivendic Desert until you come to the cursed islands of Westdyn. But none but a pirate would venture there either' he said shaking his head.

'Nevertheless, to the north is where I must go', explained Celeste, 'if you cannot guide me over the mountains could you at least tell me the best way into Midencia, for I believe I must pass through that land first?'

'That I can do' agreed Daal, 'it is quite straightforward. There are two routes, one would take you through the Strait Canyon and into Western Valdencia, from there you could carry on following follow the river Dyn and this would eventually take you north into Midencia'

'Can I get my horses through the canyon and into Valdencia?' asked Celeste

'No, it is too dangerous, the river runs swiftly and the ground underfoot is unsure, especially for beasts of burden, your other choice is to strike directly north from here, there is a road which runs up to Longfield some twenty leagues distant, the road isn't too challenging, but further north after Longfield you would have many days of travel through a very barren country with little shelter until you came to Bridgenorth where you will once again come to the River Dyn and into the East of Midencia. After that the road goes only as far as Castletown in the far north of Midencia, beyond that I have no knowledge'

'Thank you Daal, I am in your debt' she declared

'You could work for me tonight to repay me?' he ventured

'I'm sorry' she replied, 'under other circumstances I would love to stay here, I like the town and I like the people. I could happily live here. My quest takes me north though'

'Why do you have to go north Celeste?' he enquired

'I cannot say Daal, but trust me, if by chance I pass by this way on my return, I will take you up on your kind offer, and I will work for a time in this place for you, it's a promise!' she added

Daal shook his head as she turned and left, he still had much to do and soon he would have to open for lunchtime. Celeste had proved to be a welcome distraction to his busy morning, and he momentarily regretted he wasn't twenty years younger as he thought wistfully of her figure and many lost opportunities in the past.

Meanwhile Bracen had found the apothecary who was most unwelcoming, declaring Bracen to be a vagrant and furthermore stating to the departing youth that his supplies were plentiful and he was not reduced to picking not-so-rare plants from the ground. Before he left Bracen managed to take various leaves from his store without him noticing, as he served another customer. Rebuked and slightly embarrassed Bracen made for the market. A stall holder offered him one silver penny for his herbs and leafs, only a third of what he had expected. He had little choice but to accept.

Slightly depressed at his lack of success he made his way back to his room at the Inn. Tonight there would be no drinking in the Inn, what little money they had he should keep, as it might be needed again on their journey.

Chapter 5

In Lendel Pallos apologised once again to Reva

'There is nothing more I can do, you will not be allowed out of the land and back to Salint, and your papers have been withheld due to the death of the two border guards at the hands of Celeste. I have to warn you too, if she comes back to this place, she will be imprisoned and immediately put to death, without trial or defence, such is their law. I have to tell you that representations have already been made to the Codencian Council in Stanleigh asking for the two fugitives to be arrested and returned, I doubt they would want to risk confrontation with the Northmen at this time'.

He looked at Reva with pity.

'I have worked hard on your behalf, the High Elder holds you partly responsible for the murder of the two men and he sees it as a tarnish on his character that the mother of an assassin lives in his village, for now and whilst you dwell in this house, you are under my protection, but to venture out might be dangerous and ill advised!'

'So in fact I am under arrest and imprisoned in this house?' she asked sadly

'In one sense of the word yes', answered Pallos,' though I still have enough influence in my position to prevent you being arrested on my property, the few Northmen here wouldn't want to risk any kind of rebellion and rely on my good offices to keep the villagers peaceful'

Reva spoke no word but shook her bowed head and simply stared at the floor in shame.

'So you shall be my permanent guest' he said at last, 'and to have a lady in the house is not such a bad thing after all, my home has lacked a female touch since my wife died five years ago'

Reva looked up at him and replied shamefully,

'So Pallos I will dwell here under your roof as all the villages will presume I am your mistress!'

Before he could reply she continued

'So I am guilty by association for murder and guilty by association through shame, what will become of me?' she asked

'Reva, worry not about the finger wagging and gossiping women of Lendel. To save face I will announce you are to be my house-keeper and they can think what they will'

Revs lifted her face and looked at Pallos stood in front of her, his face rung with concern for his oldest of friends. She took his hands in hers and said earnestly to him.

'I thank you friend, I am blessed to have such a soul looking after my interests'

She half smiled and kissed him tenderly on the cheek.

'If I am to keep house, I must start in the morning and I will give you a household to be proud of.'

'Let it be so, I will arrange sale of your house, in fact', he said as an afterthought, 'I might just purchase it myself.

'What about my house in Salint?' asked Reva

'I can do little other than send someone out on occasion to make sure it is secure, but it is a seven day round trip and not many would want to volunteer that journey for no reason!'

'They could use it as a second home in the summer months?' she suggested

'Indeed, that might be a way we could arrange things for you benefit' observed Pallos

Chapter 6

Bracen and Celeste made ready to depart, he went to the stables to prepare and saddle the horses for the next stage of the journey. Celeste called in to see Daal.

He smiled as she entered; once again he was busy tidying up the room in preparation for the day.

'I will leave now' declared Celeste, ' I simply wanted to thank you again for your hospitality, if I meet like minded people on this journey I will be fortunate indeed!'

Daal flushed slightly and put down the cloth he was cleaning the table with.

'I have a friend in Longfield, he used to be a partner in the Inn but he married and his wife found the role of an Innkeepers wife not to her liking. He lives; I should say they live, in a small house just outside town. He has a bakery; he is good with his hands and has good natured face, he will be happy to earn a few pennies providing a nights accommodation that is if his wife hasn't worked him to death yet. They have a spare room, I am sure they will……..

'Daal slow down, you will trip over your words one of these days and fall flat on your face' insisted Celeste, 'what is your friend's name?'

'He is called Golan and his wife is Anjou, anyone in Longfield will tell you where he dwells'

Celeste thanked him once again; he was bent over a table already polishing the ale stains from the wood. She bent over and kissed his brow.

'Farewell Daal, when you least expect it maybe you and I will meet again one day!'

She closed the Inn door behind, her heart was heavy she felt at home in this place and was reluctant to start again, she paused for a moment before entering the stable, the last thing she wanted to do was show Bracen that she was not ready to continue their quest. Bracen had fed and watered the horses and packed their bags for the journey.

'Ready?' he asked

'I'm ready, come on lets go!'

They rode out of the stables and into the main thoroughfare; they rode for a few minutes until they came to another archway, this time leading out of town. The road split in two, one way went almost directly east, the other north. Keri swooped down as if called.

'Which way?' Bracen enquired

First Edit – July 2011

'North' she stated with some purpose, 'come Bracen let us put some distance between here and our camp tonight!' she rode off without looking back as Keri flew ahead. Bracen as usual following her horses hoof fall as she galloped off into the distance.

After two hours they paused, she had ridden the horses quite hard and they needed a rest, there was a small stream running down from some distant hills in the east. They didn't know it but these were the first foothills leading to the larger mountains in which the Strait Canyon flowed. Bracen had laid a blanket on the ground and was rummaging in his bag for the fruit he had saved for the last two evening meals; at least they wouldn't go hungry today. Celeste didn't seem to want to talk, the sexual chemistry which had existed only a few days before seemed to have evaporated into thin air and she seemed distracted and a little sullen

'Where are we heading now?' he asked

Celeste took a bite out of an apple and chewed forcefully,

'We are heading north' she declared

I can see that from the position of the sun' he said, 'I meant where to in particular'

She seemed to relax a little and said,

'Oh Bracen, I'm sorry we shouldn't have stayed the extra night in Kaisley, I think I liked it a little too much there. The plan is to ride north for two days; we will come to a place called Longfield. Daal told me he has a friend there who might let us stay the night'

'And what after that?' he persisted

'A lot of riding through some harsh country side, we will have a difficult few days once we leave Longfield' she observed

Keri glided down and landed on her shoulder.

Celeste looked at the falcon, it seemed disturbed somehow. It flew off to the right to where a small copse of trees lay and then immediately came back, Keri repeated this twice more.

'Bracen, I think Keri is telling us to get off the road under cover!'

'Maybe she has spotted danger ahead, come let us take shelter for a while' he replied

They led their horses under the boughs of the trees; the copse appeared to be about a furlong thick so they would be out of sight from anyone on the road. Celeste left Bracen holding the horses.

'Stay' she ordered,' I want to see what was troubling Keri.

She ran back the way they had come to the edge of the trees. She pulled herself up to one of the lower branches using only her arms for leverage, and then managed to throw her left leg over. The rest of the branches would not support her weight above so this would have to be her perch. Keri clearly was in an adjacent tree looking north. At first nothing happened, then in the distance she clearly saw dust rising from the road, then the thunder of hoofs. She lay flat on the outlaying branch just in time, as a thirty strong brigade of the Condencia Militia swept along the road. The horses were being hard ridden and they were clearly heading from Kaisley. Celeste could guess why, obviously the Northmen would not take the murder of two of their guards lightly, there was either trouble now at the border or worse still, they were looking for Bracen and herself. She waited a while before all signs of the horsemen had gone and then dropped down from the branch to the floor. She quickly ran to where Bracen was waiting. She explained what she had seen.

'So, you think either there is trouble at the border or we are being hunted?' he asked.

'I hope the former' she replied thoughtfully, 'if it's the latter then the news has travelled nearly as quickly as we have'.

'No, think!' said Bracen, we were tied up for three days at least in that fen and then idled for two days in Kaisley. I imagine that would have been time to get information from the bridge over the River Dyn to Stanleigh'

'But these horsemen were riding south' she maintained, 'the news can't have gone as far as the Codencia and Midencia border'

Celeste didn't know of the sheds outside Longfield which held the northern soldiery, paid riders who could be called on during times of strife or the method of using pigeons trained to fly between sheds where the military were posted throughout Codencia.

'I think we should go' she said urgently, 'though we have to sleep in the open tonight I want to find somewhere similar to this place but after a few more hours riding, we need to be extra careful. I have an uneasy feeling that we are now fugitives!'

'Will it be safe to go to Daal's friend then? Bracen asked

'Yes. I think so, even if we are wanted, I doubt that kind of information would have got out to ordinary people yet and besides Daal vouched for him, so I think we can trust to our luck this time'.

They led the horses back out from the copse and quickly mounted. Keri was away in the distance, she appeared to be flying away and Celeste took this as a sign that there was little or nothing on the road.

They both urged their horses into a gallop.

The sun was starting to drop eastwards signalling the afternoon was waning and they hadn't seen any further suitable place to make camp for the night. The land on either side of the road dropped down at both sides so there was nowhere to hide at all. After some time Celeste reined her horse in and stopped.

'What's wrong?' asked Bracen with some concern

'Listen!' she answered

There, unmistakably the sound of running water, surely they couldn't have gone so far east that they had come across the river Dyn again, but no, that would have taken them into Valdencia and she was sure the sun had been ahead the few hours before so in the north. She dismounted and pulled the map she had taken from Pallos's hall.

'Ah' she exclaimed, 'we have made better progress than I thought, it must be the river Vendic ahead which only puts us half a days ride from Longfield, the map shows the road has a bridge over the river, maybe we can shelter by the river under the bridge?'

They rode another four furlongs and now they could see the river, not very wide at this point as it rose only in the hills adjacent to the River Dyn in Valdencia which they had seen that morning in the east. The bridge came into sight; it was stone built and arched, obviously built for safety. Celeste guessed in time of heavy rain the river probably ran very swiftly and no doubt the stone nature of the bridge was to ensure it wasn't swept away. She looked up at the sky; Keri was overhead circling, no doubt looking for food. She could see the clouds were building and they would possibly have rain

They led their horses off the road and down to the riverside, where Bracen tethered them but with enough slack to allow them to drink from the clear and slow running water.

They ate some fruit in silence as the river quietly went by. Overhead there was a flash in the sky and a few seconds later a rumble of thunder. Both horses neighed in fright. Celeste walked over and patted her horse on the nose

'Be calm Bren, nothing can harm you here!'

Keri swept in under the bridge and settled on the bank in front of them holding a river rat in its claws as the rain started to pitter-patter on the ground outside the bridge. Soon the pitter-patter changed to a deluge as the rain hammered down. They were both mightily relieved they had managed to find this shelter, being on the road in this type of weather would have been most unpleasant. Another flash of lighting and this time almost immediately afterwards a massive clap of thunder. The horses shifted uneasily whilst Keri finished off the unfortunate rat.

Eventually the storm passed over head and the thunder became a distant rumble. Bracen moved to the horses and laid their blankets and coats on the ground. At lest they were dry and hopefully out of sight, so they ought to be reasonably comfortable.

'Reasonably comfortable?' he thought to himself, 'only if you consider a rock to be a pillow!'

They laid side by side, Bracen not daring to show his physical excitement again at this time fearing some kind of rebuke. The sound of the rushing water was peaceful and the warm nightfall was drawing in.

He woke first the next morning; Celeste had managed to curl herself into a ball under his outstretched arm. He put the arm round her protectively. She stirred.

'Morning already?' she yawned.

'Yes it is', he observed, 'the thunderstorm has cleared the air somewhat and it feels a little fresher'

He looked at the now slightly swollen river still running merrily amongst the rocks under the bridge.

'I think I will try and catch fish' he said eventually, 'I think we should delay our travel plans until after noon, since if it is only a half days ride we would approach Longfield at dusk and under some cover'

Though they had slept well the fear of possible pursuit returned to them.

'You are right' she said, 'I think I will take a chance and bathe further downstream, and don't you use this as an opportunity to spy on me again!'

'The thought never crossed my mind' he lied

She returned under the arches of the bridge some time later, Bracen had caught a couple of small fish; hardly enough to fulfil the needs of two weary travellers, but some food other than fruit at least. Celeste managed to get a small fire going under the arch and pierced both fish on a spit.

Bracen boiled some herbs from his pouch and they both sat down to eat. The fish were both bony and oily, though not inedible, at least it was warm, and this and the boiled herbs put them both in good spirits.

Celeste looked at her friend and considered what he had given up and all that he had done for her. He was a good man, despite his transparent sexual drive and sometimes sullen moods. She made up her mind to try and be nice to him for the rest of the day at least.

'Come on' she said at last,' time to move on, I hope Longfield is as hospitable as Kaisley was!'

Eventually around dusk, they saw the town in the distance; it appeared to be situated on top of a plateau on a fair sized hill. The only piece of land hereabouts which wasn't flat, no doubt which was why the place was built there in the first place. Once again Celeste explained to Keri they were going into town for the night and she would have to fend for herself. Immediately she left Celeste's arm and rose into the sky.

They approached from the south, there was a gatekeeper who simply waved them through without looking up and they entered the main street. Few people were about.

A youngster approached, running towards to gate, he slowed to a trot and then finally stopped, looking Bracen and Celeste up and down.

'Looking for somewhere to stop tonight?' he enquired, 'my fathers Inn is just around the corner to the left'

'No' said Bracen regretfully, 'do you know where Golan lives?'

'You passed it to the right of the road when you approached the gate, there was a house situated about two furlongs from the road on the right, didn't you see it?

Bracen admitted he had not

'Well then follow me, for I am going there to collect bread for my father's guests at the Inn tonight'

Chapter 7

Celeste and Bracen introduced themselves to Goran once the youngster had departed with a cheery wave. They told him they had stayed at Daal's and he had recommended Golan as a good friend.

Golan looked at them curiously.

'It's not often we get youngsters such as you riding on the road northward, are you bound for Bridgenorth?' he asked

'Further than that sir' replied Celeste, 'I make for Castletown in Midencia'

'What about your friend Bracen?'

Celeste looked and Golan and laughed heartily

'Friend?' no indeed he is no friend of mine!'

Bracen looked at her at once puzzled and with a look of hurt spreading on his face

'He's my husband' she declared, 'we were recently married at the coastal town of Salint in the South; we are riding to Castletown to start a new life there!'

Why Castletown, it is a very long way away and in another country you know? observed Golan.

'Bracen is an Apothecary, I know he doesn't look old enough, but I think he uses his potions to make himself look younger, so you know he is nearly thirty!' she said quietly into Golan's ear. 'And what is more', she said more loudly, 'we were advised there wasn't another apothecary there, so he will start a business and keep me in comfort where I can deliver many strong children to him'

Golan's eyes sparkled, 'just married eh? I can't wait to tell my wife, Anjou! Anjou!' he shouted.

Anjou appeared at the door and looked at the two visitors. 'What is it and why have you disturbed me from my cloth-making?'

'Daal recommended us my love, to these two, they want a room for the night, and they are just recently married!'

'Well stop chattering you oaf and go prepare their room, I will make them something to eat, is that alright? she asked

'You are most kind' said Celeste, 'we are indeed both hungry!

'And wet no doubt if you were caught in that thunderstorm last night, be seated and I will serve you food, it's not much, just some stew, but I expect you two young lovers will be more interested in your room?' she added with a half smile.

Anjou returned to the kitchen frowning, something didn't add up here, Bracen had hardly spoken, only the confident and strong looking Celeste. After dinner she would go see her friend Kayleighn in town, though she was the towns worst gossip she was also the one who tended to collect most news. She supposed a prostitute's life would be full of men talking way to freely under Kayleighn's skilful massage. If there was news of newlyweds up from the south, she would know about it!

Golan served the food whilst his wife excused herself with a smile explaining she was going to see her best friend in town, she casually waved as she stepped out into the yard and towards the town.

Celeste and Bracen too made their excuses and handed the baker the two silver pennies he asked for, that being the price of the accommodation and stabling for the night.

Shutting the door behind the departing Golan, Bracen turned and looked at Celeste enquiringly

'Why all the lies?' he asked

'Simple, if word is out a young man and young woman are wanted fugitives I thought it would be better to have some kind of plausible story. I thought it was well intended!' she laughed

'Indeed yes' grinned Bracen, 'I will be demanding a husbands rights in bed tonight too, really Celeste, if you are going to play this part you have to play it totally!'

Celeste smiled, he never gave up, he was at least pleasantly predictable. At last she gave in.

'Alright husband of mine, take off your clothes, and lay back with you eyes shut.
I am still shy, so no peeping'

Bracen quickly undressed and climbed into bed as ordered. Celeste looked at him; she turned the bedclothes back revealing his gangly body. His erection was evident even without her touch.

She slipped into bed by his side and kissed him fully whilst slipping her hand down towards his throbbing member. He gasped as she held it firmly.

'Celeste' he pleaded, let me please let me!'

'Shhh, shut your eyes' she said

Bracen did as he was told; Celeste squatted above him and guided his penis towards her wetness. She lowered herself gently and he entered her with a moan. She sat for a minute not moving, feeling the sensation of him inside her, she leaned forward, putting her hand over his eyes again, she started to move her hips backwards and forwards, and he responded in rhythm. Celeste sat up with her back straight using her hips to drive the movement. From deep within the sensation she had never experienced or imagined exploded as Bracen's back arched as he too exploded in orgasm.

He pulled her towards his face, kissing her fully on the lips again, whilst marvelling at the magnificence of her body, one given freely tonight to him. He could have died a happy man there and then.

Anjou banged on the door of her friends house. Kayleighn answered the door and looked with some disappointment at her friend

'Oh it's only you' she observed

'Nice welcome! I take it you were expecting someone else?' Anjou asked

'Not expecting, but hoping' laughed her friend, 'come on inside, lets have a talk'

Kayleighn told Anjou all she had heard since they last talked, how the woman next door was having an affair with someone out of town, how the towns councillor had been away and asked for a relaxation in this years tax burden (something Anjou knew already, however it didn't stop her friend repeating the fact), how many men she had bedded in the last four weeks and a whole lot of gossip taken from either the women of the town or the lax-talking men under her direct care!

'Any soldiers?' asked Anjou

'Why dear, do you want me to send some round? I don't think your husband would be too happy!'

'No I just wondered if there has been any talk of a young couple, possible runaways I think you might call them', said Anjou laughing in turn

'Now that is strange' answered Kayleighn, 'it's almost as if you knew already!'

'What?'

'Well I had a captain in my bed only about an hour before you came, and he was telling me that a contingent of the guard had gone down to the border because there had been some trouble there, you won't believe it, but it's claimed that a girl on her own murdered a whole contingent of guards on the other side of the River Dyn, down near the coast where Codencia Minor is! I believe less than half the news the men in my room tell me but he said it with some earnest, and this man who told me, you know the captain, is one of the few people who I would believe, as I think he is honest, well at least as honest as any man could ever possibly be, I know that's not saying much!'

Anjou at this point had stopped listening to her friends continued monologue and was thinking of the girl in her house, who she thought looked quite formidable (though she doubted she could take on a whole contingent of men) it might be something the Sheriff in town would like to be advised upon. Giving Kayleighn just as long as necessary for it not to appear she had only come for this bit of news, she excused herself claiming she had guests who she had to tend and promised she would come around again the next day. She rushed back out of the town gate, passed the gatekeeper without a word and ran up her path towards the door.

Golan was dozing in his chair and she shook him none too gently

'Wake up you oaf' she explained, 'I have some news!'

Golan rubbed his eyes and peered at his excitable wife

'What is it?' he enquired

Anjou related the whole story about the murder of a whole contingent of guards and hissed at her disbelieving husband, 'it's them, it's them upstairs, I would bet any price it is!'

'Now, now!' he exclaimed, 'let us not jump to conclusions, it's just a story you heard and less believable than the story those two have told us, and besides that, remember that Daal recommended them and he wouldn't be likely to set up an old friend in that way if there was any danger would he?'

'He might if he didn't know all the facts!'

'And you do Anjou?'

I'm not saying that' she answered defensively' but it might be worth reporting these two to the sheriff don't you think?'

'Maybe, but not until they have gone, I don't want any fuss or any disruption to the business, once they have left tomorrow, you can do what you like, it will no doubt come to nothing anyway' he added

Chapter 8

They both rose quite early, noting was spoken about the previous night; Bracen was still in some kind of dream, Celeste was however, now doubting the wisdom of what she/they had done. This wasn't a teenage adventure, it was a deadly serious quest and she chided herself for her lack of self respect

They excused themselves from their hosts, mounted their horses and bid them farewell, they decided to ride through the town and out of the gate at the north side. It wasn't a market day so the road through wasn't too busy there were a few occasional stalls scattered along the route and they stopped at one of these and bought some bread and plenty of fruit, they paid the stall-holder one silver penny and set off once again, no-one paid them much attention as they rode casually towards the gate. The gatekeeper signalled them through without a word and they left without looking back. In truth Celeste hadn't much cared for Longfield the way she had Kaisley, Bracen however felt the place memorable for all the right reasons!

Not far out of the gate, probably about six furlongs, Keri swooped down from the sky and landed on Celeste's shoulder.

'It frightens the life out of me every time she does that' declared Bracen

'Don't listen to him darling' said Celeste to the bird, 'he is only jealous!'

Bracen grunted and peered ahead, the land lay flat and quite dry, they were not going to get much cover for a while, the sun was too hot and it was going to be an uncomfortable days riding.

They had been out of Longfield for about three hours when a hard ridden horse came up from behind them; there was nowhere to hide, so they just continued on their journey hoping he would sweep past. The horseman slowed momentarily to look at them, but then rode off northwards without a word.

'What was all that about?' asked Bracen

'I don't want to imagine that everyone in the world is looking for us, for that way simply leads to paranoia, lets just hope it was a traveller in a hurry going in the same direction, there's nothing to show on the map between here and Bridgenorth, which is about a weeks solid riding away' she answered

'I feel exposed on this road without shelter or cover' declared Bracen 'is there no other way?'

'Not that this map shows, its looks to me that the quickest route north is by the road, which makes sense in this dry land, one thing is for certain, we are going to have to not ride the horses too hard, we have precious little to drink, certainly not enough to see us a full week, and I don't want anything to happen to Bren' she said as she patted her proud horses neck'.

'We have food enough maybe to get us to Bridgenorth if we ration ourselves, there may just be enough for the horses too. The water situation is a worry and I am already parched!' he answered shaking his head

Keri had no problems finding food however whether it was rodents or other small birds, at least she wouldn't go hungry.

It was late afternoon and Keri had once again flown off and she could be seen high up in the sky wheeling around, she swooped once again before immediately taking off, and then repeated the action twice more. Celeste reined her horse in.

'Bracen!' she called ahead, 'I think Keri is trying to tell us that we might have company again soon.'

Bracen slowed his horse and wheeled round to face Celeste, 'there's nowhere here to hide' he declared.

He looked worried.

'Yes that's true' she replied as she reached down for her sword.

If there was going to be any trouble she wanted to be ready. She pulled the bow from around her back and readied an arrow just in case. Soon they could see the tell tale signs of approaching horseman as the dust was sent spiralling up in the air.

'Go Keri' said Celeste 'keep us in sight but stay out of bowshot from any of the riders!'

The riders swept over a small hill in front of them, Celeste grasped her sword firmly, ready to do whatever necessary. Bracen looked scared, there where at lest twenty horsemen galloping towards them and not even Celeste's true aim and fiery swordplay could keep all these at bay.

'Stay your sword' he shouted at Celeste as the horseman swept past and then turned at right angles and turned again until they were encircled the riders edging their horses nearer and nearer until the were only a few feet away. Without a word they all stopped and pointed long spears directly at Bracen and Celeste. Bracen could feel his heart beating through his ribs and the sound thundered in his ears as he looked terrified at the faces of the horsemen.

One of their number leapt down from his horse and strolled to where Celeste and Bracen stood motionless.

'Name and business' he demanded.

'Give me your name and I will give you something to remember me by' said Celeste with a sneer.

'Ah so you are the spokeswoman it seems' he declared, 'see here now, I am Captain Farrier and I am tasked to look for a fugitive, someone who murdered two border guards way down south yonder', he pointed vaguely back in the direction of Longfield. 'Some reports say there is just one, whilst other say there are two, but anyway it seems likely given your appearance and your acid tongue you just might have the necessary courage to take on a couple of armed men and win. What do you think?' He turned around to ask his men

They murmured in agreement.

He nodded at her before adding 'but there are twenty of us and I don't think your silent friend will want to die pointlessly resisting arrest!'

'Arrest for what? demanded Celeste as she glared at the captain.

The answer came back immediately, 'for murder most likely'

'But why do you think that we are the fugitives you are looking for?

'We have a description of a woman, of your height and your bearing, with your hair colouring and who it is said is most formidable, I think that adequately describes you.' he answered as he looked her up and down.

'Any many others' replied Celeste, though her heart now faltered as she realised she was not going to convince this weather-hardened captain with a battle of words.

'Take them' he ordered his men 'and do not resist' he said looking directly into Celeste's brown eyes.

'Where are you taking us sir?' asked Bracen.

'To the military sheds just northeast of here, only about one hours ride' he replied

'And then? questioned Bracen again

'And then, if I can get through the day without you asking me any more fruitless and stupid questions, you will stay there, as our guests, until we can get representation from Stanleigh, I am not your judge, but others will be, and when it is time for you to be judged I warn you now, and you especially' he said as he looked again at Celeste, 'do not bandy words with the servants of the law lest its force comes crashing down around your head, if you answer with honesty you will have no problems'

They were allowed to mount their horses and they rode alongside three horsemen at either side with two ahead and two at the rear, there was no chance of any escape and the only thing they could do was fall in with their request.

'At least we may get fresh food and be able to drink tonight' thought Bracen ruefully

It was as the captain said as one hour of the day elapsed before they saw the sheds. The men all dismounted and Captain Farrier indicated to them both to do the same. There horses were taken from them along with all their personal belongings, they were none too gently pushed to what looked like a jail, and they were ushered inside and the door closed behind them with a clang.

Other than being jostled neither of them had suffered any real harm, they looked around at their cell, it seemed they were going to be housed together at any rate, though there only appeared to be one wooden pallet which might serve as a bed. There was a small window with a bar high up where the wall met the roof but it brought in little light.

'This doesn't feel like being treated as guests, any ideas?' asked Bracen

'No but I will think of something' she answered grimly.

They both sat down on the pallet in silence wondering what would now transpire, when the door opened and two men entered, they dragged Bracen up to his feet and pushed him back out of the cell.

It was the last time Celeste would see him for nearly a month.

Chapter 9

Nothing more happened, day turned into night and night into day, men came and gave her food, but no one spoke, she was given a wooden pale for her toileting needs which was emptied daily but apart from that no one spoke to her. She wondered occasionally about forcing an escape, but the men came at irregular times and she didn't know where Bracen was and in what condition he might be in. She wondered about Keri and whether there was anyway to get a message out using the falcon, but she had nothing to scribe on, and she hadn't seen her friend since she flew away when the militia had approached.

Then late one evening the door opened and someone pushed Bracen inside her cell. He was in a terrible state, his face all cuts and bruises, he had been stripped to the waist and his gaunt body too was covered in lesions and bruises. His arm was in a basic splint, no doubt it had been broken and his mouth was encrusted in blood where some teeth appeared to have been either knocked out or forcefully removed. She rushed over to him and helped him over to the pallet.

He looked up through his blood shot eyes and the speech came in gasps.

'I wouldn't tell them......they tried to make me talk......make me admit to witnessing the killings......but I told them I didn't see anything.......I told them we were just travellers wanting to get to Midencia.......oh! but Celeste, they beat me, they beat me every day, with fists and with wooden stakes, they even broke my arm and smashed my face against the wall.....I lost teeth' he said through his tears.

'The soldiers did this?' she asked

No, the first two weeks were okay, I was just locked in my cell like this.......then He came..... they said he was a Sherrif out of Longfield and he brought with him two henchmen.........'it was they that did this to me, while that bastard watched on laughing'

His breathing was laboured and he was clearly in some pain but he managed another sentence before collapsing back to the floor again

'Celeste........... they said you were next!'

Celeste put his head into her lap, her face wrung with pity for her best friend and guilt for putting in him in this position. She should have never let him come on this journey; she should have made him stay in Codencia Minor. One thing was certain however as the thought hardened inside her, she wasn't going to let them torture him any more, when they came for her, she would be ready!

Celeste cradled her friend's head all through the night as he slept, sometimes crying out in pain in his sleep, she stroked his hair whilst sitting with her back to the stone cell.

Dawn broke and Celeste who had fallen asleep sat in that position woke with a start as the door flew open. Two men entered and one of them said gruffly to Celeste.

'Come with us'

Bracen was now also awake and tried to move but he was in far too much pain

'Please don't hurt her' he groaned

The first man laughed, 'We have more novelties that can be used on this one; there are more ways to break someone than just violence'

Bracen knew exactly what he was referring to and judging by the fire in Celeste's eye so did she. The second man reached out to grasp Celeste by the arm, she didn't resist but spat in his face as he pulled her towards him. He slapped her across the face but Celeste was unmoved and showed no reaction at all. She was pushed roughly out of the cell and made to walk in her bare feet across the stony ground towards another building. If she was in pain she didn't show it.

She was thrown into another cell similar to the one which she had stayed in, except this one had a table and chair in the middle. The second man shut the door behind them and smiled to himself, this was going to be enjoyable. He walked over to Celeste who stood proudly and showing no discernible concern. He pulled with some force at her tunic exposing her right breast but Celeste still didn't move as he grabbed it and fondled her nipple.

The first man laughed and eager to join the action was taking his over trousers off, he walked over to Celeste and rubbed up against her, his manhood pressing against her thigh, his breath stank and Celeste turned her face away and shut her eyes as he pawed at her. She stiffened as he thrust his hands between her legs and tried to enter her with his grimy fingers.

The second one was now masturbating as his friend thrust his fingers further inside her. This was nothing like the sensation she had felt with Bracen, she felt sick and her head was spinning, all reason was leaving her, she decided it was time to defend herself. Her knee came up and she connected between the first mans legs; his grip loosened as he held himself in agony and sank to his knees. The second one lunged at her and attempted to pin her to the wall as the first got to his feet, his face like thunder.

'Enough' came a voice from behind them, 'bring her to me!'

The two men grasped at Celeste and shoved her roughly towards the newcomer who was stood by the table, her breast was still exposed and she made no attempt to hide her modesty.

'You two will answer for this' he indicated to Celeste, 'you were told to bring her here but not for your own sexual gratification'

'She was resisting, she wouldn't comply' complained the first

'Enough' shouted the third man again, 'your skills are for violence and not for words!'

He turned to Celeste and bowed in a mocking way

'Hopefully you will have more sense than these two, or your friend Bracen, my name is Piotr, and I am the Sherrif from Longfield'

Celeste brushed herself down and put her exposed breast back in her tunic. She wiped the sweat from her face before answering.

'Why are we being held, and why have you beaten my friend so?'

'I will ask the questions' Piotr declared forcefully 'and the form of your own punishment will go hand in hand with the answers you give me, if you lie you will be beaten. Carry on lying and I will leave you in the most capable hands of my two friends here who have little charm or wit but know how to inflict pain most effectively'

Celeste nodded and stared defiantly at the other two men.

'Now' said Piotr, 'there have been rumours of one, perhaps two fugitives, wanted in Codencia Minor, and whilst there is no love lost between this country and theirs, our leaders would not wish to antagonise them at this time. Word came to me nearly a month ago that two youngsters had stayed in Longfield and were travelling north; I ordered your detainment so I could question you. Your friend chose to be most argumentative and unwilling to speak anything but untruths and so as a result he was punished. I trust you will be more sensible?'

Piotr sat down at the table and looked up at her, she was magnificent in her bearing and he could almost understand why his men had been tempted in the way they were.

'One question then, did you kill two border guards at the bridge over the River Dyn?

Celeste looked straight into his eyes and said

'Yes, I did!'

'See' said Piotr to his men, 'see how easy it is when you introduce intelligence into the discussion'

The two men looked disappointed but said nothing in return, he stood up to leave.

'Wait' insisted Celeste, 'surely you want to hear my tale, for I believe I was justified in my actions'

He turned and faced her with a false smile

Nay young lady' replied Piotr, 'I just needed your confession, witnessed by these two, others will judge your guilt and name the time and place of your execution. Your body will then no doubt be sent back quartered to Codencia Minor in part payment for your sins.

All three then departed and Celeste was left on her own. Her head was spinning, what could she do now? She sat on the chair with her head in her hands. Nothing, no ideas came into her mind... She had condemned herself and probably Bracen to death because of her need for revenge. She needed to think! The confession would need to be scribed and witnessed by Piotr's two henchmen (if they could write) and then this would have to be taken to Stanleigh, then either the judge would come north or more likely the soldiers would transport herself and Bracen to the capital. As far as she could see that might be her only opportunity. She needed to decide a course of action.

Later in the evening when her meagre meal was brought in, Celeste asked the guard if she could speak again with Piotr. The guard shook his head and explained that Piotr and his two bodyguards had already ridden south to Stanleigh. Not to be put off she asked if she could speak to the captain of the militia, the one who had arrested them the month previously.

'I will ask' agreed the soldier, 'but I cannot guarantee he will come'

Some minutes later the door opened again and in strode the Captain Farrier who approached the table where Celeste was sat. She quickly stood up, tipping the chair over behind her in her haste.

'You wish to speak to me?' he asked

'Yes' she replied, 'I wondered if it would be possible to see Bracen? He was sorely hurt in his interrogation and I would like to bathe his wounds!'

The captain stern face softened slightly

'What you ask is not impossible, I am a reasonable man and I would not wish to see another hurt unnecessarily'

Celeste looked at him, there was something in his proud stance that indicated that though he was a military man, and followed orders to the letter, he was also fully aware of what had transpired between the Sherriff's men and Bracen, and that he didn't approve.

'Tomorrow' he said, 'I will see to it that you are housed together to await your doom'

He turned to go away

'One more thing Captain' said Celeste,' in order to tend his wounds I really need the pouch from Bracen's horse, it has leaves and herbs which can be used to tend his cuts and bruises,'

'You ask for much' observed the captain, 'however I can see no harm in your request, and I shall ensure you receive the supplies you need.'

Celeste thanked him and he turned again and walked through the door. A plan was beginning to formulate in her head. She desperately needed to see Bracen and deliver the herbs.

She slept fitfully through the night worrying about Bracen and was already awake before dawn when the door was opened and two guards told her to follow them. She did as ordered, across the stony ground again to her original cell. Bracen too was awake, propped up again the wall, supporting his left arm with his right. She rushed over to him as the door once again shut behind them.

'Bracen, I am so sorry' she said, 'why didn't you save yourself and tell the truth?'

He gave a weary half-smile and said

'I thought I was protecting you, I wanted to take the pain myself and in besides I was telling the truth to a certain extent. I only saw you kill only one of the guards, you told me of the other, so it was only a half-lie!'

Celeste held his injured hand; he winced in pain as his arm jolted slightly.

'Bracen, I have told them the truth and I am afraid I might have condemned us both to death by doing so'

Bracen nodded knowingly as if he had already guessed at events.

'But' continued Celeste, 'I have the beginning of a plan, but I will need your help. How long do you think it will take for the Sherrif to get to Stanleigh and back?

Bracen thought for a moment whilst trying to picture the map they had possessed, 'I don't know exactly but I would have thought at least six days, why?'

'So six days there, six back with a probably day in between, that gives us just under two-weeks before we are transported, how long will it take your arm to heal?'

'Usually five to six weeks depending on the break' he replied

'So your arm will be useless until then? asked Celeste miserably

'More or less, but it is my left and I am right handed, so it shouldn't inconvenience me too much so long as we bandage it tightly in this splint, it's a shame I haven't got my herbs in the pouch, I had a supply of linen in there!' he said sadly

'Well I have some good news for you my wounded soul! I got the captain to agree to let you have your pouch so I could tend your cuts and bruises, I think deep down he is an honourable man and disliked your treatment by the Sherrif's men, what is in the pouch?

'I can't fully remember' admitted Bracen, 'I am still in a lot of pain and I can't concentrate, once it's delivered I should be able to identify them.'

'Rest then' said Celeste, 'if the captain is true to his word then he should allow us the herbs, I will wake you when they arrive'

Bracen was too tired to argue and rested once again propped up against the wall, whilst Celeste paced up and down restlessly.

It must have been around an hour though to her it felt much more, that the door opened and a solider entered and without hesitation threw the pouch at Celeste, she caught it in one movement.

'Complements of the Captain' he said as he turned and retreated through the door.

She opened the pouch and looked inside, there were different compartments within all holding herbs, the flap at the front held the strips of lined Bracen had mentioned and there were a couple of strange looking leaves in a separate part of the pouch.

Bracen stirred and shifted his weight to his right, 'has it come?' he asked, 'bring it to me!' Okay, linen for my splint' he unravelled a large piece and placed it on the floor next to where he was sitting. He looked further inside; he could identify them all without emptying the contents

Basil, Rosemary and Lemon Balm, like I told you before, there is Calendula, that would be good for my cuts and bruises, Senna for constipation, not much chance of that here' he added with a painful laugh, 'Lavender, good, that helps ease headaches and something I picked up at the apothecary in Kaisley'

He pulled out a bunch of leaves wrapped in an old piece of stained linen. 'This is Sumac' he explained, 'if you handle it without care it can leave you with a most unpleasant bout of rashes and itchiness'

'Is it deadly?' asked Celeste

'Not that I know of' admitted Bracen, 'but it would be most uncomfortable for the afflicted person, Ah yes, here it is, I have some Comfrey too, that might help my bone heal easier.'

'Well let's start with that one, the one you said was for cuts and bruises'

Bracen relaxed whilst Celeste tried her best, he didn't have the nerve to tell her what she was doing was probably ineffective, or that she would be best served with water and clean linen to wash his cuts, because in truth he was enjoying the attention which was a welcome change after the brutal beatings. She did however help wrap his arm more securely within the splint and he took some of the Comfrey.

'I was thinking just now, whilst you were discussing herb-lore that we might use it somehow to force an escape, not too soon but certainly before they come to take us in less than two weeks. We certainly need to let your arm start to heal before any attempt is made, so we have some days to formulate an escape plan, and it needs to work Bracen otherwise our days are numbered!'

Chapter 10

The days past and they talked through their escape plan, the pain was easing somewhat in his arm though it was still useless, the cuts had healed and scabbed and his mouth had improved to such an extent that he could chew effectively. They had noticed that during the night the military sheds were not a hive of activity and they could hear no noises from the yard outside. They knew there was at least one guard posted at all time, there were usually two during the day.

Cendibell was a simple man, uneducated as most of the people from the small town of Lavis on the River Khain were, however he was particularly suited to military life. He took orders without question and carried them out with efficiency, believing that his captain was the wisest, fairest and most brave individual he had ever met or have the privilege to serve under. His belief in the captain was absolute he felt he was blessed to have been given this posting since it was a true honour to serve under his command. So when he had been ordered to stand guard outside the prisoner's cell for the next five nights, he did so without question and without complaint. The order had been given; there was no room for any personal regret that he wasn't spending the evening with his garrison. Whatever he thought personally of the two prisoners did not matter, the captain had told him they were dangerous fugitives who had to be guarded however he felt no personal animosity towards them, in fact the girl had for the last couple of nights spoken to him through the closed door, claiming she was restless and not able to sleep. She had asked him where he was from and he had told her proudly of his upbringing on the river as a fisherman's son. She had told him of her life, how she had lost her father at an early age, how she had lived with her mother on the coast in the south-westernmost part of Codencia. The girl had told him her name was Celeste and her injured friend was Bracen. Cendibell saw no harm in this nightly conversation and even told her his own name.

It was the fifth night since Celeste had admitted her guilt to the Sherrif and Cendibell had told her this was his last night on duty so this very evening would have to be the one where they attempted the escape.

They waited until well after midnight when the evening noises from the camp had died down. Bracen stripped to the waist and took the Pumac in his right hand; he quickly rubbed the leaf all over his torso and indicated to Celeste that she should do the same to his back, though holding the leaves with the discoloured linen to ensure she didn't have any reaction. He also added some to his face below his eyes. The result was startling, almost immediately his skin turned purple and became swollen, the desire to itch was overwhelming, his face especially looked awful as his cheeks and neck became inflamed with the poison. Celeste went over to the door

'Cendibell' she called,' you must come quickly to see my friend; I fear he has caught some horrible disease whilst we were in the fen in the south of the county some weeks ago. He has been complaining for the last few days of terrible headaches which is why I left him sleeping nightly'.

Cendibell opened the door, and pointed to Celeste, 'you stand there by his side where I can see you, no tricks okay?'

'Don't get too near warned Celeste, his disease looks highly contagious to me, I need to be housed in another cell'

Cendibell looked in some sympathy at the prostate men, he looked terrible and close to death, if indeed this disease was so contagious it might be best to get the girl out of the cell as she asked. He move slightly closer to get a better view, he would not touch him but he needed to get all the facts before he reported this to his captain.

That was his last thought as he buckled under the blow to his head from Celeste.

'Have you killed him?' asked Bracen sitting up

No, but quickly I have another idea, use more of the leaf, spread it over his body and into his face. Have you anything that could keep him out like this?

'Lobelia would probably poison him enough to keep him under for a short while; I am told it slows the heart'. He carefully mixed the herb in some water and administered into Cendibell's mouth whilst still unconscious, the soldier gave a small cough and involuntary swallowed as the liquid was poured in.

Bracen was rubbing Lemon Balm vigorously to his rashes.

'I hope this works the way I hope it should otherwise I am going to be in agony for days!'

Quickly Celeste rubbed more on his back and into other areas he couldn't reach with his broken arm. She looked at Cendibell on the floor and shook her head; it was a pity to treat him so, since he had seemed a decent enough man.

They moved to the door, Celeste peered outside, there was no visible movement.

Carefully and silently the moved away from where they knew the men were housed, they had already discussed the fact that if they managed to escape they would be much safer as far away from the road as possible, in fact it was their intention to strike directly east since that would be the direction they would be least expected to go. They made it to the perimeter of the shed complex and still they heard no one. They had nothing however, they dare not try and go for their horses lest a guard was on duty in the stables and furthermore they had no weapons. They had to escape with stealth and trust totally to luck. They scrambled in the darkness between rocks and boulders, the land was dry and so they would leave no footprints as such. After an hour they stopped to rest, they were by now well out of sight from the sheds and they listened intently for any sound of pursuit but none came. So far they seemed to have fortune on their side

In the sheds, another soldier ambled over to the cell where Cendibell was posted, it was his turn to stand guard until mid-morning, yawning he wandered towards the building.

'Where was Cendibell? He certainly wasn't outside the door, it was not his style to abandon his post, something must be very wrong. He pushed open the door; the prisoners were clearly not there. A half-unconscious Cendibell was on the floor, he looked in a terrible state, and in fact he looked bloody diseased.

Cendibell half lifted his arm as if to ask for help but the other soldier had already turned tail and left, running across the yard he barged into his captain's accommodation without the usual courtesy of knocking first. His captain was awake in fact already dressed for the day.

'Captain Sir, it's the prisoners, they are gone!'

'What!' roared the captain, 'who was on duty last night?'

'It was Cendibell sir, but he looks terrible, I think they infected him with some terrible disease, I think he will die'

'If he is responsible for their escape he most certainly will' barked the captain. 'Go fetch someone with some healing expertise and meet me at the cell.'

Minutes later they had Cendibell fully conscious, the soldier with some healing expertise had quickly seen the abandoned leaf and linen which had been used and guessed correctly what had happened.

The captain was beside himself with rage,

'Leave him in the cell,' he ordered, and the rest of you split up I want a small contingent south and a larger one north since we know that is the way they were travelling, they won't get far, the boy Bracen is too badly hurt and their horses haven't been taken or their weapons. When you find them, bring them straight back to me here. I fully expect Cendibell to have company in the next eight hours!'

Dawn broke on the two weary escapees, they could see hills in the distance, no doubt the north-side of the Strait Canyons, and if they could make it there undetected they would be safe. About two hours later they made it to the foothill the mountains in front would provide the cover they needed. Celeste told Bracen to rest for a few minutes before they started to climb

Bracen sat with his good hand cradling his chin in thought

'Where is that bird of yours?'

Celeste looked at the floor and then at Bracen,

'I feel in my heart she is gone forever, probably looked and found a mate. She will have been confused that we didn't reappear and she has a self protecting instinct as all birds of prey do'

'Don't despair, she is a Mountain Falcon after all, maybe she found somewhere in the Strait Canyons down there' he waved vaguely south-east in the direction of the largest peaks in the mountain range.

A faint glimmer of hope came into Celeste's heart, maybe Bracen was correct.

'Come' she said, 'I would like to make the river before nightfall'

Bracen got wearily to his feet and Celeste looked at him again with some pity.

'When we get there, we will find somewhere to make camp and I promise you Bracen, we are not venturing any further until your arm is fit to use and you have regained both your physical and inner strength'

It was approaching dusk when they finally started to descend down a steep slope, they could see the fast moving river below them and Bracen was finding it difficult to keep his feet daring not to over-balance onto his broken left side. Eventually they made it down to the side of the river where they both stood surveying the area.

'We need to cross this' pointed Celeste to the wide river 'but you cannot swim in this flow,'

'What then?' asked Bracen, 'we have no sword or knife to cut wood and nothing to bind anything together so a raft is out of the question, how will we manage it?' he asked glumly.

'I don't know yet' answered Celeste, 'but we must cross this river for I believe that the other side is the country of Valdencia so we ought to be safe from pursuit there. For now I need you to rest, sleep if you can but out of sight somewhere for I am going to explore the riverside up there' she added as she pointed northwards.

Bracen had fallen asleep with his back to a tree by the river when Celeste returned some hours later. She gently shook him awake.

'I have a plan' she explained 'not far from here there is a strange substance growing from the ground, it is like a tree but it has no branches, it is some way back from the river but there is lots of it, sticking straight up into the air'

'Probably bamboo' observed Bracen

'Never heard of it' admitted Celeste, 'however I tried to pull one out of the ground but I fear they are too deep rooted. I found this one on the floor rotten nearby'

Bracen nodded, 'I think this is bamboo, do you plan to build a raft?'

'Yes' she answered, 'and I think I know how I can chop it down without a knife! It seems very dry so I will start a fire nearby then use the embers of some strips of wood to burn it at the base, have you seen? It's hollow, so it will be good to get us across the river and all I need to do then is to make it wide enough for you to lay on, I can swim at the back of the raft pushing it forward. The river's current though fast is I believe traversable and I plan to try and get to the hills at the other side!'

'Is all this necessary?' asked Bracen, 'couldn't we just stay this side of the river?'

Celeste shook her head, 'no we dare not risk it, for if they look for us in this direction which they must do eventually then we would not be safe. I would prefer to cross the river into Valdencia'

'Do you think any pursuit would respect the border?' asked Bracen

'I know not', she replied, 'but I will feel safer if we cross the water, if they come looking for us with dogs then the river will mask the scent.'

They made camp for the rest of the day, Celeste stripped the one piece of bamboo she had brought back, and she planned to use the strands of the substance to bind the raft together. It didn't need to be too sturdy, so long as it held Bracen's weight she was confident the current in the deep wide river wouldn't be too challenging for her.

They spent a restless night on the banks of the river, always fearful of pursuit. The dawn broke to an overcast day, which wasn't what Celeste had hoped for. She had planned to use the dryness of the morning sun to help start a fire near the bamboo by now she would have to try and find enough dry leaves and twigs to make this possible. Bracen helped in the gathering of the material to burn as he felt the need to contribute though once enough was gathered it was left to Celeste to create the spark using hard stones which she rubbed together. It took a while but eventually a small fire was started and they added to the burning grasses and twigs with larger pieces of bark and fallen branches. Within an hour they had a fire burning merrily though Celeste was concerned that too much smoke might lead their pursuers to where they were. Nevertheless her plan worked and the bamboo came away from it roots easily once burnt. It took the best part of the day but eventually she had enough for her needs and started to bind them together. It was approaching dusk again by the time Celeste was satisfied the raft was good enough for their purposes.

She looked again at the river in the gathering gloom, it looked at least four furlongs across.

'So Bracen, let us attempt this now before darkness properly descends' she declared

Bracen walked over to the dying fire and tried to kick the burning embers aside so as not to leave a signal of where they had camped. Celeste joined him until they had at least stopped the smoking in the fire. There wasn't enough time to properly hide the fire. If it was discovered she hoped the pursuers might think they had struck north at this side of the river.

They both waded out to the shallow sides of the river Celeste pulling the raft behind her. She helped Bracen on with some difficulty since he only had the one useful arm to haul himself on board. She kicked away from the bank and slowly pushed the boat forward using her strong legs to propel them to the bank at the other side. Bracen felt hopeless he couldn't even help, at one point he tried to use his good arm to paddle but this only made the raft veer to one side as there was no counter-stroke at the other side.

'Stop it you idiot' laughed Celeste as she paused for a moment holding onto the raft. 'How far is there to go do you think?'

'I would guess we are more than half way across so it shouldn't take too long' answered Bracen

Eventually they made landfall at the other side and Celeste hauled the raft up out of the water. The riverside had a small copse which would provide shelter for the night, the next day they could explore further to find a more appropriate camp to make their base until Bracen recovered.

Chapter 11

The next day dawned bright and they set about exploring further inland towards the hills which were the north side of the Strait Canyon. They scrambled about the rocks for some time, Bracen lower down whilst Celeste made for the tops of the hills to see if she could get a better picture in her head of precisely where they were. Eventually she made it to the top of the largest of the hills, the land to the east appeared fairly flat and she could make out some settlements in the distance which must be part of Valdencia. To the south the river narrowed until it ran through the canyon, she couldn't see any further than this. To the north the river wound out of sight though there appeared to be trees on either side of the river as far as the eye could see, she thought in the distance she could see a far away range of mountains. Turning her eyes west, she surveyed the route they had taken after escaping. She could see no obvious movement or signs of pursuit but she knew in her heart their captors would definitely be searching for them both.

She felt rather exposed on the top of the hill so carefully made her way back down to where she had left Bracen earlier. She found him looking very pleased with himself.

'Well something has cheered you up this morning' she declared

'I found a cave' he replied, 'just north of here, it has a large bush in front of it so offers some protection I think it would be ideal!'

Bracen took Celeste by the hand and led her up a small incline, there at the start of the foothills of the canyon she saw the bush Bracen had described. It was difficult to see anything behind it so if the cave was deep enough then it would indeed suit their purposes. They squeezed through past the bush. The cave was narrow at the front but opened out into a large cavern. The light failed some way in so they could tell exactly how far back the cave went, they would have to get used to the darkness within the cave to explore further. The floor was dry but there were definite indications at least one person had been in the cave at some point in the past as there was a discarded water pouch and the bones of some animal which had no doubt been eaten. It was impossible to tell how long ago the cave had been inhabited though Celeste guessed it wasn't recent since the bones were very dry as was the container. They spread the rest of their few belongings on the floor of the cave, they had no weapons to hunt with and the only useful thing they still had was the bag of herbs which had served them so well in the prison.

'Food and water are going to be necessary' said Celeste, 'I am going to have to try and fashion some kind of weapon to hunt with'

'I can fish' replied Bracen, 'I only need the one good arm, I'm sure we will not starve, I feel I could eat enough for two today!'

'Don't' laughed Celeste ' you will only make it worse, I need to find some way of getting a good supply of water back to the cave and I need to find some food to eat, I think we may be hungry today! I also need to bathe, I have no clothes other than the one's I am stood in and I hate being dirty!'

She looked over at Bracen and smiled 'this is not an invitation!'

Bracen stood up and took her by the hand; he looked deeply into her eyes and said to her seriously.

'Celeste, I thought we had come much further than that!'

She sighed and shook her head slightly. Bracen suddenly felt the cold hand of doubt reaching out for him. He spoke nervously.

'That night in Longfield it meant so much to me, I thought……well I thought we had something, I thought when we made love, it would mean as much to you as it did to me……I thought you kindness these last few days, the way you have looked after me since I had my arm broken……Have I been so blind and stupid to think you might love me?'

Celeste looked sadly back at him.

'Bracen, my actions in the river before we got to Kaisley were wrong, my submission to your desires in Longfield were a mistake but please don't think I didn't care when we made love, it was my first time and I wouldn't have wanted to share the experience with anyone else but you. You mean so much to me, really you do, you always have, ever since I was a little girl, but I fear this quest means even more and I want nothing to get in the way of finding my father! It's not that I don't want you; the truth is I don't want anybody and in the long term pretending to love you the way you want me to would only drive a barrier between us. You are the best friend I ever had, yes we made love too, but please let us put that experience behind us for now?'

Bracen looked miserable and said 'So no kind of contact at all, just friends?'

'I'm sorry Bracen, truly I am, I can see the way you look at me and I can feel your love and in any other circumstances I would have been happy to be yours, yes even to marry someday, but these aren't normal circumstances and neither of us knows where this quest will lead. I will say no more on the matter, I need to explore around the camp'.

She turned her back towards the cave front so Bracen could not see the anguish on her face. She had just destroyed the hopes of the only person she had ever had any kind of feeling for other than her parents, and she felt totally wretched.

Another wretched soul too was regretting his actions, still locked in the cell the captain had harshly had him locked in since the two youngsters escape, Cendibell now asked to speak to his captain once more.

He was brought shaking before the stern officer who of course demanded answers:

'Well, what have you to say for yourself? Tell me why I shouldn't have you tried right now for your incompetence?'

Cendibell looked at his captain with fear and found the words difficult to say, he was so afraid of what might be the consequences of misplaced words.

'Sir, I admit…..I was foolish……I thought the girl was interested in my life, where I was from, what kind of family I had…..she seemed to care and only wanted some company…..you know through the night……when I was on duty. If there is anyway I can make amends for my stupidity?

The captain looked at his quaking subordinate and frowned.

'Your stupidity is a lesson for all men; I think nine out of ten would have been distracted with those breasts and those long legs. I think maybe I have been too harsh, so I am going to propose something to assuage your guilt and guarantee your freedom from the noose'

'The noose?' said Cendibell alarmed

'Yes the noose, you would be hung for your incompetence under any other captain's rule, but I have another plan for you. We have sent parties north south up and down the road between Bridgenorth and Longfield and there had been no sign of either of them. I can't imagine they have split up given the young mans condition. There is nothing to recommend the journey west though I have just sent a search party that way, but it is my guess they headed east towards the river and then maybe turned north following the path by the river side. I have posted men at Bridgenorth since they would have to cross the bridge there to get into Midencia, your task will be to hunt them from the south. Take six men of your choice, and take three dogs also. Find me the fugitives and your life is spared. You can bring them back dead or alive I really don't care. Fail me however and you will go to the gallows….do you understand?'

Cendibell could find no words to thank his captain for his clemency, the threat of the noose and the gallows had quite unnerved him. The captain turned and left for his daily duties leaving Cendibell in an utter state of shock.

By dusk on the next day Cendibell with his men and his team of dogs had picked up some kind of scent and they were being drawn further east towards the river just as the captain had suspected. Before nightfall they found evidence of a fire which had its traces kicked over however at this point the dogs seemed confused and appeared to have lost track.

Cendibell considered for a moment two possible courses of action, they could cross the river into Valdencia and though there was no conflict between the two countries such an act would be illegal and could bring additional problems to him and his men if they were caught. The other option was to blindly strike north as his captain had suggested. He made up his mind to follow the river northwards, he knew his life was at risk whatever he did, fail in the task and it was the gallows, should he find the fugitives…..well the girls reputation for violence was evident and he had no desire to feel death from a woman's hand. He had another choice, one he might take if the search northwards didn't come to fruition. He would have to escape in the night across the river, forever condemning himself to death if he ever returned to Codencia. He would remain an outcast in a strange land but at least he would be alive. Deep down Cendibell knew which of the choices he would probably have to make!

He made camp for the night right at the spot Celeste and Bracen had crossed the water, tomorrow he would issue orders to go north and he would send one of the soldiers back to the captain to report on his actions, this would also mean less soldiers to deceive if he did feel the need to escape before they reached Bridgenorth. A watch was posted and Cendibell tried to sleep, but sleep didn't come easily for the simple man from Lavis. He knew he was unlikely to see any of his family again whatever the outcome.

'

Chapter 12

A kind of routine settled in with the two fugitives. Bracen would spend the day trying to catch fish, sometimes successfully but more often than not the one's he caught were both bitter and oily. Celeste had managed to snare rabbits had also shown a good talent for fishing but the catch which set them up after only day two of the exile in the cave was the killing of a deer. She had managed to fashion a spear of sorts using a straight enough branch from a tree which she spent time cutting down using some sharp stones she found down by the rivers edge. Fortune had been kind, the deer had clearly been injured in some way previously and seemed reluctant to run when Celeste approached. The kill was easy she was only a few steps away when she struck the deer in its flank with the spear. The kill was quick and she picked up the deer by its legs and put it around her neck. Not a pleasant smell but the hunger overcame the vanity of a pungent Celeste. They ate well that night and managed to make the meat last for more than a fortnight. In between times they had eaten fish and rabbit and Bracen had even managed to gather some mushrooms and herbs from the side of the river. It was clear anyway they were not going to starve.

Two weeks into their time in the cave in Valdencia Bracen showed the first signs that his arm was healing. He had by now used the entire supply of Comfrey and he asked Celeste to remove the splint and simply bandage the arm tightly with the same cloth. In truth and under normal circumstances this ought to have required fresh linen, but they had none so had to make use of what they had.

Bracen had suggested they should make for one of the nearest settlements which Celeste had seen from the hill top previously, but she was against the idea just in case the chase had indeed gone over the river. She preferred to stay hidden for now. She calculated it would probably be another two weeks before they set off again and she planned to keep their hiding place a secret. She was to be proved wrong!

Early the next morning they were both sat at the river bank, fear of pursuit had now left them; they were quiet as they tried to catch the fish using branches with strips of bamboo for a line. Celeste stiffened as her keen ears caught the sound of movement to the north of where they sat at the bank

'Quick Bracen' she hissed, 'behind that tree, who knows who this is passing?'

Whoever it was seemed to be making straight for them and wasn't being quiet about it. The person, clearly a man was passing beneath the trees to their right, he passed the tree where they were both hidden without a backward glance and Celeste pounced. She struck the unfortunate traveller behind the knee as she dived forward, he went down straight away and Celeste was quickly on top of his using her weight and strength to pin him to the ground. When she realised who it was she almost laughed.

'Bracen, look who we have here, the unfortunate Cendibell!'. She slapped him across the face as her mood changed quickly, 'Now tell me how many more of your kind are in pursuit?'

Cendibell struggled to throw her from him but days of weary travelling without much to eat and the worry of exile had taken their toll on the soldier. Celeste grabbed him with one hand around the neck the other hand grasping his crotch.

'Now I can break you windpipe or break stop your ability to father children, the choice is yours!'

'Please' gasped Cendibell, 'I am on my own, I left the rest of the soldiers over a week ago much further north' he pointed vaguely back from the direction he had come. I'm a fugitive like you are now!'

Celeste relaxed her grip and stood up. She brushed the dust from her dirty clothing.

'Tell me what happened!' she demanded

'I will' he agreed, 'but first I need to rest and eat if you have any provision to spare. I have not faired too well this last week on the river bank'.

Celeste, whose mood was softening towards the man she had duped in the prison and violently attacked from behind, indicated to Bracen to come forward.

'See here Cendibell we have maybe another fortnight in this place before my friend Bracen here is fully fit to continue. We are willing to share our hideout and our provision so long as you help us in the quest to find food daily!'

Cendibell could do nothing but to accept, he knew this formidable girl was far too strong for him, even if he was fully fit. He suspected she would have no problem carrying out the threat to his windpipe or his manhood for that matter and didn't want to test himself against her. He picked himself up from the floor.

'I have no reason to love either of you' he declared, 'since your actions have cost me my life if I ever return to Codencia, but I will follow you to your hideout and upon my word I will not betray you to anyone!'

Celeste looked at his face; he had honesty in his eyes. Turning around to Bracen she said, 'Are you willing to share our hideout with him? I haven't consulted you as to your feelings!'

Bracen looked at the floor and muttered 'my feelings are the last thing on your mind presently', however Celeste clearly didn't hear (or want to hear) and took his lack of actual vocal objection as an affirmative.

Back at the cave and now fed, Cendibell explained what had happened.

'When the captain found you were gone, I was kept imprisoned in your cell as a consequence of my stupidity in falling for your attempts to befriend me'

Celeste made to speak, but Cendibell held up his hand to stop her

'Please let me tell you the whole story, I know why you did what you did, and in your position I might have attempted the same. Anyway the captain immediately sent teams north towards Bridgenorth and South down to Longfield in an attempt to waylay you; the majority of the force went north as it was generally believed that is where you were heading. Scouts came back after a day or two's searching without results. The captain sent another team west again with no results. Fearing for my life I asked to speak to him to apologise for my actions, he thought he was being generous when he told me that he would save me from the gallows if I could find you and bring you back to camp either dead or alive. It was his belief that you must have gone east to the river, there he thought you would turn north and try to get to Bridgenorth on the west side of the river, a large contingent of men was posted there, to intercept you if you attempted the river crossing from west to east at that place. I don't think it occurred to him you might cross the river and lay low. After a day or two I think I found evidence of your escape as I found an old camp fire along with some bamboo. I guessed you have either used the bamboo for fire or you had used it to cross the river, knowing your boyfriend's arm was badly broken. I took the men north after sending one back to the captain to report. The dogs had lost all trail of your scent which further convinced me that you had indeed crossed the river. It was clear I could not get to Bridgenorth otherwise my fate was sealed. So about one day south of the bridge I took the decision to desert my post and I managed to swim across the river during the night when it was my turn to watch. I have wandered south on this side of the river for over a week now, and had little to eat. I was worn out but tried to keep myself positive. I had seen no one else on my travels south, not a soul'

Celeste remained thoughtful, she was sure Cendibell was telling the truth but she knew that the hunt would still be on. If the captain guessed that he had crossed the river he might put all other political considerations to the side and take a band of men across the river to look for him and for them at the same time.

'We must go everywhere in pairs for now' she declared, 'whichever two go out, one should remain in the cave, this way we stand a better chance of remaining hidden even if one or more are caught'.

Bracen and Cendibell both nodded in agreement.

'For now, until you are rested, Bracen and I will find the food for today whilst you regain your strength, tomorrow's need may be greater!'

Celeste and Bracen returned to the riverside to continue their attempts to catch fish. Throughout the day they were reasonably successful, certainly enough for the three of them though a change of diet would have been welcomed, especially by Celeste, who had never been a lover of fish anyway.

They made their way back to the cave, Bracen carrying the fish with his good arm, Celeste carrying the spear she had fashioned the weeks previously. They pushed the bush back to squeeze inside. As usual the light was dim towards the back of the cave. Something alerted Celeste that something was amiss. She could see Cendibell sat with his back to the cave entrance, surely deeper in the cave she could make out the shadow of another. Immediately the fear of pursuit rekindled, gripping the spear in her right hand she approached the figure.

'Stay your spear' said the figure, 'I am no threat to you'

'Who are you and what are you doing in our cave?' demanded Celeste

'My name is Malic, and as to my right to be in this cave, I think you will have discovered that I was here some time before you were!'

'Go on' said Celeste warily

'I have been on a quest to the south, I passed this way at least half a year ago, once the winter months had departed from my land' explained Malic

'Where do you live and what is the quest you speak about?'

'So many questions, from a girl only armed with a badly made spear' he replied, 'I live in a place called Castletown in Midencia, as to my quest, that is my business and not yours, I will tell you however I have spent half the year for the last few years on this quest and I have searched the lands south, west and east. I am a seasoned traveller and used to walking in the wild. I am on my way back to my dwelling now, which is many leagues hence to the north. Will you try to bar my way?'

'I have no quarrel with you sir', answered Celeste, 'we too will soon push northwards on a quest of our own, at least me and Bracen. The other who you have already met travels south away from this land and is a chance companion whom we met on the road'

Malic laughed heartily

Me and Cendibell here have already exchanged words so I know you are both fugitives and so is he. It's a strange story and I wonder what brings two youngsters so far from their homeland and into the kind of trouble they found?'

Celeste relaxed and sat down beside Bracen, who appeared nervous as to the turn of events.

'Malic, if your quest is to remain secret then so is ours, needless to say we appear to be travelling in the same direction, or at least would be, as I fear we have a week or so to wait before my friend Bracen here is fit to go, Cendibell however flees from the noose and needs to get as far away from Codencia as possible!'

Malic considered this for a moment before replying.

'He could come to Midencia, I could find him employment and he would be safe there!'

Cendibell looked hopeful at this turn of events but realised they would still need to get past the soldiers stationed at Bridgenorth. Malic seemed to read his mind.

'I have weapons I can and will spare, if we move stealthily and under the cover of night I believe we could get to the bridge un-noticed. I have the necessary papers to travel however, but I guess you two haven't?' He pointed towards Celeste and Bracen

'So we need to be prepared' as he spoke Malic's keen eyes fell hungrily upon Celeste and her magnificent body, she however didn't notice his gaze. The ever protective Bracen did however and he spoke to the stranger for the first time.

'Why should we trust you? How do we know you are who you say you are?

Malic approached him and Bracen backed away slightly whilst Celeste stood her ground. Now pointing his sword towards them both he said.

'If I wanted I could kill you all now, I am well armed and well fed, I believe you are not. You have one over there too exhausted to even stand up, you are still carrying your arm and I doubt you could even lift a sword at this point'. That leaves you' he said as he looked again at Celeste. 'For some reason best known to the Gods I am moved to help you, whether it's for your formidable appearance or your obvious beauty under your tattered and dirty clothing, I know not. What I will promise though is a friendship you should not easily cast away. I am strong and extremely skilful with the bow. Are you willing to accept my friendship?'

He held out his hand, Bracen took it with some trepidation but Celeste seemed satisfied and shook his hand warmly.

'It is good we have another to add to our party. I feel with your knowledge of the paths we are set to tread then we have little to fear!'

'It is agreed then' said Malic, 'tomorrow we will plan the rest of our journey!'

Chapter 13

It was decided the next morning. They would wait one further week before striking north, Cendibell had agreed to follow them too, and in a way Celeste was relieved as she still felt guilt over the way she had treated him and felt she owed him some protection.

Now furnished with appropriate weapons hunger would not be a factor. Bracen spent the day getting used to the feel of a sword again. His shoulder ached due to the muscle not being used for the previous month but he was sure he would regain his strength. Cendibell after being fed and having rested also felt much better and the change in his persona was quite striking. He was now confident and seemed full of purpose. Malic and Celeste practiced sword play. Malic was amazed not only at her strength but also with the skill she clearly possessed with a blade. She explained she had carried her father's swords from being fourteen and was used to its weight in her hand, the sword Malic had given her was not quite as heavy and the balance of the blade slightly different, but this posed no problem to her as she expertly drove him back in their parleys. She was quite an effective archer too but found she had more than met her match in Malic whose accuracy even when moving was startling. She asked where he had learned this skills, he simply shrugged his shoulders and claimed he had been born that way and as far back as he could remember could loose an arrow at any object within range and hit it dead centre.

Celeste and Malic went off hunting mid morning leaving Cendibell and Bracen at the cave entrance. Cendibell looked at Bracen and asked,

'What did they do to you back at the sheds?'

Bracen shivered internally not liking the reminder of what had happened.

'For the first couple of weeks, nothing happened; I was simply split up from the cell Celeste was in. I didn't really know what was going to happen. The soldiers who guarded me were not very talkative so I did not know what to expect. Then one day a table and chair were brought in and at first I thought the harsh conditions of the cell were being relaxed but I quickly found out these were not for my benefit. That afternoon another man entered the cell, with one of your soldiers standing guard. He seemed reasonable enough. He explained he was the Sherrif of Longfield and simply wanted to know the truth of our situation as fugitives escaping from Codencia Minor had been reported and as such any persons without a good reason for travelling were to be detained. I told him the story Celeste had made up whilst we were in Longfield, I claimed we were married and seeking a new life and were on our way to Midencia and that I knew nothing about the fugitives he spoke about.'

'What then?' asked Cendibell

'He left without further questions and I thought we might be released, but the next day he returned with two others. I could see what kind they were and their purpose was to inflict pain. He asked me again about our travels but this time told me to leave out the lie about Celeste and me being married. I repeated my tale. That's when the violence started. It went on for days, first the two henchmen would come into the cell and beat me, then the Sherrif would ask the same question, each day he left unanswered and so the beatings continued but got much worse. One day when I was in no position to defend myself I was bundled to the floor and they took turns at kicking me in the face. I lost a number of teeth and my mouth inside was just a mass of cuts and blood. I felt like I was going to die. Worse was to follow though. The very next day all three came in at once and the Sherrif asked the question again. He got the same answer. He nodded to his men, one held and pinned me from behind, and the other had my arm against the table. The Sherrif repeatedly stamped on it until it broke, then they subjected me to the most horrible beating I had up to then. If I had wanted to tell them at that point I couldn't have. I was delirious and thought that I was probably going to lose my life as a result of the loss of blood. Then two of your soldiers came for me and put me back in the cell with Celeste. I know she told the Sheriff the truth but I don't know what they subjected her to for this information'

Cendibell looked at Bracen and shook his head.

'Captain Farrier claimed the woman answered the question simply and factually when asked and as a result condemned her and possible you, as an accomplice to death. It is said the captain disapproved of your treatment but there was little he could do in the way of intervention. I know he tried to make you both reasonably comfortable after your ordeal, but you repaid him with dishonour!'

'Oh come now' said Bracen, 'what would you have us do? Simply sit there and wait for the noose to tighten round our necks. I doubt Celeste would ever accept death in such a manner. We did what we had to do; I know she regrets her actions with regards to you, for she told me you were a decent and honest man!'

Cendibell didn't answer and remained silent for a few minutes staring at the floor. He looked up again at Bracen.

'She is your woman?'

'No' admitted Bracen, ' I thought in my heart she was, but she says not, she doesn't want me in that way, but she clearly loves me, it is so confusing!'

'You need to watch that Malic, I have seen the way he looks at her, I think you might have some competition for her favour!'

He nodded in agreement, 'Yes I have seen this, but she claims she wants no man, so want can I do?'

To this Cendibell had no answer, he had never been successful with the fairer sex himself and as such had been easy prey for Celeste and her now obviously false interest in his life whilst he had been on guard.

Shortly afterwards Malic and Celeste emerged with a young wild boar. They would eat well tonight and tomorrow at least!

Chapter 14

Six days later they were ready to leave. The removed all evidence of their stay in the cave and buried the bones of the animals they had eaten. The evening before Bracen, whose arm was nearly fully recovered had burnt the raft with which they had crossed the river. Malic had explained and Cendibell confirmed, that the river was much narrower further north and though the current was swift it was possible to swim across. All four were armed, Bracen and Celeste having been given swords and bows by Malic whilst Cendibell had kept his own soldiers sword. They had discovered he had a very unsteady hand when it came to the bow so he wasn't trusted with one.

They walked down the bank to the river, the plan was to follow the river north on the east side, all the time remaining in Valdencia. It would be doubtful anyone would attempt to waylay four well armed travellers but they all felt it wise to try wherever possible to travel under the boughs of the trees which seemed to march on endlessly on both sides of the river as far as the eye could see northwards.

Malic walked confidently in front, it was clear he must have used this route on more than one occasion. Behind him Celeste and Bracen walked together with Cendibell bringing up the rearguard.

As they made camp for the night and ate a rather frugal meal of berries which had been picked on their travels Bracen was feeling the weakest of them all. He gave a loud sigh.

Celeste looked across at him, she was sat next to Malic who have been explaining the lay of the land northwards.

'What's wrong Bracen?' she asked

'Nothing really' he replied, 'I think I just got used to not travelling and found the days walking a bit of a trial. I suppose my fitness will return but I must admit to feeling very weary today!'

Malic looked quizzically at Celeste. She quickly explained everything that had happened whilst they had been held captive and their subsequent flight to the east side of the river.

'It is little wonder you feel as you do Bracen' said Malic, 'you had an ordeal many men could not have managed. I think you must be stronger than you look!'

'Only in spirit' laughed Bracen grimly, 'I leave all trials of strength to Celeste!'

'Even so' Malic insisted, 'you have suffered cruelly in Codencia and deserve some peace when we reach our goal!'

'I doubt Celeste will agree to any kind of delay, even when we reach Midencia. Her quest is all important and she will not be gainsaid!'

Malic pulled his coat up around his shoulders and looked at Celeste who appeared to be lost in thought staring into the camp fire.

'As we travel further north' he observed, 'you will find the temperature drops, if you haven't noticed already, when the autumn leaves us and winter falls, there will be no point in carrying on your quest until the following year. The lands in Midencia will be covered in snow and the temperature will make the water freeze and the rivers ice'.

Neither Bracen nor Celeste had seen snow and so could have no real understanding of how difficult it would be to travel in such conditions. Cendibell simply nodded his head in agreement as if he had guessed at this too.

'So without knowing fully the details of your quest, I fear you may need to remain in Midencia until the spring next year. It is my hope you will all accompany me back to Castletown where I dwell'.

He looked at them both, neither Celeste or Bracen gave any reaction, so he pressed them still further.

'It is my belief that you make for the Cynric Mountains and the Northlands beyond. Not many dare tread that path, the passes are supposed to be high and treacherous at any time of the year, though it is true in times past Northmen came in the other direction, most invaded from the west and east coasts when the pack ice dispersed for the first time, it is said'.

Bracen said nothing and looked at Celeste; she seemed to be weighing decisions up in her mind. Presently she too looked back at Malic and said.

'Your guesses are shrewd and yet you cannot possess all knowledge especially since it seems to me you have never tried those passes yourself. However I feel you may be correct about the weather. It would be pointless risking our lives over the highest of those mountains in the north if we have little chance of traversing them. It may be then we are forced to do as you say and stay somewhere in Midencia until the quest can continue. Beyond that my foresight seems to fail me'

Bracen joined in the conversation. 'I think you are all looking too far forward! Have you all forgotten we have to find a way to get across the bridge a few days hence. This isn't going to be straightforward, after that, supposing we are successful, then that would be time to make plans for the future.... but not now!'

'Bracen is quite right,' observed Malic,' but we cannot plan against what is not known. We need to get to the bridge and find out how many hold it against us. We will need an effective scout and some kind of plan of action. My heart tells me we are not going to get across without a fight!

Bracen looked quizzically at Malic then at Celeste who still looked deep in thought herself.

'You risk much, and I start to wonder why that should be? You have admitted to many years of travelling the lands on your own undisclosed quest, but you are setting yourself up for problems in the future if you attach yourself to us. You could simply walk up to the guards and hand over your pass. They would certainly let you through. Why risk your neck on our behalf? You will condemn yourself to never being allowed to travel south through Codencia again if you align yourself to Celeste and me. I am sure you realise this?'

Celeste looked up at this point is if the realisation had hit her too, the looked keenly at Malic.

'Bracen speaks the truth, why would you do this?'

Malic stood up and paced about the fire before answering.

'I told you before, something moves me to help you I don't not fully understand why'

Cendibell coughed gently and Bracen looked over to him and nodded, they both felt they knew the reason for his interest.

Celeste however was insistent.

'Come Malic; explain more, why would you risk this venture when you have made this journey so many times?'

You have all but answered the question yourself' explained Malic, 'my travels south are well documented at home and I feel I have exhausted all the possible avenues open to me. I have travelled extensively west too, nearly as far as the Mountain of Dyn near to your homeland without finding any indications that I am close to finding what I search for. This only leaves Westendencia and the Northlands. I will decide in the winter where I will go. However I feel my time in the south is over! Does that answer your question Bracen?' he asked as he looked at Celeste for her reaction.

Bracen was still unmoved.

'It answers everything but the risk,' he replied, 'if it was just me and Cendibell on the road would you put yourself in this position? I think not, and therein lays the answer. I think this is more for Celeste than it is to help the three of us generally'.

'Of course you can think what you will Bracen, replied Malic, 'but be careful not to make enemies out of friends when their only guilt is trying to help you without asking for any payment in return!'

Celeste's eyes were now smouldering and she looked angrily at Bracen.

'Once again you push things too far Bracen, all Malic here has tried to do is show true friendship yet we treat him with disrespect. I consider myself answered and for your sake I hope you do too',

Bracen reluctantly accepted Celeste's rebuke and held out his hand to Malic.

Malic without hesitation took Bracen hand and shook it whilst at the same time looking directly in his face. Bracen looked away unable to stare at his recent adversary, but as he did he noticed a glimpse, nothing more, of cold amusement within Malic's eyes. He clearly wasn't revealing everything and would need to be watched.

A few minutes awkward silence ensued until Malic looked up as if struck by an idea.

'Bracen, thanks to you I have the beginnings of a plan! You said quite correctly I could walk up to any of the guards on the bridge, show my identification and would be allowed through. This may be some way we can get you all across. If I can somehow distract them enough, maybe you could, all three of you, make a run for it and get over to the other side?

The other three looked at each other

'It's not much of a plan yet, I admit, but it gives us something we can work on. If Bracen here can bend his mind to this plan rather than looking for imaginary problems with me, then we might yet succeed'

Once again Bracen saw the cold amusement on Malic's face, but this time played along.

'I ask your pardon Malic, I spoke foolishly and from my heart rather than from my head before. I agree it is the start of a plan, as we travel further north we can discuss other contingencies for we do not know how many will hold the bridge against us. We may need more than one plan of action'

Celeste seemed satisfied both Bracen and Malic had put their quarrel behind them, but both men knew that there was going to be further strife ahead. Bracen knew the reason for Malic's interest and Malic himself planned to drive a barrier between Bracen and Celeste for his own purposes. There would need to be an uneasy alliance.

Chapter 15

The next day dawned and there remained an uneasy truce between the two antagonists. Cendibell throughout it all kept his counsel. There was no need and indeed no point to make things any worse. He just hoped the two of them could refrain form their true feelings for long enough to enable him to get into Midencia and into comparative safety. They walked again all morning, through the trees by the river. At no point had they seen anyone and the land seemed quiet enough.

Malic had confirmed the night before that the reason there were no settlements as would normally have been expected on either side of the river was indeed that the river flooded annually in the winter so any townships and villages tended to be some way from the river. Valdencia anyway was sparsely populated in its northern region though according to Malic possessed big settlements further south and an almost constant state of conflict along its border with Westendcia. This would no doubt explain why they had come across no soldiery at this side of the river on their travels.

They were hungry; the roasted boar seemed a distant memory so a decision was made to spend the afternoon fishing. They had seen no other wild life except rodents for the last two days and they needed sustenance.

Bracen and Cendibell were tasked with catching the fish. Bracen felt this was a convenient excuse for Malic to have Celeste to himself for the afternoon, but at no time had she seemed to notice is interest in her obvious charms. He supposed she could look after herself and he further doubted he would be stupid enough to try anything uninvited. Still he couldn't shake the feeling that he had been despatched to the riverside for a reason.

Back at the campsite Malic sat down next to Celeste who was sharpening her blade. He absent-mindedly picked at the feathers on the arrows he was carrying. He had few left and this worried him. Turning towards Celeste as she put down the sword he had given her.

'You know, I think I have an idea, which that boy Bracen has put into my head'

Celeste frowned at him.

'Please Malic, don't call him thus, he has shown himself truly to be a man in the last few months!'

He paused to consider her statement; could she mean they were romantically entwined? He dismissed the thought; she had shown no indications of love towards Bracen during the last few days though it was obvious there was genuine affection there.

'I'm sorry' he said, 'but he does still look like a boy of no more than eighteen summers to me'

'Which is precisely what we both are' admitted Celeste, 'though we have seen more adventures than most greybeards could boast in their life! What was the idea you spoke of?'

'Bracen was correct; I could walk up to the guards on the bridge without causing any kind of suspicion, though they are bound to be wary under the present circumstances. My thought was I could pass through unchallenged then lay low on the Midencia side. We are both excellent archers and with me on one side of the bridge and you on the other we could do a lot of damage to anyone who was exposed, hopefully then you three can make a run for it without having to resort to much swordplay'.

Celeste admitted it was the best plan they had come up with so far but would need agreement of the other two.

Malic sighed 'asking for Bracen's blessing to the plan might not be easy, he seems to want to take the opposite point of view to everything I suggest!'

'You have to give him some leeway' she suggested, 'after all he is simply trying to protect me the only way he knows how.'

'Are you lovers?' asked Malic

Celeste looked at him with some doubt, why would he want to know this, still it was better she told the truth as she didn't want any further conflict between them.

'No, apart from one time by my weakness, though I have to tell you that I love Bracen, but I think more like a sister would love a brother'.

'It is how it should be then, you both put each others welfare first and I respect that of him and of you'

Some time later Bracen and Cendibell returned with their haul. They had been quite successful and the fish they had caught meant they would feel no hunger for the remainder of the day. After eating Malic put forward his plan and was surprised to find no objection from Bracen, in fact he seemed quite enthusiastic.

'Of course, this is all dependent on how many are posted around the bridge, but I have no better plan in mind' added Malic

They settled down for the night, Bracen next to Celeste put a protective arm around her as they lay down. Celeste smiled inwardly at his attempts at chivalry. Bracen smiled too that she didn't object. The last things she saw was Malic hunched with his back to the wind lighting a pipe. It occurred to her that she hadn't seen him smoking before, but the thought passed as she fell into a peaceful slumber.

Eventually one week later the travellers reached the point which Cendibell had crossed the river. He pointed out that officially they had left Valdencia and were now once again in Codencia but only in an uninhabited enclave on the east side of the river. He explained the Grey Hills ahead were on both sides of the river but the range was much higher on the east side where they were known as the Grey Mountains and the crossing he attempted was the only place it was possible south of Codencia's most northern outpost of Bridgenorth. It would be possible of course to walk around the Grey Hills to the west eventually reaching Midencia at the confluence or the rivers Vendic and Cynric but that would take many weeks on foot. Malic confirmed there were no passes over these mountains that he knew of and the mountains were in effect just a southern spur of the even larger range of the Cynric Mountains further to the north. They had no choice but to attempt to cross the bridge.

It took a further day to reach the bridge, the last few hours had been worrying as they were now by the open road which ran from Longfield to Bridgenorth and there was little cover by day. They tried to stay slightly to the east of the road and therefore by the river bank. The hills in front were getting much closer and they began to see a gap where the river must flow through.

'The town and the bridge are not far ahead' confirmed Malic. 'The bridge itself is about four furlongs out of the north gate. It is possible to bypass the town to the east and come to the bridge hopefully unseen'. The town is quite a size indeed the biggest settlement in Codencia except Stanleigh itself. The river doesn't run through the town so we should get past unnoticed

Celeste looked about her, she felt concerned.

'We are exposed here so near to the road. I think we should camp now by the riverside and wait for darkness to fall before we make our move'

Bracen looked worried too and chewed his fingernails. Looking up he asked,

'But if we expect to cross the bridge under cover of darkness how does that leave our plan. Surely if and when he gets to the other side he won't be able to see his quarry?

Celeste nodded but assured Bracen

'I don't think you need to fear, I have seen Malic's skills with the bow and I doubt there is anyone in the land, who could match his prowess,'

Bracen couldn't help but feel deflated, it was clear from her reaction she admired Malic and he couldn't help but give in to the jealousy which was raging inside.

As darkness fell they made for the bridge, the busy town even at night seemed busy even at this time of the evening and Bracen especially regretted the missed opportunity of a well earned ale, struggling on they noticed the hills were rising which meant they were above the bridge looking down as they approached. Malic pointed to the trees on the other side of the bridge.

'That's where I will hide up, Celeste once I start letting off my arrows no doubt they will all face the trees and let loose their own arrows. This will give you an added chance to pick some off from behind. Exactly how many men are posted here is unknown and we will have to think on our feet, then if you two can stop the escape of any other soldiers from inside the gatehouse I think we might be successful.

'Are we all agreed?' asked Celeste.

Bracen and then Cendibell, who looked the most nervous of them all nodded in agreement.

'I will make my move then' said Malic, 'be prepared!'

There was no need for stealth on Malic's part as he had to act as normal. He made his way up the steep river bank then across the half a furlong distance to the road. No one appeared to be coming up the road from the south from the town of Bridgenorth. He walked with purpose towards the bridge. There was an expected barrier across and a gate house which of course he knew from his travels previously. If he was lucky some soldiers might be posted who had seen him before on occasion. As he approached the barrier one man stood up and gently tapped another on the shoulder who it appeared was taking a break. The man shouted towards the gatehouse whereupon another two appeared and stationed themselves by the barrier.

Malic walked nonchalantly up to them. In the darkness he couldn't make out whether he recognised any of the four and they certainly showed no indications that they had seen him previously either.

'Identification!' said the first guard

'A little abrupt if you don't mind me saying!' said Malic back to the guard, 'the welcome travelling from Midencia into your country has always been most evident!'

'You speak as someone who is a regular traveller between our two countries, my apologies sir, all the guard is on alert as we have been told fugitives from the south might be making their way to the bridge'.

'Well I am no fugitive,' laughed Malic, 'you can see from my identification and your own records that I have travelled this way many times in the last few years. Malic handed over the parchment with his details which the soldier took into the gatehouse no doubt to check his story'

The soldier stood his ground and still blocked Malic's route to the barrier.

'What was your business in Codencia?' he asked

'Not that is any business of yours' replied Malic, 'but to save argument and unnecessary conflict, I should tell you I am a man of leisure, indeed a Lord in my own country. I own the fortress in Castletown and have capable people running my estate. I travel extensively in the summer months for my own amusement. I winter in the castle for I do not enjoy walking in the snow and ice, are you answered?'

'Maybe' said the guard, 'if your story can be verified, why it is you walk on foot?'

'My horse was made lame attempting the Canyons of Dyn', he explained. 'I have walked through Valdencia and up into northern Codencia even as you see me. I have no constraints, time is my own and I have little to look forward to other than snow in Castletown when I return. So it was of no concern.

The second guard came out of the gatehouse and saluted to the first

Everything in order sir!

'…and besides' laughed Malic warm-heartedly, 'the walking will do me no harm; I have put on too much around here these last few years!' he said pointing to his stomach.

'The same could be said of many of us!' laughed the soldier in agreement as he relaxed his stance. 'Forgive my questioning; it is a portent of the times I fear when friends are set against friends when there is no need. I wish you a speedy journey and a warm winter in the north!'

Malic thanked him as the barrier was raised. He hoped the other three behind him and above where he was walking could see he had made it through. So far so good, their plan was working out. The barrier on the other side was manned too, but only by a single guard who he recognised immediately.

'Wrightson!' good to see you' he declared

'And you sir'

'Come, I need a favour' said Malic, 'this is going to seem a strange request but I want you to sit inside the guard house and don't come out, you might hear things which you think you need to address, but in reality you don't need to, I will see to everything.'

'As you wish' said Wrightson, if he thought the request was strange he wasn't going to argue with someone of Malic's reputation. It was said he was the most charming of friends and the most hideous of enemies and he knew which side he preferred to be on. If the Lord of Castletown had business he preferred him not to see, then he would do as instructed without question.

'Now Wrightson, if you please, I have something I need to attend to unseen!'

Wrightson retreated into the guardhouse, he had promised not to interfere which meant not looking. He could not think what kind of business he might have, surely not smuggling, not someone of his standing?

Malic quickly found cover within the trees at the far end of the bridge; he had a clear view of the four guards still on the bridge and could see Celeste further up the bank on the other side. He wasn't too sure if she would have marked where he had hidden though it didn't matter. She would know what to do. He waited, he could see movement, and clearly Cendibell and Bracen were stealthily approaching the bridge but still unseen to the soldiers. They stopped and waited. Malic had his supply of arrows ready and fitted the first to the bow. If he had any regret about shooting men in cold blood he didn't show it as he let go the first arrow which flew straight and without deflection into the throat of one of the soldiers. He couldn't make out which it was, he could see panic ensue, words were shouted, he let loose another which pierced a second soldier in the heart. He fell forward already dead. In the confusion Bracen and Cendibell had crept onto the bridge and to the guard house. Now the two remaining soldiers tried to take cover at the side of the bridge as they tried to fire arrows back in the general direction where Malic was hidden. They crashed harmlessly through the trees to the right of him. Celeste fired her first from the back of the soldiers, her arrow struck the third soldier in his shoulder and he cried out in pain. As more guards tried to get out of the guard house they were hewn down from each side by Cendibell and Bracen, four fell to their swords; the wounded soldier was sat in the middle of the bridge whilst the final soldier held up his hands in surrender.

Bracen walked forward whilst Cendibell checked the guard house, there was no one within. Bracen took the sword and bow from the unhurt soldier as Celeste made her way onto the bridge. She joined Bracen and checked the soldier further for hidden weapons. As Cendibell walked up to join them, in a last act of desperation the injured guard tripped him as he passed and stabbed him three times in the stomach before Celeste realised what had transpired. Running back to Cendibell she almost decapitated his injured foe such was the venom and strength of her attack. Cendibell was sat with his back to the side of the bridge holding his stomach.

'Go you fools, my time is spent, but I beg you to finish me here, I cannot be taken back to Codencia as a prisoner, my fate would be worse than death if I survived this'

Celeste shook her head, 'No you can make it, and you must try'

He looked down at his stomach his tunic already covered in blood, his breath was laboured and he knew the pain would hit him soon once the adrenaline of the fight wore off.

'I cannot, I am too weak, please Celeste, finish it now but finish it quickly!' He shut his eyes.

In pain herself with the thought of what she had to do she raised her sword, and cleanly pierced her friend cleanly through the heart. He sank further to the ground without a sound.

Celeste was beside herself with anger. She walked away from the dead body of Cendibell and up to the soldier who still stood with his arms up in surrender. Pointing her sword at him she spoke no word as he looked on in terror. Bracen too couldn't believe what he was seeing as Celeste deftly thrust the sword into the mans throat and then made a sweeping action to cut off his head. The sword crunched against his spinal cord but he was already dead as his head was left precariously hung from his shoulders.

Looking behind at the figure of Cendibell lying in his own blood on the bridge she walked to the Midencian side to be greeted by a grim Malic who had seen all the action before coming down from his perch in the tree. The three looked at each other as if they were trying to decide what to do next. Malic spoke first.

'Arrange all the Codencian militia in a rough semi circle around where Cendibell lays, it will appear that they all died at his hand as he tried to escape his fate which was decided by his captain last month'.

'Surely they will realise some died from bow shot and Cendibell possessed no such bow' declared Bracen

That is true' said Malic, 'but hopefully within the confusion they will not look too carefully and maybe guess that he had some kind of accomplice. I doubt they would want to admit to the government in Stanleigh that they believe their fugitives had escaped, and anyway I will have a witness to testify that he didn't see a young man and certainly no impressive and formidable woman during the conflict'.

He looked around and shouted

'Wrightson, you can come out now!'

The Midencian border guard crept out of the gate house and onto the bridge. He looked in amazement at the carnage just yards away.

Malic looked at him sternly

'I wasn't here' he stated and pointed at Bracen and Celeste 'and neither were these two!'

'I understand sir', he answered, and 'it was too dark to see what was going on and I did not want to concern myself with an internal conflict within the Codencian militia' he added with a grin.

'Let it be so then' said Malic, 'I will personally see to it you are rewarded for your silence on this matter.'

Wrightson bowed as the three crossed fully into Midencia and safety.

Part Five

Solace and Distress

Chapter 1

They camped for the night just inside the Midencian border, Malic was confident there would be no incursion into this land.

Celeste was not talking and was clearly hurt, not in a physical sense but for Cendibell. She felt responsible for all of his recent problems, her attack on him originally, his imprisonment, his exile and now his death. She counted in her head, two men killed at the start of their journey, now another nine including her friend. Eleven souls lost to their families and friends. She was wanted for murder in Codencia Minor and was a fugitive in Codencia itself with no doubt a death penalty as a reward for any bounty hunter. Bracen too was no doubt sentenced in his absence as an accomplice. Was it all worth it? She felt much older than her eighteen years and right at that moment wanted the comfort of her mother's arms. Now she wondered about Reva and a long overdue thought for the welfare of her mother took shape in her mind. Something she foolishly hadn't considered amidst her murderess actions on the border of Codencia Minor and her subsequent flight through Codencia and Valdencia. A fleeting moment of guilt entered her thoughts as she hadn't considered what her actions would mean for her mother. Hopefully Pallos could find a way to protect her. She snapped herself out of her melancholy, after all her mother had caused this by keeping her fathers story secret from her through her teenage years.

'How far is Castletown?' she asked Malic

Seven days walk, though I don't intend walking much further. I think you would appreciate horses for the last stage of your journey. Tomorrow morning we will come to the small border village of Newvale. I can borrow three horses, and then it is a steady three day ride until I can get you both housed in Castletown

'Tell me about your dwelling' said Celeste

Malic smiled at her, 'you will see it soon enough, I trust you will find it to your liking'

Malic and Celeste talked further into the night the dubious excitement of the day had served to keep them awake. Bracen appeared to be sleeping.

'Tell me of your quest' ventured Malic

'I cannot yet' answered Celeste, 'something holds me back, I don't not know why!'

'Do you not trust me yet?' said Malic

'I have grown very fond of you, I think instinctively you know this, but I have destroyed one person's hopes this journey, it is not my intention to make this two'

'I am not a forlorn teenager like Bracen, I am as you see me, can you not love me?'

'I look for love from no man' she answered sadly

'Yet you know there are two here who think they do, does that not tell you something?'

Celeste considered this for a moment before replying.

'It tells me I have been too transparent with my own actions and I am clearly giving the impression I am looking for something else other than.......'

She stopped herself speaking further

Malic looked at her curiously, 'other than what?' he asked

'It matters not Malic, my heart for now is not mine to give, I have told Bracen this and now I must tell you. If I live past my quest I cannot foresee my path though I doubt somehow it will be to happiness!'

Malic took her hand; she hesitated slightly but didn't pull hers away.

'You are too hard on yourself Celeste, you are young and strong and you should afford yourself some excitement other than that you find in battle'

She pulled her hand away but not abruptly.

'I know what it is you want Malic, Bracen desires it too, will I have you both fight over me? I tell you now I would rather have no one than see the two people I trust in conflict over me'

Malic stood up and brushed his tunic free of dust. 'So then, it shall be as you say, and we will speak no more of it whilst you have the love of two individuals. I bid you goodnight!'

He cast himself on the ground and at once fell into a deep sleep. Only yards away Bracen lay, his eyes wide open, his face enraged.

Eventually Celeste too found the need to sleep though she was awake at dawn, she must have only had a few hours sleep but she felt somewhat refreshed as if the guilt of the day before had been washed out of her in the morning rain.

Malic and Bracen awoke at the same time; neither said a word to the other. Malic shouldered his bow and sheathed his sword, Celeste did likewise. He strode off northwards without a word, Celeste and Bracen following.

Soon they reached Newvale; it was indeed a small village. Malic appeared to know what he was doing so they dutifully followed. He disappeared into the first house on the road and they waited for a few minutes before he appeared from the back of the house with three horses, saddled and freshly groomed.

Each mounted a horse and they set off without much haste. Malic still leading, Celeste and Bracen still following. An uneasy silence prevailed.

At noon Celeste had heard enough, or rather not enough. She slowed her horse down and then stopped and dismounted.

From behind Bracen called to Malic to halt. He did and trotted back to where Celeste stood with her hand on her hip

'I will go no further until this is resolved' she declared

'What?' asked Bracen and Malic together.

'You two and your childish behaviour, I tell you now; if you both do love me as you claim then you will put your argument to one side, not just today but for the rest of your lives. If you cannot agree to this I can go no further with either of you!'

Bracen looked somewhat sheepish and looked up at Malic. A smile appeared on his adversary's face. 'Come Bracen, let us be friends, we both know Celeste will not give herself to either of us, so why do we fight?'

Bracen held out his hand to Malic. 'I can do that for Celeste'

'Do it for yourself', growled Celeste

'….and for me' agreed Bracen

'Good' declared Malic, 'we are one big happy family again, let us stay that way!'

'We will ride together' declared Celeste

They remounted their horses and moved onwards with a little more urgency. For the rest of the day they rode without a break and well into the evening. Malic provided bread he had purchased in Newvale and they both marvelled at how long it had been since they had eaten anything other than fish, meat and berries.

The next day dawned with a curtain of rain; it felt much colder in Midencia than they were used to. They rode again through the day, however now they saw many people on the road, some on foot some on horseback, they passed through a number of villages the second day and Bracen and Celeste were amazed at how many people seemed to know Malic.

On the third day they came to a small hill, they rode to the top at Malic's insistence though there was a path evident round the base of the hill. Once they got to the top they could appreciate why Malic had insisted. Below them lay a vast dale, the air had cleared and the visibility was good. Celeste felt like she had walked into a dream.

'It's stunning' she declared.

'Those mountains far off in the distance, they look vast, what are they?'

They are the Cynric Mountains and almost impassable by foot. Long they served as a barrier between Midencia and the wild Northmen. See over there slightly to the northwest?

Celeste and Bracen shielded their eyes against the sun.

'I can see a town' suggested Bracen

'Indeed my friend you can. You see Castletown and that is where I dwell. It is but one days ride from here and we have only one more night under the stars before I can promise you a degree of comfort.

'Neither of us will object to that, it has been weeks since we have felt a pillow under our heads!'

They rode on, Bracen and Malic together Celeste felt almost forgotten at the back. She wondered how long this false friendship would be maintained for her benefit. Eventually they made camp; they all were tired and slept well. Tomorrow promised to be another clear day.

Chapter 2

They rose late for a change; the town was only half a day's ride and Celeste was keen to breathe in the clean fragrant air of the late summer morning. She loved this place, after the barren and arid lands they had ridden through after Kaisley and their month in the cave, this made a welcome change.

They followed a fast flowing stream they had picked up the night before, as the morning wore on the stream became wider and deeper causing the water to flow more slowly. Stream turned into river and flowed through a delightful wood full of wild deer and other bountiful animals. The trees hid them from the morning sun and the floor was a canopy of newly fallen leaves.

'It may be summer still in the south, declared Malic, 'but here autumn has already started and before long we may even see snow'.

'Hard to imagine Malic, replied Bracen, 'neither Celeste nor I have ever seen snow or felt its texture.'

'You will experience it soon enough' Malic laughed.

They rode on, soon they could see an opening ahead, which must have meant the end of the wood. A minute later they cleared the last of the trees. The river wound its way through a small valley and towards Castletown which they could see only a short distance away. Even from here it looked bigger than any town Celeste or Bracen had ever experienced, certainly bigger than Southaven, which was the largest town in their own country. Towering over the town to the north was a huge castle, its size evident even this far away. Bracen and Celeste looked in awe at the immensity of the town fast approaching.

Eventually they made their way to a gate, which was already opened. Again people all spoke to Malic as if they all knew him and Celeste wondered at this. It was market day and the town was busy, Malic however was keen to get back to his home. Against the protestations of both his companions he travelled on.

Eventually Celeste asked, 'which is your dwelling?'

'Not much further, just out of town to the north' grinned Malic

They passed over a small tributary to the river, the castle rose in front of them, Malic headed straight for it. It dawned on them both at once.

Celeste laughed out loud, 'No never, surely not!'

'It is so', declared Malic smiling,' the castle is my home and I am lord of these lands. Once we are eaten and watered and maybe slept in a bed for the first time in months, then tomorrow I will tell you a tale. A tale of how an orphan with no mother could become a lord with his own castle'

Bracen was slightly taken aback, to have someone of his obvious standing as a rival for Celeste's affections was going to be awkward. Nevertheless he welcomed the thought of comfortable surroundings. If Malic was correct and the snows came early in the north then Celeste might be persuaded not to attempt the mountains until the following spring.

They rode in, Malic shouted some instructions as they dismounted, the horses were taken away to be sent back to the border.

'Now I must leave you for a while, said Malic, 'I have to see the capable lieutenant who has been running things in my absence. Being a lord is no easy task and the estate on which this castle stands is both wealthy and extensive. Come I will introduce you both to his daughter. She can find you individual rooms which you will be welcome to stay in as long as you like'

Bracen noted the words 'individual rooms' but said nothing as he stared about in wonder at the splendour of their surroundings.

A small but pretty young woman approached and bowed

'Ah just who I was looking for!' declared Malic, 'this is Keigan and she will house you and look after your immediate needs whilst I am gone for a few hours. I leave it to all three of you to make you own introductions. I must attend to my estate'.

He turned and walked back over the courtyard and towards the gate. Keigan looked at them with wonder and if she thought their travelling clothes were a touch dirty and pungent she had the manners not to say anything. She led them into the castle itself and through a large dining area. She led them up a flight of stairs and there at the top along an open corridor which overlooked the dining hall were a number of doors.

'These are the guest rooms. I will allocate one for each of you. You will find the beds are clean and freshly laundered. There are baths in each and I will arrange for boiling water to be brought to you both for your bathing needs. Firstly you sir' she motioned Bracen to follow her inside.

'Make yourself comfortable and rest for a while, dinner will be served tonight in the hall we passed through. I have no word from my Lord, but Malic will I suppose want to eat well on the day of his return. The window looks north towards the mountains.

Bracen thanked her and paused to consider her as she busied herself with his cushions. She was small with lightly coloured hair, not a blonde the legends spoke of but very light compared to Celeste's almost black hair. She was much smaller than he probably a good head shorter but she left the impression of sweetness in her demeanour. He shook himself from his thoughts just in time to thank her as she left the room.

Celeste had waited patiently outside and was shown her room. It was delightful, even more luxurious then the one she had stayed in Lendel at the Pallos residence.

Keigan had explained the same as she had to Bracen about the evening meal but looked at Celeste with some concern.

'You will no doubt need fresh clothes after you bathe, for your friend next door this should be easy to arrange, I have a brother who is similar in build and will not miss a couple of items until something more permanent can be arranged, but for you, I'm afraid our sizes are definitely not similar.'

She smiled at Celeste who returned the same.

Celeste sighed, 'Keigan I must tell you, though I suppose you might have guessed it, I have travelled for months in only the clothes you see before you and though I have bathed in rivers and tried to wash my clothes. I have to admit new clothes would definitely be appreciated if anyone can be found of my size. I am Celeste, my travelling partner is Bracen

Keigan looked at her doubtfully for a moment. 'I am not sure I know of anyone in this town who would match your stature but I imagine I can find a skirt to fit your waist and maybe a tunic. I will personally go to market to see if I can find anything appropriate.

Celeste looked at her unhappily. 'I cannot pay you for the clothes I'm afraid, our money was taken when we were imprisoned in Codencia!'

'Imprisoned! I can see there are strange tales woven around you and I am eager to learn more, for now I bid you not to fear, I can personally buy the clothes and my Lord will fully restore my purse!

'I cannot thank you enough' said Celeste, 'I hope we become good friends during our stay'

'I hope that too and I hope your lover Bracen also feels the same.'

'No' laughed Celeste,' he is my travelling partner only. And though I am very fond of him and have known him many years, I fear a relationship of that kind is not for Bracen and me'.

'Pardon my impertinence' said Keigan at once, 'I thought……well I imagined….to be honest I presumed…….'

'Your pardon is granted' said Celeste with some amusement, 'but you must not tell Bracen what I said. It is true he thinks he loves me, but I don't actually think he has experienced real love. Maybe he might find it here?

Keigan smiled back sweetly, 'I will return later with clothes, rest now for tonight there will be food and drink in plenty!

Celeste took off her clothes and quickly washed herself in the cold water of the bath. She didn't need warmth yet but she was eager to lay down on something comfortable for a change. Having quickly performed the necessary she cast herself onto the bed. It felt wonderful against her naked body. She looked to the window alarmed that someone might see in before she realised the castle was on top of a hill and she was above floor level in the castle. She lay there for a moment then walked to the window and peered out. They had been housed above the castle's battlements, she looked towards the mountains and her heart sank. Soon she would have to cross those impenetrable passes to the other side and to whatever fate would befall her. Suddenly she caught her breath. A falcon dropped from the sky and landed on the keep. For a brief moment she though it was Keri but realised this was a smaller male. She felt for her lost friend, her one and only true companion when growing up. She wondered idly where she was now and how long she had waited for her after the capture and imprisonment. Sadly she shook her head and returned to the comfort of the bed. She closed her eyes....

Chapter 3

Celeste woke with a start as she realised someone was in her room. She relaxed when she saw it was Keigan.

'I'm sorry to wake you Mistress, but you have slept the afternoon and dinner will be served for you and Bracen in one hour. I have prepared your bath and there is fresh linen to dry yourself with. I managed to find something for you.' She held up a skirt, made of some hide which Celeste could not identify still it looked new and clean which was more than she could say of her old clothes. 'I struggled with a tunic at such short notice so I borrowed a shirt of my brother, if you tuck it into your skirt and wear it in a loose style you will look presentable for dinner. I hope this is all alright for you!'

'My dear Keigan, it leaves me deep in your debt!'

Keigan stayed in her room and helped her bathe and dress. Celeste had never had anyone take care of her like this and it felt strange but she didn't want to hurt the girl's feelings especially since she had done so much for her in the last few hours.

Finally they were ready and Keigan led Celeste down the stairs. Bracen and Malic were waiting. It appeared they had both been drinking wine in her absence, still the mood was light and there was no sign of the conflict from the days before. It was no feast and only the tree travellers dined whilst Keigan waited on the table, but the food was plentiful and the wine free flowing.

Eventually the three travellers and Keigan were sat at the table. Keigan especially seemed eager to hear any news her lord would impart. It was she who set the conversation going.

'Celeste, tell me of your imprisonment!'

'Nay Keigan', said Malic, 'let them start at the beginning. Their tale needs to be told in the correct order!'

Celeste looked to Bracen who signalled his approval, no doubt helped by the free flowing red wine. Celeste explained how she and Bracen had met again having once been childhood friends; she told of the fight at the River Dyn where she had killed two soldiers, her own wound and how Bracen had tended her with his medicinal skills. She told of the stinking fens and their eventual visit to Kaisley which she enjoyed, then on to Longfield, followed by their imprisonment. Celeste explained the Codencian Government were to try them and deliver them back to the Northmen in Codencia Minor. She told of their escape and how they fooled Cendibell and escaped over the river to Valdencia. From there they stumbled once again on Cendibell who they took pity on.

Celeste looked kindly at Malic and then told Keigan that they had met the day after Cendibell and her lord had assisted them on their travels. She wisely left out the details of the fight over the river at Bridgenorth.

Keigan listened intently, but Malic ventured a question at last.

'Celeste, you still have left out the reason for your journey north. Can you not tell me now I have proved my trust?'

Something melted within Celeste like an icicle in the spring sunshine. She looked again at Bracen who showed no sign of objection.

'I will tell you of my quest if you will tell me of yours' she stated

'So be it' said Malic,' who shall go first?'

'I will start' said Celeste, 'it is easy to explain, I should have no secrets from my friends. My first memories are of my father and though strangely I cannot see his face anymore I know I had a very close relationship with him. I remember him taking me to the Volcano before it erupted and to the Geyser in the area, it's one of my first memories. I remember when we were away my Grandmother died though I cannot admit to remembering much about her other than what I have been told. My best friend was always Bracen here and we spent much of our early childhood together. One day the volcano I mentioned erupted and covered the land with a thick blanket of ash. We were fortunate as we had a second house on the southern coast of Codencia and we escaped there. I remember bidding my father farewell as I expected to see him shortly once the mountain had stopped and the clean up had finished. I was told that that my father had travelled to Southaven for some kind of summit with Lendel, who was the Elder of our village. My mother told me some time later that my father had been killed in a raid and the Northmen who still occupy my country had killed him. I can't remember my feelings; I was alone with mother and somehow felt I had to be brave for her. I grew up in Salint on the south coast, we didn't return to the village of my birth until I was eighteen years old. That was only a few months ago. On the way into my country the border guards stopped mother and me and made some disgusting comments about what they would like to do to me. Eventually they let us go unharmed and we made our way to the village. I met Bracen again and we had a lot to catch up on! Whilst we were staying there, mother had been forced to return to oversee the sale of our original house; she told me the truth about my father claiming she had lied to me to protect me in my childhood and youth. She told me he had been taken away north, probably on a ship because the sea ice had broken in the unusually warm weather of that year. Obviously I was upset with my mother and vowed to find my father despite her efforts to persuade me otherwise. I told Bracen, he was keen to help me so we arranged our quest and set off the next day. When we reached the border again two of the guards who had taunted me so much when I had arrived were still stationed there. I am afraid to report that the reason we were imprisoned was true, I killed the guards out of temper and revenge and though I was injured myself, Bracen tended my wounds.

Bracen interrupted

'Celeste you haven't mentioned your bird!'

Celeste looked sorrowful and said, 'Yes that is true, when I was about fourteen I found a young chick, a Falcon by the side of the cliffs near where I lived. I helped her recover and regain her strength. I called her Keri and when she was well again she didn't leave but made her home in the barn of my home. She followed me everywhere and on our quest too. She helped me by attacking a third guard at the border'

'Where is she now?' asked Keigan

'I do not know' admitted Celeste, sadly shaking her head, 'I think she will have waited for some time whilst we were imprisoned, but a wild bird has to fend for itself and it's my belief after all those years she finally succumbed for the need to find a mate. I hoped she might have been in the canyons where we found the cave but there was never ever any sign of her. I fear I have lost her forever'

'So your quest will take you further north and over the mountains?' said Malic finally.

'Unless there is another way that is the path I have to follow'

Malic considered this for a moment. 'You could go round the mountains but such a journey might take many months. How will you expect to find your father within the wild land of the Northmen?'

I haven't given that any thought at all, admitted Celeste, 'but I am young and have time on my side, believe me when I tell you that I will find him!'

Celeste turned to Malic and asked, 'what of your tale?'

'Nothing so romantic as yours Celeste, I simply look for the murderer of my father and I shall not rest until I have hunted him down'

'Malic you promised more, you said you would tell us of your lucky promotion to a Lord!'

'I am not sure about lucky' laughed Malic, 'alright, that is a tale worth telling; though like you I cannot really remember my humble beginnings. My first memories were of being on horseback all the time; father belonged to the Codencian militia, who would never talk of my mother so I grew up almost totally in the company of men. I too remember the mountain exploding and it covered much of Codencia with the same ash. Father decided he needed to settle down and brought me here to Midencia. He was a capable soldier and quickly found favour of the lord of this castle. He arranged the Midencian militia which stood them in good stead when the Northmen eventually attacked from east and west around the Cynric Mountains. He insisted as many people as possible should be housed within the castle and in such a way the people around here were saved from the worst atrocities. The Northmen had no stomach for a siege and wanted easy pickings and they quickly moved south almost to the borders of Codencia itself. Father used the castle and likewise other castles in the north of our country to arrange counter moves again the over-stretched Northmen and the tactic worked as after a number of years they retreated back to whence they came. He eventually married the daughter of the Lord and after he died not long afterwards was made Regent. She too died of some pestilence which affected the land at that time and with no capable overlord to take charge of the castle it fell almost by accident to my father. He never forgot his beginnings though, and like me now, was more happy in the company of the men in the Inns in town rather than behaving like a Lord which he had in truth never aspired to. One night on the way, or on the way back from town, I do not know which, he was murdered. The mercenaries left his head attached to a stake and I think stole my family's heirloom. When I find the man who wears this I know I will have found the murderer!'

'Why do you think he was murdered?' asked Bracen

'I know not' replied Malic, 'and truth be told I have given it little thought. He was not only my father but my liege-lord and his death has to be avenged. For a number of years I have travelled the land south, west and east but have had no luck in my quest. I think like you Celeste I am forced to consider the northlands as my next venture, but I warn you now that any attempt to travel over the Cynric Mountain range should not be made until the spring. It is a dangerous, if not fatal road at any time, but to attempt the passing in the winter would be suicide and would result in the failure of your quest! For my part I was going to travel to the west coast and go around the mountains but admittedly such a journey might take too long and I would be forced from my estate for longer than I would wish'.

He looked keenly at Celeste and Bracen, 'Perhaps we should pool our resources and attempt the mountain passes in the spring once the snow has cleared, since both quests seem to take us north?'

'Where Celeste leads I will follow' said Bracen grimly, 'until death takes me or Celeste dismisses me from her side!'

Celeste looked at Bracen, she could not have wished for a more loyal partner on her quest. Why was it then she felt she had to take Malic up on his suggestion?

'Enough of the sombre tales' said Keigan, 'let us drink and be merry, who knows what tomorrow may bring!'

As she spoke the words she looked at Bracen with smiling eyes. For the first time he noticed her gaze and returned the smile, maybe staying the winter in the comfort of the castle might not be a bad thing, since Celeste had decided on chastity, maybe there might be other options for fun. He was only approaching nineteen after all!

Chapter 4

The weeks went by, the late summer turned to autumn followed quickly by the first snow flurries. Both Bracen and Celeste delighted to see this for the first time in their lives. If they found it unbearably cold they said nothing. Bracen was spending more and more time in the company of Keigan and since she too dwelt within the castle they were often found in each others company. Celeste felt torn, part of her was happy that Bracen had found someone to love but the other more unreasonable part of her was jealous. Not that she wanted Bracen in that way, but jealous that their friendship and yes it had to be said, their shared love of each other had been affected. Celeste felt their relationship had now come to an impasse. Malic was often away during the day on his estate's business though they all tended to dine together on an evening. Since Bracen and Keigan were so comfortable with each others company naturally Malic and Celeste were forced together for the evening meal, which she didn't mind at all since she had become very fond of their host

The month before they had celebrated Bracen's nineteenth birthday and Celeste was again pained to see how little attention she was now receiving from Bracen, his sole focus seemed to be on Keigan. Her own birthday was coming up just before the winter solstice and she was truly not looking forward to it. She felt that once the holiday was over she could count the days again to the continuation of her quest. What bothered her most about this was she was going to have to split Bracen up from Keigan if he was to stand by his word. She desperately didn't want to hurt him again but she knew he was a proud man and a keeper of promises so unless she released him, she would be forcing him down the road to unhappiness. On the other hand she didn't want to appear she was abandoning him simply because he had found someone in his life. It was impossible and she really didn't know what to do.

One evening after their meal, Bracen and Keigan made their excuses and went to Bracen's room, this again left Celeste in the company of Malic.

'I have a problem' she said

Malic looked up and simply said 'tell me'

She explained her predicament with Bracen's feelings. She knew he would want to stay but would feel duty bound to follow her on her quest. She wanted to release him but didn't know the best way to address this. She didn't want him to feel she didn't need him anymore and wanted him to understand what she was doing was for him…..and for Keigan.

Malic nodded as if he understood, 'so we need to find a way that would suit all, let me think!'

They sat for a few minutes by the open fire in the great dining hall, their movements echoed within the large chamber.

'I have a plan', said Malic at last, 'I have the need of an apothecary in town, and since old Oran died last year the town has been without one. I could set him and Keigan up in business with a small rental, they could then marry and he could stay in the town. Everyone wins, Keigan get's her man, I get a share in a business venture, the town gets an apothecary again and you get to release your friend from his promise! What do you think?'

Celeste was in fact suspicious of how quickly this idea had occurred to him, she was cynical enough to think that this had long been in thought and planning and could be considered a ruse to get Bracen out of the way so he could pursue his affections with her.

'We will need to speak to Bracen, this needs handling carefully and we should do it sooner rather than later!'

'Tomorrow at dinner?' he asked

Celeste nodded, why did she feel so uncertain, was it jealousy again? If it was she only had herself to blame, Bracen had offered himself freely to her months before and she had rejected him out of hand to concentrate on the task at hand. The quest however had been stalled by the weather and mountains and now she certainly felt a tinge of regret as she thought of the day they played in the river before they arrived in Kaisley and their night of lovemaking in Longfield. It seemed an age ago though in truth it was less than half a year. She looked again at Malic who seemed deep in thought, he was certainly a handsome, if not a somewhat rugged man, he was quick to laugh but also moved to anger far too easily. Maybe they were too similar and joining together on the quest might prove problematic for that reason alone. He had raven black hair, like her own, was slightly taller than she (and not many could claim that) and had dark brown piercing eyes. As she considered all this she realised she was staring at him and he was staring back with just as much thought. At first when she had met him, she had found him to be all too transparent with his obvious desire of her body, but lately she had not witnessed any of this, in fact since the argument with Bracen on the way to Castletown he had treated her with total respect. What was going on behind those eyes she didn't know? The more he showed her the respect however the more she would crave something more. Was it therefore possible to love two men at the same time?

What in the name of the Gods was wrong with her? Because she couldn't have the love of her childhood friend she should throw herself at the first man who shows her kindness. She reproached herself, there was a name for women of that nature and it was not something she would have ever ascribed to.

Shaking herself from her thoughts she excused herself claiming she was over-tired, but something pulled at her inside and she yearned for him to follow her. When she reached the top of the stairs she turned round but Malic had already gone.

The next day dawned and she had half forgotten the previously night as she realised today was indeed her birthday. Keigan had brought her a gift in the early morning. It was a necklace of polished stone. In truth she had never really felt feminine enough to wear trinkets like that and much preferred a sword, dagger and bow for ornaments, but it was a nice thought. She had seen Bracen around midday and being a boy he had totally forgotten that this was her special day. Celeste realised it was another pointer to the change in their relationship. They agreed to meet as usual for the evening meal; Celeste planned to spend the day in the market. It was time to start preparing for the journey and warm clothes were going to be a necessity. Malic had given her a handsome gift of thirty sliver pennies which was more money than she had ever held in her hand before. This would go a long way. She needed a better sword than the one he had lent her and the dagger was only fit for skinning animals. She had a bow which was suitable for her needs. She felt rusty and needed to feel the weight of a sword in her hand once more. Her first stop then would be to the forge, she knew exactly what she wanted.

It was pointless the forgemaster arguing, the impressive girl in front of him was insistent on the length of the blade, where its balance should be and moreover how much it ought to weigh. Now he had prepared many such blades in his lifetime but only for the strongest of men and never one to these specifications for a woman.

She stood before him adamant with hand on her hip and a total lack of respect for his opinion.

'I have the money' she held out her hand with fifteen silver pennies which indeed was more than enough to cover his costs and secure a health profit as well.

'I am not the type of man who would take advantage of a woman no matter how impressive she looks'

Celeste gave him the kind of withering look that all women learn from an early age and reserve for the most special of occasions.

'I have a sword similar to your specifications which I would prefer you to try; if you can wield it effectively then I will relent.

'As you wish' said Celeste with cold amusement.

The forgemaster produced a sword and handed it to Celeste hilt first. She wrapped her fingers around it lifting it without difficulty then she made swift cutting actions to the left and to the right of the astonished forgemaster, her hand speed even with this weighty blade was a blur and she finished by holding the extended blade to his heart.

'A nice child's sword but not the real thing so give me what I require by noon on the winter solstice and I will give you an order for an effective dagger too. Do we have a deal?'

'We have a deal' said the stunned forgemaster.

'Good here are four pennies as a deposit. Do not fail me!'

She wandered off satisfied by her purchase, buying armoury was much more preferable to looking for clothes in her eyes, but the latter was now a necessity and in the last few months she had been surprised and more than a little pleased to see the market holders providing clothing which fit her frame. She would need furs for the journey so that would need to be her next stop.

When she returned to the castle she found no one around, and she felt a childish pang of regret that she could not boast of her dealings with the forgemaster. She climbed the stairs to her room. After a while with freshly washed hair and perfume given to her by Keigan she changed into what for her was a very feminine outfit, a very short skirt with a white blouse which in truth showed way too much cleavage, which was just what she wanted for the occasion.

Keigan knocked on her door and smiled that Celeste was wearing her gift.

'I will turn you into a lady before you leave here', she laughed

'I doubt it' laughed Celeste in turn, 'I remain too much of a warriors daughter, still I think I will pass inspection don't you think?

'That would depend on who is doing the inspecting, come Celeste I have a surprise for you!'

They walked down the stairs into the dining hall. Malic was sat on his own smiling as he looked in appreciation at Celeste's attempt to make herself look more sensual.

'Where is Bracen?' she asked

'I'm here' said Bracen and he entered with a tray of specially prepared food. Two other servants stood behind him.

'I know you thought I had forgotten your special day, but I was trying to keep this a secret. Keigan and these two charming ladies have been instructing me in the art of cookery, and today my best of friends I have prepared your meal. In fact I have prepared everyone's meal!'

A girl came in through the entrance of the dining hall. As Bracen was serving with Celeste smiling like she had never smiled before the girl started to sing. The words were strange to Celeste but the tune was haunting and she found herself transfixed.

The girl bowed to leave but Celeste insisted she stayed for a while longer.

'Sing me another beautiful song!' she insisted.

The girl sang again, a different tune but the same unfamiliar language and this time the tune more uplifting.

All four applauded noisily when she finished and this time she was allowed to leave.

'Who was that and what were the strange words she spoke?'

'The girl is a minstrel I do not know her name' admitted Bracen, 'but she was recommended to me by our friend Malic, this was his idea for the evening which we have secretly been planning for some time now! The language is of ancient Midencia, only spoken in the north east now and by very few.

'I shall never trust either one of you again!' said Celeste indignantly, but laughed when she realised they thought she was being serious.

The wine flowed freely as it had on the first night of their stay in Castletown and Keigan made as if to clear the crockery away.

'Keigan sit down, Malic and I have a suggestion for you and Bracen'

Keigan and Bracen looked at each other and both shook their heads indicating they didn't know what was going to be said.

'There is no need to worry' Celeste walked around the table and kissed Bracen tenderly on the brow, 'I have come to a decision with the help of Malic who also has a proposition for you'

Malic stood up, rather formally with his hand behind his back as if addressing an audience, it was clear to Celeste he had been rehearsing this, such was his desire to say the right thing.

'Celeste and I have noticed the obvious attraction between you and Keigan, now she has a suggestion and I have a proposition, the two go hand in hand but you may refuse either if you want!'

'You are both talking in riddles' complained Bracen

Bracen I need an apothecary in town, I know of your expertise in this field, furthermore I can see the love in your eyes for Keigan and I can see the same in hers too. My suggestion is, you start your own business here in Castletown, I will set you up with the necessary funds and you can pay me back a percentage of your profits. Keigan will leave her duties here and go with you.

'Go with me? I had planned to follow Celeste on her journey north, how can I take you up on your very kind offer?'

'You can and you must' declared Celeste, Bracen my dearest and most loyal friend; I release you from your promise! Consider it my wedding gift to you!'

'Wedding gift?' stuttered Bracen

'Yes you idiot, can't you see the love in her eyes and realise the feeling in your heart, do you duty and propose to her now!'

Bracen looked at Celeste and then at Keigan who was stood with tears in her eyes, not for sadness but for joy that all her wishes were coming true

Bracen knelt down on one knee

'Keigan, I have no ring to give you, I have no dwelling to house you, I have no dowry to give to your family, but what I can give is my total love and devotion. Will you take me as your husband?'

Keigan smiled at him sweetly

'Bracen I have loved you since the first day I saw you, the promise of a life by your side is everything I could have dreamt of. Yes I accept and I will become your bride!'

'Good' said Malic as he clapped his hands. 'Do not burden yourself with the worry of a house, the old apothecary has enough room to house you both and any babies which might happen along the way!

'We must make the arrangements; we haven't had a good wedding celebration in this castle for ages past.' He winked at Celeste who smiled knowingly back at him.

'Come Celeste, let us leave these two lovebirds in piece, will you walk with me?

'I will but I fear I am not dressed for a venture in the snow!'

'I will find a fur, I want to go no further than town tonight, and I plan to leave the castle to these two for the evening!'

They walked on the battlements for a few minutes whilst Celeste gazed at the snow covered mountains which they would soon have to cross. She shivered, more because of the task she still had to face, not because she actually felt cold. Malic noticed and he put his arm around her, she didn't resist. He pulled her still closer and turned to look at her, she looked back at his handsome rugged face. She buried her head into his chest.

'Hold me Malic' she pleaded

Chapter 5

The arrangements were made and Bracen and Keigan were married on the first day of the fourth week of the New Year, they preferred not to go away to celebrate but instead spent their time making the shop right and sorting out their accommodation ready. The whole town celebrated not just the wedding but for the newly discovered medicine man who could hopefully cure their many ailments.

Celeste had been Keigan's helper on the day and she genuinely looked happy for them both, but Bracen could not help but to notice over the next few weeks how she slipped out of the events of the town and spent most of her time in her room in the castle. Malic too was away a great deal, ordering the estate in preparation for his annual departure. His worry was that he possibly might lose his friend forever if something awful should befall her in the north.

Mid March came and the first appearance of daffodils, Bracen needed to see Celeste as he had some news to tell her and he wanted her to be the first to know.

He found her in her room, looking over ancient maps of the north, she had her new sword and dagger laid out, it was clear she had been sharpening it.

'Bracen my friend how is married life today?'

'More wonderful than you could imagine Celeste, I have come today to impart great news. Keigan is with child and I am to be a father!'

'Oh Bracen I am truly delighted for you', she hugged him tightly. Bracen too felt the warmth of her love towards him. He broke free from her and looked deeply into her eyes.

'Celeste, I never meant for any of this to happen, I would have followed you to the tops of the mountains the depths of the sundering seas and to the end of the world'

'I know it Bracen and no words can ever describe the feelings of love we have for each other, but you now have other responsibilities and one day you will have to take them both on the journey to see your parents. Leadel and Cirard need to know they are grandparents! You may have to go in disguise however if you are to travel through Codencia!'

'I doubt I would have any trouble getting through if you were not by my side, it is for you they search!'

Celeste hugged him again, not wanting to let him go, they both knew that soon she would embark on her quest and it was possible neither would ever see each other again. The thought of this tore at her heart as it did at Bracen's.

'Go' insisted Celeste, 'you have a wife and unborn child to worry about. I will be alright I promise!'

'I need to see you alone before you go' insisted Bracen

'You will' she said

Celeste had no intentions of honouring her promise however as she felt the sorrowful parting would be too painful for both of them. She even considered leaving the castle and striking out on her own without telling Malic whilst he was on estate business, but something told her he now had a part to play though her foresight failed her as to precisely what. She had nearly succumbed to him on her birthday, whether it had been the wine or not she didn't care to imagine. They had kissed under the stars and she had been held close, so close in fact that she could distinctly feel his hardness through his garments. She so wanted him at that moment, but something held her back, something niggled at the back of her mind that this was wrong, she couldn't put her finger on it, maybe the age difference since he was in his mid-thirties, though she was very mature, she was still only a teenager in after all

Malic had not tried again and gone back to his charming self when they ate their occasional evening meals together, lately however he had been away a great deal and she had preferred her own company as she prepared herself for what she hoped would be the last stage of her adventure.

Celeste awoke one spring morning as if called. She looked out of the window, the visible mountains which had been covered in snow for the last six months were now clear. It was time for her to go; she decided she must find out where Malic was.

She didn't have to look far; it was almost as if he had felt the call too. He was giving instructions to Keigan's father in the dining room when he noticed Celeste looking at him from the overlooking balcony.

'We should go soon' shouted Malic

Celeste put her finger over her mouth to indicate she wanted their departure to go unnoticed. Malic having satisfied himself the castle was once again in good hands bounded up the stairway to where she stood.

'You want secrecy?' he asked

'I can't bear to have a final farewell alone with Bracen; I think we should leave soon!'

'I agree, the snows appeared to have gone, though in the heart of the mountain range we may still find the weather challenging. We should have a last dinner tonight and get Bracen and Keigan over together. They don't need to know why. You can then say the farewells in your heart. I know we disagreed over you Celeste, but I have grown to respect your gangly friend. He will be a very useful addition to the town!'

Celeste agreed, she would be partly keeping her promise that way. She would see him but not alone, that she simply could not bear. She remembered her promise to herself when her father had hit her when she was eight years old that she would never ever cry again. A bitter sweet parting from Bracen might force her to break down at last and she didn't want that scenario

So it was the four friends had there last meal together, it was a fairly upbeat occasion as the newlyweds were keen to talk about their soon-to-be addition to their family. Celeste did her best to join in as they talked of their plans of their future. Eventually it was time to go, Celeste bowed and kissed Keigan on the brow then hugging Bracen like a long lost brother told him to watch her steps that night, it had been raining and she didn't want any accidents in her condition.

Celeste looked at her friend depart and without a word to Malic walked up to her room for the last time. Malic knew not to interfere; he could guess the pain she suffered.

She surveyed her belongings she intended to take along, the bow, the sword, the dagger. She would take more clothes this time, warmer ones too, the one thing she had disliked out about north east Midencia was that it was so much colder than her homeland. She looked out of her window for the last time at the castle below, all was quiet. At that moment all she wanted was to curl up on her bed and forget her stupid quest, she yearned to stay in the peaceful castle and amongst the wonderful people of the town. What drove her so to find her father? Maybe it was as her mother had said, that she would find her was indeed dead and that all her journey had been wasted.

The enormity of the task ahead hit her hard as she realised that her truest of friends would no longer be watching her back. She cast herself onto the bed; this might be the last occasion for some considerable time that she would feel the comfort of a bed and the softness of a pillow. She was comfortable but sleep was hard to find that night.

As they walked back towards town Bracen stopped suddenly as he approached the bridge.

'What is it my love?' asked Keigan frowning

'I have just seen my dearest friend for the last time'

He broke down in tears, sobbing for all he was worth as Keigan struggled to find the appropriate words to ease his pain.

Part Six

The Northlands

Chapter 1

Celeste and Malic were up before the break of dawn. They had enough supplies but all they had they had to carry. He had inspected her clothing before they set off and seemed secure in the knowledge she would have some degree of warmth in the cold mountains. They ate a very healthy breakfast and packed plenty of fruit and cold meats for their journey.

A cockerel crowed as they left the east facing gate of the castle. Walking down as if making to town they then veered off when they came to the bridge. Though the River Dyn was not much more than a wide stream this far north, Malic's plan was to follow it to its source in the foothills of the Cynric Mountains.

They made good progress along the stream; Malic's plan was to strike for Northorpe by nightfall. At least there they could find shelter in one of the villages three Inns after that there would only be the northern outpost of Penworth a further two days hike which was as far as the Midencian authority stretched.

They rested for a while by the free flowing stream at lunchtime; the morning walk had been very pleasant in the crisp spring air.

'Have you any idea of how far it is across the mountains?' asked Celeste.

Malic looked north at the already imposing peaks, he shook his head.

'No not really, but legend claims they are more than a hundred leagues across. Up in that vast range we might take two days to walk where we would take three on the level, and that's if we encounter no problems. There will be no clear pathway and so I expect the journey to take perhaps six to eight weeks. We will need to replenish our food before reaching the mountains so I have brought money so we can add to our supplies in Penworth.'

'How high are they?

'The tallest on the maps away to the northwest is one and three-quarter leagues high' he said as he saw Celeste's alarmed expression, 'but I would hope we can find our way through without going above half a league up, otherwise the air will be too thin and we may struggle to breath in those conditions with the excess weight in food and clothing we are carrying.'

'It's going to be a tough journey, are you sure you want to strike over the mountains with me? she asked

'I made a pledge and like Bracen, I too am a man of my word!'

Approaching dusk they eventually saw a small village in the distance.

'Northorpe!' said Malic, 'or at least I hope it is' he laughed

'You have never been here?'

'No' he admitted, 'my estates do not stretch this far and though it is less than a days ride on horseback I have never had the need to travel this far north before'

Eventually they arrived, the place was not large enough to warrant any kind of entrance gate and the village started with a few remote homesteads near the road side followed by more straw roofed houses by the river side. They came in due course to the first inn and paid the two silver pennies which was the rate for accommodation for two for one night. Malic decided a few drinks were the order of the evening but Celeste preferred to stay in her room. He had at least been enough of a gentleman to order two rooms!

After breakfast the next morning they set off again, once more the air was clear and crisp and there had been a slight ground frost the previous evening. The cobwebs sparkling in the hedgerows were a novelty and a beautiful sight for Celeste to behold.

The stream was narrowing still further and was now no more than eight Ells across but its vigour was evident from the melted snow in the uplands. They again lunched by the river and then had there first night under the stars half way to Penworth. They found shelter in an old disused croft and though it was stark and uncomfortable it at least offered some protection for the second overnight frost of their journey.

Day three started bright and sunny but clouded over toward lunchtime, by Malic's reckoning they were only about three hours away from Penworth when the rain started. At first it was a gentle pitter-patter on the leaves of the canopy of trees above their heads but gradually it increased in strength. The final part of their journey to Penworth was miserable and wet and neither spoke but hurried on as fast as they could in order to make it to the last village in the north.

They arrived bedraggled just before dusk and eventually found accommodation again in an inn (the only one of the town, since passing trade was not something they experienced, the place was nearly always used just by the locals). On this occasion Celeste agreed to go and join the throng after she had picked up further provisions for their travel. The Innkeeper was clearly delighted as his small room had more than doubled it normal intake due to the news travellers were in town.

They found themselves answering a bewildering number of questions when in truth all they wanted was to relax from their awful afternoons walking.

One 'old timer' by the name of Forlan who had up to that point been the quietest acknowledged to his nodding neighbours.

First Edit – July 2011   Page 166

'Unless you have been given misleading maps I think you ventured on the road to nowhere!'

Malic laughed, 'Nay, it is not so, to you I say, and for those of you who have already guessed it, me and my partner here are to attempt to cross the mountain range'

A stunned silence befell the gathering and then all the men-folk started talking at once. The warnings were stark from everyone, no one, but no one ever tried the mountain passes anymore, even the Northmen didn't try that route when they invaded.

Malic however heard the phrase 'mountain passes' and asked

Is there rumour of a pass over the mountains?

The men grew silent, but Forlan gave a dire warning

'Many have tried in the past, and a few other rash adventurers have attempted the mountains since the weather became warmer these last few years, thinking the snows would be fully melted and the path easier to travel. None have ever returned!' he added almost in a whisper.

'There could be any number of reasons for that' declared Malic, 'they could have made it through and liked it so much in the Northlands that they did not want to return!

'More likely that if they made it through they were done in by the murderous bastards of the north. I remember their kind very well', he answered

Malic however was unmoved, 'we shall attempt the crossing nevertheless and one day will return to allay your fears!'

Later as time was called and the men-folk made to depart to their individual dwellings Forlan (who had left and retuned again) approached Malic.

'You might need this' he said as he passed him a parchment

'I thank you' he said as he guessed what had been given to him

'Good luck, you will both need it' came back the answer.

Malic retired to his room, he opened the parchment and studied its faint scribbling. It was a map of the Northlands on one side, on the other was an unmistakable path winding through the mountain passes.

Chapter 2

News travelled fast and the next morning the village was lined with people to see them off. Many shook their heads as they passed. Celeste did not like the attention but Malic was adamant this was the best way to go to avoid anyone surreptitiously trying to follow them out of curiosity.

They followed the stream northwards and the few stragglers (mostly inquisitive children) who had thought it would be an adventure to follow them out of the village soon gave up and they were once again on their own.

Malic peered again at the faint map, 'we follow the river to its source, from there need to travel a couple of leagues to the west, according to the map this is where the mountain pass starts'

By noon the stream had narrowed to the width a man could jump across in the mid afternoon they found the source, a small hill from which the infant river emerged from the hillside destined to flow the hundreds of leagues through the continent to the sea. They decided this was as good a place as any to spend their fourth night of their journey, once again it would be in the open, but tonight at least the weather though cloudy was a good deal warmer and with that the threat of any frost had disappeared.

After their evening meal of cold meat and wholesome bread Celeste asked to look at the map, Malic handed it over somewhat reluctantly she thought. It appeared to be very old, she turned it over. In the failing light she could make out the writing and drawing. The north, it seemed was split into various lands just as the south was. The names of these places were most archaic in her eyes and the map would mean nothing until they had managed the pass and come down the other side. What they would find in the wild north she couldn't even guess. She handed the map back to Malic and studied him as he prepared his place to sleep. He was definitely unpredictable, twice he had made very obvious passes at her but twice he had simply gone back to his usual demeanour, sometimes he could be very eloquent and well spoken whilst other times like today hardly saying a word. Some days he ate like a pig at the trough, but other days hardly seemed to need any sustenance. She had never heard him complain, before or since Castletown.

'Malic, as we travel further into the mountains and through the higher passes we will encounter intolerable cold, we should prepare for that.'

'I have given it some thought' he admitted, ' I know you do not want to get to close to me, for whatever reason you think that is good and proper, but the path we must now tread will mean we will be forced into each others arms, we will welcome each others body warmth!'

'Does this disturb you' she asked

'No not at all, its one of the key survival aids in the cold, it is you who turns away from me when I try and get close to you'

Celeste sighed, what he said was the truth, and she thought he deserved an explanation.

I grew up in a protective environment, I live with my mother through my teenage years on the coast, I had little opportunity to experiment sexually as young people of that age would. I found when the rare opportunity presented itself, for some reason I scared the boys off. I have only had three sexual encounters in my life, twice with Bracen before we were imprisoned and once with the dirty and grubby pawing hands of my captors. The times with Bracen were a joy, but he was and still is my best friend in the whole world and I didn't want any complications to come between us. Falling out over sex could do that, besides which, I used the convenient excuse that my quest was more important than my own desires, which has a grain of truth to it after all. The time with the guards in my cell was disgusting' she shivered at the thought 'one of the men was touching himself whist the other roughly put his fingers inside me, it was horrible. I would have killed them both with my bare hands if I had not been imprisoned!'

'It doesn't have to be that way, it shouldn't be that way!' he replied

'I'm not ready yet' she lamented, 'one day perhaps once I forget the memory of the time in prison'

'Let us talk no more about it then, be happy in the knowledge I can give you my warmth without you having to worry about my own sexual frustrations'.

He stopped conversation for a moment whilst looking at Celeste, and then he continued. '

I have to say Celeste unlike you, I have had many experiences in my life with a variety of women of different ages and sizes, and too many, some might say. Still I have the advantage of possessing a multitude of techniques and positions to keep even the most insatiable sexual appetite satisfied. I do not brag, it is a fact!'

He studied her face further for a reaction but when none was forthcoming he said. 'As a result I never settled down because up to this point in my life I had never found anyone before who I felt was an equal'

At this point Celeste looked over to him

'You consider me an equal?'

'I do' he said

Though she had said she was not ready every essence of her being cried out for the promise of what Malic could deliver. Celeste however was stubborn even with herself.

'No, not yet, not until the task is complete, then I will willingly give myself to him' she thought

As it was that particular night was not cold under the starts and though a cold wind could be felt from the approaching mountain it was far from unbearable.

The next day they rose early and trekked northwest as the map indicated, as they ventured away from the source of the river the ground began to rise, moor after moor of uplands as they struggled their way through the heather and bracken. The Cynric Mountains now towered over them, their immensity more than taking up half the sky northward. They both knew that what they saw wasn't half the picture that further within the range the mountains peaked at unspeakable heights where no man could ever venture. Hoisting their packs again after a short rest they set off again. By nightfall the moors had cleared and vast cliffs soared above their heads. This was not the time of day to look for the path they needed, they would be better served in the morning.

The next day they scrambled about the rocky tops of the hills trying to find an obvious sign of the path they needed, all the morning without any luck. Celeste was going to suggest they doubled back just in case they had missed the obvious opening when Malic whistled her over. She half ran up the brow of an adjacent hill to where he stood.

'There' he pointed, 'do you see? Clearly there is a path, see how it winds up to the mountain face!'

'I wonder who made it and for what purpose?' asked Celeste

'I don't think we will ever know, however it seems clear to me this is the path the map indicates, come let us strive for the start of the mountain pass ere nightfall'

Malic felt as if they had achieved a small victory and had some sense of optimism, Celeste though looked at the formidable mountains and wondered if they were indeed traversable.

Down the hill they went then the ground began to rise again though this time more steeply. This was more difficult and before long they were forced to take regular breaks such was the gradient of the lower slopes of the mountain into which the path ran.

By dusk they were amazed to see how far up they had travelled, the lower foothills lay a long way beneath them and much of North East Midencia could be seen from this height. They decided they had gone far enough, they found shelter of sorts between a cleft in the mountain side and thought this offered some protection from the whistling winds which sounded so eerie to their unaccustomed ears. It rained through the night, not a nice pleasant shower which would leave steam rising from the grassy plains below, but a cold northerly downpour which held the suggestion of snow and certainly more difficult days ahead. They tried to sleep with their back against the wall their coats covering their heads, but the wind howled round the north side of the cleft they quickly realised they were more exposed than they first perceived. The rain eventually abated but the cold wind did not and they both suffered from a distinct lack of sleep the first night on the mountain.

The next day dawned but they both felt tired and the mood was somewhat sullen. They trudged on the path keeping its gradient as it wound its way between two very tall peaks. Mid morning they saw the first signs of winter snow still laying on the mountains higher up and without a word both knew that they were going to have to face this additional burden before they got much higher. By lunchtime they felt the first flakes of snow against their faces as the wind eventually died away. Malic peered upwards at the gathering clouds, they held the promised of much more snow and they needed to find more effective shelter for the night if they were going to survive on the mountain side. Before long the snow was falling much heavier and the going became difficult as they trudged ever upwards into the snow capped mountains. Then mid afternoon the path seemed to level out slightly. They would have welcomed this more heartily if the snow hadn't been coming down so heavily.

Eventually they came to a large drift which had settled into another cleft in the mountain side. Without a word they both stopped, as if they realised independently they could go no further this day.

Malic surveyed the sky above; this snow storm didn't look like stopping anytime soon.

'I will make a shelter' he shouted to Celeste

He began to tunnel out a hole in the snow, when she realised what he was doing she joined in.

' No' he insisted, ' you cannot help yet, we need to leave only a small entrance, once I have made enough space for two inside then we can tunnel further and make the snow cave bigger.'

'This will keep us warm?' she asked questioningly

'If not warm it will certainly keep us out of the wind, with our warm clothes it shouldn't prove too much of a challenge. We will both need to change inside to get out of these wet clothes.'

Soon Malic had moved enough snow using his broad sword to dig out the harder packed ice, he motioned to Celeste to get in too, and they both spent the next hour digging snow out and removing it outside. It was tiring work, but eventually they felt their little snow cave was indeed big enough.

He dragged in his pack from outside, at least the clothes inside would be dry; he was shivering violently as he removed his top. Celeste tried to use her hands to warm him up but she was so cold herself couldn't manage more than a few minutes. Malic indicated she should change too. Frankly at that point she couldn't have cared less whether anyone was watching. She removed warm clothing from her pack which she then sat upon.

Removing her fur lined coat and tunic she quickly changed and though she didn't feel that much warmer at this point she was at least dry. Malic meanwhile did the same and before long they both had a small pile of wet clothes in front of them.

'Nowhere to dry these' he laughed, 'to the bottom of the pack they will have to go, maybe the warmth of the other clothes will dry them out eventually!'

Celeste crawled to the entrance and peered out, she could hardly see anything such was the intensity of the snowfall but at least they were protected from the worst effects of the wind. Malic pulled out food from his pack, only fruit and bread but it was most pleasing, a hot drink at that time would have been even more welcome. They ate without a further word and eventually lay on the cold floor of the ice cave. Malic edged up to Celeste so they could both enjoy what little body warmth the other was transmitting. They were both exhausted from their ordeal and despite the cold quickly fell asleep.

The next morning dawned; they rose somewhat later to find the snow still coming down hard. Travel any further would be impossible that day and they resigned themselves to another night and day in their little cave.

Morning turned to lunchtime and then to afternoon. They had both eaten and dozed with their backs against the snow cave wall. Sleeping seemed to stave off the worst feelings of desperation in the cold. About an hour before dawn Celeste suddenly woke from her cold induced slumber and crawled again to the entrance.

'It seems to have stopped' she observed.

She slid herself fully out of the shelter and looked around her. All the mountains as far as she could see were covered in snow, but the temperature did feel somewhat warmer.

She crawled back inside

'The storm has passed, but the pathway is blocked by heavy drifts, we will not be able to travel further unless this melts'

Malic nodded sombrely, unless things improved markedly he knew they could go no further and the mountain range would have defeated them. A dark mood enveloped him and he spoke no further words that evening, Celeste had to hug the back of him to get the much needed warmth she needed through the night.

The next day dawned and the change in the weather was startling, the sun was up and the air was clear. The temperature many degrees above freezing as Celeste looked out of their shelter.

'Malic, you will not believe the difference out here' she shouted back into him cheerfully

Eventually he crawled out, eyes blinking against the bright sunshine. He was amazed at what he saw. It was as if the mountain had decided to throw the worst weather she possibly could against them in the hope it would drive them back. When they did not move it appeared she had relented and gave in to their continued trek.

He looked at the fast melting snow and observed their own cave showing signs of liquefying.

'We can't stay here another night' he said grimly, 'let us hope that the weather holds and we find another place to shelter'

He crawled back inside and quickly pulled out their packs. He handed Celeste hers and hoisted his own upon his back.

They trudged on, as the snow covered path started to melt, they stayed as near to the cliff side as they could, trusting to luck that the path followed the same route. After a couple of hours the increased warmth was really noticeable even this high up and the ground beneath them started showing through the snow.

They were not to know it but they had reached a plateau and the first stage of the mountain journey was behind them. As afternoon waned they were lucky to find a small cave within the side of the cliff, it was hardly big enough to house them both but it was dry and moreover would protect them from the possibility of avalanche since the snow was still in rapid melt.

The next day the path levelled out again and they found themselves besides what looked like a huge cliff made entirely of ice. Had they come as far as they could? The path seemed to have disappeared. They looked about them there only choice was to somehow get to the top of this ice sheet to see how far it ran into the mountain range. They looked at the ice face; it appeared to have sufficient toe hold to climb though they couldn't ascertain how high it was. They had rope however and they tied themselves together for the climb.

'I will go first' declared Malic, 'I have made my way up rock faces before and this should be no different'.

He pulled out his dagger which he used to stab into the ice face and use as a lever to hoist himself up a few feet once he found an appropriate toe hold, then he repeated the manoeuvre. Celeste waited until he was twice her height before attempting the same; she followed up the face of the ice, using her dagger to find a handhold where none could be found. Before long the backs of her legs were burning with the effort, Malic looked down at her as he felt the rope tense as she appeared to have stopped.

'Keep going Celeste, stopping is the worst thing you can do, the trick is not to look up or down but only at the cliff face in front of you'

A grim determination washed over her as she determined not to let Malic see her weakness on the ice. Stabbing her dagger into the ice above she once again hauled herself upwards.

Eventually, her breath coming in gasps she looked up to see Malic only a few feet above holding his hand out to her, she grasped at it whilst he pulled her up. They had done it; they were on top of the ice sheet.

She gasped as she surveyed the scene. The mountain range they had climbed initially was only the start of their troubles, further north, many many leagues away and only just visible was another row of mountain tops. In-between as far as the eye could see there was nothing, just league after league of snow on top of ice. There would be no shelter from any adverse weather. They would have to move on and hope, or go back and admit defeat!

Chapter 3

Going back wasn't an option for Celeste; she would complete this quest or die in the attempt to do so. Malic seemed determined too as if some other will than that of his own was driving him on.

Furlong after furlong, league after league they trudged on, walking throughout the daylight and only stopping between dusk and dawn. They were never warm during the night but the weather stayed calm and bright. After seven days the mountain tops behind them looked about as far away as the ones in front. They couldn't have known it but they were travelling on top of the continents biggest glacier. If they had died where they stood, eventually after thousands of years their frozen bodies would have eventually been transported to the glaciers edge as it moved inch by inch throughout the years. The journey was much quicker however, and though they spoke little to each other through the bright days and cold nights each found comfort in the others presence. It was doubtful either would have had the will to carry on without the others silent support during this time.

Another six days and nights passed when finally the weather turned again, they were well and truly exposed this time and there was nothing else they could do but to carry on walking through the night as the snow came down. They were both feeling very cheerless but the extra nights journey through the dark and snowy conditions meant that as dawn broke they realised they had come to the edge of the ice sheet. Only a few furlongs ahead the dark top of a mountain peered out from its snowy grave. With added hope and vigour they drove on, eventually the ice sheet narrowed and cracked giving way to bare rock. The were of course still very high up and still exposed to the worst effects of the cold weather but they both felt heartened by their success thus far.

They scrambled about the side of the mountain for the afternoon; they were both exhausted from lack of sleep the night before and the unending journey across the unforgiving glacier. Eventually worn out they cast themselves down on the floor beneath the overhand of a cliff wall and fell at once into a long and satisfying sleep.

They slept the whole evening and throughout the night, over twelve hours in total. The effects of this prolonged sleep gave them extra strength of mind to move on again the next day. They were clearly moving downwards, only slightly at first, but eventually a path of sorts could be made out, similar to the one at the other side to the mountain range they had climbed in that it hugged a cliff side on its descent. It looked to have been carved out especially for their purposes. Walking downhill also presented problems as the gradient became steeper. They soldiered on through the north end of the range; sometimes rising again as they traversed one mountain side only to be confronted with another, but each one became less steep until eventually two days later they came upon a valley. Here the first signs of life were evident as a swift mountain stream sprang from the rocks to start its journey down the fertile valley below.

They were still quite high up but below they could see a forest, it was hard to see how wide it was from north to south, certainly from east to west it hugged the mountains side as far as they could see. Beyond the forest Celeste whose eyes seemed the keenest at long distances thought she could see a grass land stretching away into the distance.

The next morning they made it to the forest, this was a welcome change to the bleak glacier in the mountains and they delighted in the life which had sprung about them. The forest itself also was warmer than the upland meadows and vales. They had spent so much time in the cold they now found the apparent warmth of the forest slightly oppressive. Had they known it the temperature this far north was about the same as they had been used to in Midencia only a couple of months before. The stillness of the forest meant they could dry out their wet clothes much more effectively and a day spent relaxing at the north end of this woodland made them feel so much more at ease

'Well we made it where all said we would not' observed Celeste.

'We did indeed', he answered, 'but now we must turn our thoughts as to where we go next, our paths are likely to part soon enough'

Celeste's heart jumped slightly, she hadn't really considered this, selfishly she had just presumed Malic would follow her to whatever end as Bracen had been willing to do, but now she realised once again that his quest was so much different to hers.

'We certainly need to find a small village for now', he continued 'we need to get as much information about these strange lands as possible. Finding your father in such a wide and unfamiliar land will be a challenge which could last many years. For my part I can only give myself another few months. If I had known how long it would take to cross the mountain maybe I wouldn't have attempted it. So it is unlikely I will find my fathers killer in such a short space of time!'

'But if you go back to Midencia, surely you can come back next year by the same path?

'Nay Celeste, I think during the long trek over the mountains the realisation has hit me that my year by year quests to find my fathers murderer are futile, to find one man amongst millions of individuals is a hopeless task. For now I will accompany you to the nearest settlement from there I will make a decision. I do not look for hope at the end of my quest though and I will dread the journey back to Midencia alone'.

She looked at him with some pity, he had given his promise in Castletown and he had seen it through, she could not have asked for more. She walked over and hugged him. She studied his weather-worn face as if looking for clues to how much further he would go. She kissed him, not the long slow kiss of a lover but enough for her to realise she still liked the half forgotten feeling. 'Come Malic; let us find the nearest village'

They wandered for a time amongst the trees of the forest; the ground was still descending slightly as the forest started on the up-slope of the foothills to the mountains themselves. Once again they came across the small stream, slightly wider now but no more than a man's leap across. They determined to follow this stream as it would no doubt find its way out of the forest and find other tributaries, it was a well known fact that people built their villages where the water flowed so they were reasonably confident they would find habitation soon. A further day started under the canopy of leaves but mid morning the trees thinned out then failed altogether. The green fields of the northern land rolled away into the distance. So far they could see no other sign of life so they walked on briskly. The stream was now slowing which indicated either it was getting wider or the slope was less pronounced. In the event both were true. They followed it though steep banks actually forced on two occasions to walk in the stream itself. The cold water on their tired feet was a delight, eventually the river emptied into a small mere and there at the opposite end they could see the first sign of habitation. It was only a small house, made of wood it appeared (as to be expected being so near to the forest). Encouraged they strode on until they came to a well kept field and delightful garden full of growing vegetables and plants.

No one was obviously visible so Celeste volunteered to investigate further whilst Malic looked about the immediate surroundings.

She walked up the path and knocked twice on the door.

'Wait' said a voice from inside.

Presently the door opened, Celeste found herself looking at a middle aged man, probably in his mid fifties by his greying hair. She could see however that he must have been very tall and vigorous in times past and his badly trimmed beard had held out against time and still held on to its darkish blonde colour. Celeste stood in amazement (having never seen a blonde man before). The occupier of the house was no less astonished to see a formidable, olive skinned beauty at his door.

Celeste was the first to speak again, 'I have travelled far with my companion, we wondered if we could shelter for the night'

'You can, yes of course you can, and you say you have travelled far? Then I fear you have been misled as this road leads nowhere unless you can sprout wings and fly over the mountains yonder!'

'No sir, we have not been misled, we have indeed come over the mountains on your border the journey was long and the hardship great.'

I can see strange tales are woven about you, he said in amazement 'where is the other you speak of?'

At this point Malic appeared round the corner of the house, he nodded to the occupant.

'Forgive the manner of my arrival, we are in strange lands and was unsure of the welcome'.

'It is forgiven; such is my delight to see two travellers thus. Although I am not too far away from the nearest village the road here leads no further so few ever some here unless they are tax collectors' he laughed, 'please come inside, I will prepare something to eat. There is a small room to your left with cold water for bathing; I will prepare you something to drink! I am Tharel and my house is yours!' he added with meaning.

'I am Celeste, my companion is Malic' she replied

Sometime later both cleaned and wearing cleaner clothes they approached their host again. His home was basically one room with a small bathing annexe to one side. It was clear he lived and slept in this one room. It appeared he cooked mainly outside, he had a structure which was stone built over which sat an iron grill which he turned his meat on. The food was plentiful, the few vegetables seemed just an afterthought to the generous portions of different meat. He poured a drink; it was in a very small cup and looked clear. Expecting something like white wine they both drank down their cups quickly. Both coughed suddenly as they realised the strength of the beverage given to them.

'What is this?' asked Malic, 'I have travelled far in my life but never have I tasted anything so potent!'

'It is made from potatoes, I do not know how; I trade it for meats for I have cattle a-plenty, certainly for my meagre needs.

Malic looked doubtfully at his host, with his not too small stomach hanging over his trousers he thought 'meagre' wasn't the appropriate word, though he said nothing.

'Well whatever it's called it certainly warms the inside' he declared

'Then you should drink your fill' said Tharel, 'then we have tales to tell, yours more interesting than mine I should imagine!'

They settled down for the evening feeling both warm and relaxed from the alcohol and open fire burning in the corner.

Celeste told of her tale and quest to find her father, leaving out the flight from Codencia Minor and the border problem (he was after all a Northman like they) and also the imprisonment. She talked of meeting Malic and their journey to Castletown where his true identity became known.

Malic too told of his own quest, how his father had been murdered and how he had scoured all the lands looking for his foe, but to no avail.

Tharel was a good host, and did not question either too deeply, preferring to let them both tell their tale in the manner they chose, but he was wily enough to know there was more to this magnificent young lady sat on his rug and her equally impressive travelling companion, than they were admitting.

Finally he stood up and looked kindly at them, 'the tales were well told, and though I do not doubt you have told me only what you believe I should know, the reward for you should be comfort for this night within my walls. I have many furs and rugs, so you need not fear the cold'

He looked at Celeste, 'tell me of your father' he asked

Celeste explained what was truly known to her but admitted much was hearsay and other parts were small snippets of memories from her childhood.

Tharel shook his head, 'there was much commotion some years past, and for a time all the lands were joined as one' He hesitated before plunging on 'I will tell you of the north, the tale is long and though difficult to understand the reasoning by outsiders it will contain some of the information you need to carry on with your quest. You are indeed fortunate to happen upon this place, for in the past I lived elsewhere and I was a recorder of deeds!'

'The lands in the north are not one country as you might think, they never have been. They are split into three larger states, Wostenland, Ostenland and Sorland, in each state there are seven smaller confederations, each independent from one another. Our maps show us the mountains you crossed as the most southern area; further to the north there are no borders to speak of. There as the land becomes colder and snow covers all the land throughout the year, we are told the nighttimes' last a half year and the daylight also. It is also claimed the men who live there do so in ice houses, though I only half believe these tales! Still for many generations we have lived in the north in relative peace, though members of the smaller confederations do argue and sometimes come to arms, the other members would always intervene to find a way forward without too much blood being shed. The peoples of the coastal areas of Wostenland and Ostenland are and always have been the most fierce and war-like. They are also the only ones to build boats but it had always been very hard to sail anywhere but in the most sheltered bays because the sea was ice bound virtually the whole year. In the summer months short journeys could be managed but any journeys of more than a few weeks were deemed too risky and as a result never undertaken. Some twenty or so years ago our weather started to change, we had one very warm summer and the ice around our bays was seen to melt for some time. People started to talk about the lands in the south, rumour had it these places were warm the whole year round, the land was ripe and the life there pleasant. People started to grumble about the way we were restricted by the mountain and ice and voices started to be heard claiming the south could be taken for our own purposes. Year after year the weather remained milder than usual and some fifteen years ago a grand assembly of all the states was called to discuss the possibilities of invasion of the southern lands. Scouts were sent out to each of the states in the south, their mission was to conduct some kind of census, to see firstly what opposition their might be and what the spoils of war might bare fruit. When the first scouts returned agreement for a joint force could not be agreed, the coastal areas wished for invasion, the states furthest from the sea tended towards caution. Then one day a scout came back by way of the islands of Dyn, he spoke of the melted sea that a clear passage could be found throughout the islands to the land in the south. More scouts were sent, especially to the coastal areas of the south as leaders of the confederation made plans to invade. Another couple of years passed and still the seas froze in the winter and melted in the summer, each melting phase seemed longer than the years previously. Then one came back who had been exploring a land to the southwest. He told of a great volcanic explosion which had covered much of the land with a choking ash. At this point many of the confederates would have turned their back on any plans for invasion; the prospect of ash covered estates was far from appealing. But the more powerful costal confederations replied that the lands would be easy pickings, that the militia of the southern states would be unprepared and the people would not want to risk war in that time of strife. The next year was spent arming the population, every able bodied man was drafted and hundred of ships built in the harbours of the coast. The attack was going to be two-pronged by sea and by invasion at the lowest points of the mountain by the sea. We had already had emissaries from the southern land of Westendcia who would want to join our attack on its richer and more powerful neighbours. Then some ten years ago, I think that would be right, yes about ten, the invasion went into full swing. Thousands of armed men crossed into the southern land by the coastal areas and they suffered little opposition. The boats sailed southwest and lay off the coast of that land. Under cover of nightfall they made landfall and another invasion started there. The plan was to split the enemy into three, so war in the north, west and east'.

Tharel paused for a moment before returning to his story

'The problem was that there was little agreement between the generals on the ground, arguments started about the best way to proceed. At first there had been little resistance, but then one by one their forces began to fight back. It was hard enough fighting the battles as the armies moved ever southwards, but behind groups of men who had been hidden inside the castles started to disrupt our line of communications. We suffered some defeats and were forced to fall back, still the attacks behind our lines continued until eventually the promise of plunder and greater living space in the south was tempered by the realities of war and the losses we were suffering. Dissent grew within the individual armies and our forces started to fall out amongst themselves making the oppositions fighters more optimistic. No one called for a retreat, it just happened, the soldiers were unconvinced of the promise of plunder, and the opposition had been burning all their fields as they at first retreated leaving nothing but burned ground and deserted towns. So the great invasion failed, the Northmen retreated to their lands to lick their wounds'

'They didn't retreat everywhere' replied Celeste, 'they still occupy my homeland!'

'Now that is the strangest tale of all' replied Tharel, ' for it is the people of this confederation, the furthest from the coasts at each side of the continent and the most peaceful of the tribes of the northlands who still occupy that far off land.

'Tell me what you know' demanded Celeste

'The confederation here is called Mozile and is furthest away from the lands away south, unless you go over the mountains as you did, consequently we did not have the desire for plunder and invasion as some of our more war-like neighbours. However with all the other twenty confederations against us we were forced against our better judgement to agree. Our own leaders were insistent though that we would not be in the vanguard of any invasion whether overland or by sea. We agreed we would supply an occupying force once the lands had been liberated and we would provide the means to supply the armies in the south. The plan was that we would follow the invasion and replace the soldiers, consolidating the gains made and winning over the local inhabitants. Their leaders who I believe were all pre-identified and slain in the first attack were then replaced by our own men. From what I am given to understand the forces from Mozile are the only one's still in the southlands and the small occupied land carries on as normal in the way it always did'

'Do you know the name if this occupied land? she questioned

'I believe it goes by the name of Codencia Minor'

'There is truth in your words and though I have no reason to love the peoples of the north having destroyed my countries peace and splitting up my family, I can see that you have no part to play in all this' said Celeste

Tharel considered the statement for a moment before responding cautiously

'I had a small part as I told you, I am or rather was a recorder of deeds. Once the invasion and occupation was complete I was given the task of scribing events from a Mozilian perspective!'

'So you were sent to Celeste's homeland?' asked Malic

'No, indeed not, I had the stories of both our own wounded soldiers and also those of some captured men who were brought back to the north in the belief they might prove useful especially since a lot of the skills needed to live in this place were now with men conducting warfare in the south.'

At this point Celeste rose out of her chair in a threatening manner her eyes blazing.

'So man of the north, you have told us much, indeed enough to give me hope my father still lives as it is likely his skill as an Archer and Fletcher would have marked him out thus. You endanger yourself Tharel by speaking as you have you may have assisted an enemy in her quest and maybe those in your own confederation might question the wisdom of imparting news in this way!'

'Why an enemy and what is it to me anyway? I owe my government nothing; I completed my task and asked to be released back to my small farm and simple way of life'

'If you haven't guessed it already my homeland is Codencia Minor and I am of the belief my father was taken away by Northmen ten years ago. I always refused to believe he was dead. My quest has been and still is, to find him!'

'You have travelled far in your quest, and must have suffered much discomfort on the way, as a token of my friendship and repayment for your family's loss all I can do is offer this place for you to dwell in until you regain your strength to carry on'

Celeste's mood lightened slightly as she could see the man meant neither her nor Malic any harm.

'Is there anything further to report, news maybe of men from the south still imprisoned?

'I can tell you what I know which is not much but may be a starting point for you, I cannot speak for all the confederate states but all the prisoners in Mozile were freed within two years of arriving here. Many were disinclined to walk through the northlands and within the borders of other confederate states in the belief they would be recaptured and put to work as slaves again, none dared venture the mountains so those who survived the first couple of years slavery settled down mainly in this area.'

Fresh hope came to Celeste as she probed him further

'Where did they settle, all in one place or spread amongst all the towns and villages of your land?'

'I cannot speak for them all, I no longer record or scribe, however the main town in this land is called Mocrambe and my belief is you should start your search there. I must warn you to try and stay within the border of Mozile, your accents are strange to my ears and your skin colouring Celeste is not what you would expect in the north. Your presence would be challenged in other places especially in Wostenland and Ostenland and even in some of the less accommodating places in Sorland'

Celeste sat back down and looked at Malic

'It seems Mocrambe would be the most likely place for me to start, are you willing to travel at lest to that place?'

'Three months at most is all I have if I am to return from whence I came, for all that time my sword and bow are yours'.

'I thank you Malic once again,' said Celeste,' maybe you will also find news of your quarry in that place?'

'I doubt it, my own quest is surely over and I have failed my father!'

Chapter 4

They spent a comfortable night in the Northman's house and decided that another day would be beneficial as they rested and regained strength after their ordeal on the mountain. Tharel busied himself in and around his small house, disappearing occasionally to tend to his animals. They sat and talked about the next step of their journey. Tharel had supplied a map and told them the town they sought was about seven days easy walk from his home, three on a horse, before adding somewhat forlornly that he didn't have horses to spare! The map showed that the small stream they followed was a tributary for the main river which flowed through Mozile and the rest of Sorland before turning west and meandering through Wostenland to the sea, Tharel told them the river only flowed freely four months of the year the rest of the times it was frozen solid.

At lunchtime Celeste asked a question of their host

'Tharel, when Malic and I left Midencia hundred of leagues south of here it was colder than it appears to be at your homestead, how can this be possible since you are much further north?

Tharel nodded his head as if agreeing with her statement.

'You are right of course, you would normally expect the lands this far north to be much colder as indeed they are on the coasts and where you are travelling to. The mountains have something to do with the local weather conditions. You can see my place is situated between two prominences in a valley protected somewhat especially from easterly or westerly winds. When the weather comes from the north however there is no such protection and in the winter, this place is one of the coldest there is in all the lands save the ice-fields of the furthest northern regions. As you travel north from here you will quickly lose the mountains protective influence and you will find the weather becomes increasingly bitter. Only in the three summer months does it rise above freezing at all and the nights are still frosty more often than not. You wouldn't want to be out in the open at night time during our winter months!' he added with a shudder.

'We have travelled in colder places' remarked Malic, 'though I thank you for your wisdom and care, it is clear it will be at least a week before we find comfort in Mocrambe'

'It need not be so' said Tharel,' the river flows by many villages, surely that would be preferable to sleeping in the open?'

Maybe' admitted Malic, 'but could you give reassurances that everyone we met on our journey would now be as accommodating as you have been? I think not! Sometimes it is safer to keep away from prying eyes, especially as you say if our accents and bearing give us away as strangers not of this land.'

Tharel coughed as one going to apologise, which he was!

'Malic, I don't think you would need to fear, your own colouring is not much darker than the locals and your accent almost neutral. It is Celeste who would cause most indignation!'

'If that is so' said Malic to Celeste, 'you had better let me do most of the talking when we leave here!'

Celeste made as if to answer but Malic held his hand up to stop her then in a whisper so their host couldn't hear added 'it is wise to keep you so disguised Celeste, have you considered the news of the border crossing might have come this far north, as especially since the men you killed might have come from this part of the north!

It was true, she hadn't considered that possibility

'As you like, I care not' she lied

Malic called to Tharel who was preparing, or pretending to prepare a meal for the evening.

'Tomorrow we will set off for Mocrambe, tonight we should partake of the drink you gave us last night!'

So it was at dawn the next morning they left Tharel alone once again to tend his animals on his farm. They followed the river ever northwards, its size increased by the melting of the winter snows high up in the mountains further south. Tharel was correct, there were many villages and small towns on their journey, they were forced each time to go the long way around and skirt the inhabited areas as Malic especially did not want to subject Celeste to any unnecessary questioning especially given her short temper. Each day seemed like the last, any stray travellers they met on the way they either ignored or Malic alone would hold any necessary conversation, Celeste kept her mouth shut and her face covered whenever possible which was advisable since the weather had indeed turned much colder as they followed the path away from the mountain.

Celeste and Malic finally one evening some six days out from Tharel's small home came within sight of Mocrambe. It certainly looked from afar as if it held many thousands of inhabitants. They camped by the riverside which was now turning west as it reached to plains of the northlands destined to wind it way through the cold lands and down to the half frozen sea. They made their final plans.

'We will need somewhere to stay' declared Celeste, 'you can use a story I once did with Bracen, you could claim we are married, that you married a enslaved girl from the south, that way you might not be questioned so much'

'It's a good idea', he admitted, 'only you will have to play the part of a downtrodden slave girl not one of the fierce warrior princess you like to portray'

'I'm no Princess and would have no desire to be, I am a warriors daughter maybe and as such have his blood running through me'

She thought for a moment before continuing

'You are correct again though Malic, it seems clear to me from speaking with Tharel and listening to you talk to other northerners on our travels through this land, that the women-folk are no better than slaves themselves. I suppose I can play the part but it goes against my very nature to do so!'

'It is agreed then, you shall play the part of my dutiful wife and we can at least try and find an Inn to make our base for our enquiries. I have plenty of money on my person, of course, if we cannot find your father as seems very likely, within the short time allotted to me, we are going to have to formulate another plan, how will we explain you stopping on in this place without me by your side?'

'I don't know' she admitted, 'let us hope it doesn't come to that!'

'I have one last comment to make on the subject' said Malic finally, 'wherever we stay we have to play the part of man and wife, which means one room and more likely than not, one bed'

Celeste laughed; by his word he hadn't tried this with her for some time.

'One can sleep on the floor?' she suggested

'I will not do that' said Malic forcefully,' not whilst there is an adequate bed in the room'

'I did not say *the one* was you! I have slept in worse places recently than the hard floor of a nameless Inn.'

Malic grunted his agreement and settled down for the night, tomorrow's journey would be a short one but he felt tired and weary from his travels, maybe this was one journey too many.

He woke during the night; Celeste had not settled and was sat cross legged with her sword and dagger on her lap. It was clear to him she must have been sharpening them not for the first time in the last week. Obviously she had some portent of trouble ahead.

Chapter 5

The next morning the dawn broke but the two travellers rose later; they had little distance to travel. It was less than two hours from leaving their camp by the river that they finally approached the town's southern gate. Celeste kept her head down as Malic did the talking. He confirmed they were two married travellers with a desire to witness the greatness which was Mocrambe, famed throughout all the lands. This seemed to satisfy the self importance of the gate-keeper who let them through without further questions.

'Too easy' muttered Celeste

They strode on; they reached the centre of the town which was indeed huge by any standards. By the market square there were a number of large taverns. Malic chose the smallest as his first choice. Leaving Celeste outside for a moment he made his way inside. The interior was typical of any inn anywhere in the world, it was filled predominantly with men, playing card games, smoking and drinking and no doubt putting the world to rights. He approached the inn-keeper

'Do you have a spare room' he enquired

'Indeed yes, is it for you alone?' asked the innkeeper.

'Nay' said Malic, 'my wife is outside, awaiting my instruction'.

'Then bring her in, you will be most welcome!'

'She will not come thus into a room of men, she is shy and not used to the ways of men.'

'In that case I will show you both to your room' he said

Malic showed his head through the door and indicated to Celeste to follow him. She fell in behind, acting the part of the subservient wife, saying nothing and keeping her eyes fixed to the floor in front of her.

The room was not overly large but certainly would suit their purposes. There was a large bucket in the corner, filled with cold water, no doubt for their benefit, so at least they would be clean and comfortable, even if there was little privacy.

Once settled the innkeeper returned to the bar to tend to his flock of eager drinkers. Malic sat on the bed testing its softness.

'Are you sure about the floor Celeste?' he grinned

She ignored this remark, instead asking him a question instead

'How will we start our search?'

'The inns would be a good starting place' he said, 'clearly I can get much information from the loose tongues of drunken men. It would be more advisable for you to stay in the room'

'And play the demure and silent wife? I find this role difficult!'

'Only for this night, let me see what I can find out this evening, in the meantime rest, we can take it in turns to use the bedroom facilities. I was not serious you should sleep on the floor all the time!'

'What will you do?' she enquired

'I will take it in turns to use the bed of course' he stated

'No not that, I mean this evening, when you seek information'

Ah I see, well that is easy, I am a man in search of a well brewed ale, I can visit each one of the hostelries within the square and maybe more further afield. Men have a tendency to talk once they have a few drinks, I can ask relevant questions without raising suspicion. We just need to know if there are many southerners in this town, and if so where they might eat and drink if not in their own homes'

It was eight hours later in the early hours of the morning that Malic staggered back into the room and without a word cast himself on the bed next to Celeste; too drunk to talk she knew any news would have to wait until the morning.

When the sun rose, Malic rose much later, Celeste had already washed and changed before he managed to raise his head from the pillow.

'Well?' asked Celeste

Malic sat up and immediately regretted his decision, his head was thumping and he felt decidedly ill. Without a word and without answering Celeste he stumbled naked over to the pale in the corner whereupon he thrust his head into the cold water. He repeated this twice before drying his head.

'Better' he exclaimed as he made his way back to the bed. He lay flat with his head propped up on the pillow. He made no attempt to hide his modesty.

Celeste, as much as she might try, could not help but admire his body, without a trace of excess weight his shoulders and chest were broad and his stomach flat and muscle hardened, but it was not this which distracted her. She looked half longingly at his manhood, he was huge, and she only had Bracen and a grubby soldier as a previous experience .

Shaking herself from her musings she threw a towel at him.

'Here, cover yourself up, I have no interest in such things!' she lied, 'now tell me, what did you discover last night?'

Malic had seen her interest and despite the denial he knew that she had been spellbound by his nakedness. Drying himself further with the towel he made more of drying the lower half of his body, laughing inside at her obvious discomfort at her own feelings. Finally he slipped on his clothing and ran his fingers through his wet hair.

'I learned much, it was an easy task, too easy as I felt myself drawn into the comforts of many ale-houses. It seems our friend Tharel was correct; there are a few 'southerners' in town. As is normal when in foreign places people tend to be drawn to each other if they have similar cultures or backgrounds so a few dozen of these men who had originally been kidnapped from your homeland were indeed set free and settled in this place'.

'Did you find out where in this town they lived?' she demanded

'Apparently they don't live in a group; it seems they have integrated into the Mocrambe daily life though I am told that many of them drink at a place near the north gate'

'You didn't think to go and investigate?' she asked

Malic laughed, 'no indeed, I didn't, I found the general ambience and comfort of the last inn I visited too much of a temptation!'

'So you found yourself a whore and deemed this more important than our quest?' she said shaking her head in disgust.

'Celeste, I am here of my own free will, my quest is not yours, and since I am forced to keep my hands to myself as far as you are concerned, I am forced down other paths as far as women are concerned.....and besides, she wasn't a whore and no money changed hands! Sometimes women like to bed me for reasons of their own!'

Considering what she had seen that morning she wasn't at all surprised if this was true, she backed of slightly and apologised.

'I'm sorry Malic, of course your own business is just that....your own, I was simply desperate for news. I feel I am, rather we are getting closer!'

'We will venture there tonight, for now I will take some more rest and I suggest you do the same'

Not caring that he had claimed the bed and as such only left the option that she lay down next to him, he lay his head on the pillow and smiled despite the pain in his head.

For now Celeste felt imprisoned, it was clearly not wise for her to leave the room and go into town on her own but she had nothing else she could do other than what Malic had suggested. She waited until his breathing deepened then slipped onto the bed next to him and closed her eyes.

It was early afternoon before Malic once again opened his eyes, Celeste had been awake a couple of hours though of course he had no idea that she had been laid next to him.

'We should go soon' observed Celeste, 'how are you feeling now?'

'I feel like my head has declared war on the rest of my body but it is nothing another ale won't cure'

'Good but you need to keep your wits about you today, remember we are playing a part you the husband, me the dutiful wife. I will wear a cloak for I feel we both ought to be armed!'

Malic put on the rest of his clothing and sheathed his dagger and hung it from his belt, his sword would be visible carried the way all northerners seemed to carry theirs, on the right hand side and at an angle which the sword could be drawn in haste. Celeste once again had the type of clothing she was fond of wearing, unlaced blouse, and short leather skirt but this time overlaid with a long coat her own sword hidden beneath.

The made their way out of the Inn, it was some kind of market day and the square was busy with traders and buyers, the same scene would have been repeated in many parts of the lands both north and south. In truth they had discovered that life here, though much colder, was in no way different to life in their own respective homelands. They made their way steadily northwards, stopping at a few stalls to browse like any other married couple might. Eventually they left the market behind and continued on the road which would take them to the north gate. Celeste looked from side to side trying to find an obvious ale-house but she could see nothing but dwelling places of the local inhabitants, then just as the gate approached there was a little side passage, further down they could see an old sign hung loosely over the entrance. They walked down the passage, the sign was faded but they could make out the name 'The Northgate Inn'

Celeste's heart was pounding, she felt this was it, the possible end to her quest, in her haste she pushed open the door before Malic, which wouldn't have been normal in these parts, realising her mistake she stood and let Malic pass as they made their way in.

It was a typical ale-house, wooden beer stained tables with benches to sit on, the place was dimly lit and smoke filled despite the fact that apart from one other patron there was no one else but the bartender inside.

Celeste couldn't help but feel disappointed though it was in truth only the late afternoon and wouldn't normally fill up until the evening; still she was being forced to wait longer than she had hoped.

Malic indicated she should sit down; she did as instructed, picking a table in the corner where she could get a view out of the window and an equally clear view of the whole room, Malic came over with a tankard of ale and a small tumbler of wine for Celeste. The room despite being dusty and smoky was at least warm with an open fire roaring in the opposite corner from where they were sat. Celeste could not sit with her coat on through the night like this and despite Malic's disapproving look shed her coat making sure she kept her weapon hidden within.

'Hardly the most modest look' Malic indicated to her revealing blouse.

'My skirt will be well hidden', she answered as she laced up her blouse.

'It will have to do', he admitted, I would think that women in these types of establishments rarely come in with their husbands and those that do are likely to be looking for some recompense!'

'What? So now you want me to act like a common whore?

'It's just an option if awkward questions are asked, for now there is no one here, but the bartender indicated to me that the place fills up in the early evening before men head home to their wives. Later in the evening once fed many will return.'

Listening to Malic talk of food made her realise she had eaten nothing since the day before. 'I'm hungry!' she exclaimed

Malic drained his tankard and made his way to the bar, in the quiet room she heard him ask whether food was available, the bartender nodded in agreement. Malic made his way back to their table, 'he will provide cheese fruit and bread which should be good enough for us'

Eventually the bartender came over with a wooden platter which he placed on the table without a word; then he looked at Celeste and winked before turning back to his own business.

'What was that about?' she asked quietly as she sipped her red wine somewhat suspiciously.

'I told him you were my slave girl and I was of a mind to sell you, I sort of indicated this could be a short term or longer term engagement', he admitted

'If any man puts his grimy hands upon me he may or may not live to regret it', she hissed.

'Stay your anger, if I am right, the old timer who was listening to our conversation will soon leave the inn, I would imagine, men being men, that word will quickly spread amongst those who frequent this place. It was just a ruse to get as many in as I could'

Celeste unbuttoned her blouse again and kicked out a chair in front of her to show her long bronzed legs. 'Seems I should advertise myself' she said looking at Malic with some anger, though in truth this was a much more comfortable act to portray than that of a dutiful wife.

She ate slowly especially favouring the cheese, which she hadn't tasted since Castletown, slowly men started to appear in the bar, some cast glances over to where they both sat though none approached leaving the pair of them somewhat conspicuous in the corner. Soon however the room filled to such an extent that men were forced nearer and nearer. Many of these could not help but notice and stare somewhat wistfully at the magnificent specimen of womanhood who was in their bar!

She refused further offers of drinks as she wanted to keep her wits about her, Malic too was drinking much slower than would be expected though whether this was a result of the hangover or his own wish to stay alert she wasn't sure.

People came and went, there were definite Codencian accents Celeste identified, each time she hear a familiar accent she strained to see who was talking. Early evening came and went as did many of the men-folk, no doubt back to their wives to be fed. Some would return. The Inn had emptied somewhat when the door opened again. Three men entered one taller than the other two.

Suddenly and without a word to Malic, Celeste stood up quickly, scattering the stool she had her feet on. She walked with purpose to the other end of the bar as Malic looked on in some bewilderment. The tall man had his back to her and didn't see her approach. She put her hand on his shoulder and forcefully turned him around.

She knew those eyes, and though his hair was greyer than she remembered, everything else was so familiar; all the memories came back in a flood of emotion as she threw her arms around him

'Father!' she gasped

Chapter 6

Carig's two drinking partners looked on in amusement as he broke Celeste's hold and looked deeply into her eyes.

'Upon my life, I never thought I would look into your eyes again, how have you found me, how did you get here? I have so much to ask!'

'As I have too, we need somewhere to talk in private, I need to introduce you to my travelling companion Malic, and together we have undertaken a great quest to bring me here' she said

Carig indicated for the bartender to come to him. Putting his cleaned tankards down he sidled over to where they stood

'I need a room for a while, this is my daughter and we have much talking to do!'

The Inkeeper motioned to the back of the bar, 'you can use in there, it's my room but I won't be using it tonight until the bar is empty again'

Carig made to go behind the bar but Celeste grasped his arm

'Wait father, I must bring Malic over'

Eyes shining she walked back to where he sat in the corner. She smiled and said 'Malic, it's him, I found him…I mean we found him, come let me introduce you!'

The three entered the dimly lit room at the back of the bar.

'No good' said Carig 'after all these years I need a clearer view and more comfortable surrounding than this'

He paused for a second before continuing.

'Come, you shall come to my dwelling, it is only at the end of the row which this Inn stands on, there we can talk in more comfort'

To this Celeste agreed readily, Malic was content to give his support too as he picked up their belongings from the table in the bar. The three of them stepped outside into the cold night air. They walked only about one quarter furlong before they came to his dwelling. He ushered them both inside.

Celeste was at once suspicious, the place was too well kept and tidy to be one mans residence, surely here was an indication of a woman's presence. She shuddered internally as she thought of her mother and Carig's wife, thousands of leagues away in Codencia Minor. Dark thoughts started to enter her head as she looked around his home.

'Sit down' he ordered, 'where shall we start?'

Celeste looked around the room then directly at him, 'lets start father with the questions why you never came back, why you never sent word, why you forced your only daughter to grow up in the belief that you were dead, try explaining that!'

Carig looked at her sadly, all she said was true, the joy of seeing his long lost daughter evaporated as he realised he had some hard questions to answer; none of them would be to her liking.

'What do you know already?' he asked

My mother, your wife, whom you seem to have abandoned so readily, told me last year. Up to then it had been my belief you had been killed in Southaven when the Northmen invaded. She said she kept the secret from me to protect me growing up, but I grew angry and vowed to find you after she told me the truth. Tell me now, what happened and how did you end up here so far from your home?'

He looked at the floor as if considering his options; finally he looked up again at her.

'Celeste, what I am about to tell you wont be easy to hear though I beg you to try and understand from my point of view'

'I cannot promise that' she answered, 'but continue your story!'

'It was as your mother told you up to a point, Southaven was invaded. I had gone with Lendel as a guard and I had taken along Naiden for companionship, both died the first night. I was taken captive. When I regained consciousness after falling to a blow to the head I found myself chained and was soon taken aboard a ship. I was forced to row when the wind was against going ever northwards into the cold and unforgiving waters of the ocean. We traversed the Islands of Dyn and eventually made landfall. There we were imprisoned awaiting a very uncertain fate. Our captors left and another group of Northmen took their place. These were less vicious and were to be the rearguard of the invasion. We the slaves were to replace their men on the farms of their own land of Mozile. After maybe a year the invasion faltered and many men returned to the north but some remained in Codencia Minor I believe'

'It is still occupied' said Celeste angrily, 'but would not be so if the men of that land were not akin to lambs!'

Ignoring her remark Carig continued

'The confederate of Mozile lost it appetite for thraldom when they realised the captured men were more useful as paid workers than obstinate slaves. Many were set free but on the understanding they settled the land. It was made plain to us all that to be caught walking through any other land other than Mozile would probably result in imprisonment or worse'

Carig looked at his daughter almost with pleading eyes, begging her to understand his plight

'So it was I gained my freedom and made my living partly on the farms and more lately as a Fletcher in my own right'

'You miss out three important facts father' said Celeste with some indignation, 'firstly this place has a woman's touch, don't bother to deny it I can sense her presence as any woman would, secondly you were and still are a coward, you could have and should have attempted the mountains to get back to your family!'

'It is said they are impassable' he answered.

'Yet my companion Malic here and me, we managed the journey you were too scared to make, or was it more that your woman kept you here?'

Now it was Carig's turn to grow angry, 'you forget to whom you speak my daughter, I will not be spoken to in such a manner, I deserve some respect at least…..'

'……..you deserve nothing' interrupted Celeste

She rose from her seat and picked up her sword, Carig rose more slowly from his chair; he wondered what his errant child was going to say or do next. As he stood the pendant round his neck slipped into view from behind his tunic.

Malic who had up to this point sat quietly listening to all that was said, jumped up with such force that for a moment it surprised them both. Unsheathing his sword he pointed it at Carig.

Carig looked in surprise at Celeste's companion and said forcefully, 'this argument is not yours!'

'Neither is that pendant around your neck you murdering bastard! Celeste, it is he whom I have been seeking, this is the man who viciously murdered my father!'

'Stay your sword' ordered Celeste as he approached Carig, she moved in front of her father.

'Do not come between me and my own quest Celeste'

'To kill him, you must get through me first' she snarled.

Malic took a step back and lowered his sword. 'For now it will be as you wish, but now I know who my fathers murderer is there will be no peace for him unless you plan to stand in front of him for the rest of your life

'I will if necessary' she answered

'Even knowing how he abandoned you'

Carig pushed himself momentarily in front of his daughter. 'I need no girl to defend me, not even my daughter'

Celeste stepped to the side; her sword still raised pointing at her companion. Carig continued

'It is true, I took your fathers head and took back what was rightfully mine!'

Malic took a step forward again, his sword circling, 'rightfully yours, how so?'

'Because your father raped my mother many years ago, you are the product of that barbarous act, this pendant she wore round her neck'

Malic's sword wavered slightly as he heard this news as Carig still spoke

'So, my half brother, we some to an impasse, I believe your father deserved death for the rape of my mother and the butchering of my fathers body, you believe I should die in payment for your fathers stricken head which I delighted in taking, then we have my daughter, who says she will defend me against any onslaught from you. From what I see and the way she carries a mans' sword, I wager she has some skill with the blade. Will you take us both on?'

Malic eyes blazing jumped forward, 'there will be no defence from you my brother unarmed as you are'

Celeste once again stepped in front of her father, this time with a look in her eyes Malic had never seen before.

He pointed his sword at her chest 'are you sure you want to defend the murderer of my father?'

'It is my duty' she answered firmly

Malic made the first move as Carig retreated to the back of the room. He made a feint with his sword to her shoulder then changed the angle of attack as if to strike her diagonally from the shoulder to hip. Celeste was much too clever to be fooled thus as she matched his attack with equal ferocity. He tried again this time lunging, she parleyed and again expertly countered. Malic was breathing hard, not from the exertion; he was a fit man after all, but from the confusion of Celeste's defence. He had never been equalled like this, his strength had always been enough to beat down the most vigorous defence yet here was a woman whose sword-play was his equal.

Celeste having beat of his attack then started to move forward herself, Malic took a step back, then she began her own move.

Her hand and arm speed were a blur, never before had he seen a sword handled in such a way, it was if he was fighting three men at once. Try as he might he could not stop her forcing him backwards to the wall of the room, he caught sight of Carig behind now approaching; he too had armed himself in the melee. It was now or never, he made a quick counter attack which took Celeste by surprise as she pressed forward, his sword nicked her face as she just moved to one side in time. This enraged her even more. Her attack came back, even quicker and even stronger; his last vision was of his long time companion bearing down on him with a feral grin on her face. He never saw the final lunge as she pierced his chest. He was dead before he hit the floor.

Celeste put her foot on her fallen adversary's chest and pulled out the blood covered blade. She sheathed it back into the scabbard. Without a further word to her father she walked over to the nearest chair and collapsed upon it, and then finally after eleven long years she wept.

She cried for her lost childhood and for her mother, long abandoned by her husband, she cried for the loss of Bracen her first love, she cried for the men who had died as a result of her quest, Cendibell especially for whom she felt such remorse, but most of all she cried as now she realised the awful truth. The man whom she had loved and had now slain, was in fact her own uncle, the shame was too much for her to bear.

Carig quietly went over to where he sat and tried to comfort her

'Take your hands from me you bastard!' she snarled

Carig was taken aback by her outburst; before he could answer she continued her spiteful attack.

'Betrayer of your wife, family and country, did you honestly think I would want anything to do with you now I finally know the truth? Nothing you could say or do could ever assuage the depth of anger now burning inside me! And now it comes to my mind there was another lie, since you must have travelled over the mountains to murder his father!' she pointed to the broken form of Malic

'It is true' he admitted, 'you have snared me with my own falsehood yet in my defence, I made the journey with difficulty and lost two companions to the glacier, I would have been crazy to attempt that journey again!'

'You could have come south even then' she shouted at him, 'but no, you had your new woman to return to, you cared not for me or my mother!'

Carig looked at his angry daughter sadly 'Yet you still defended me though you knew the truth, there must be still some love there!'

'There is a fine line between love and hatred and right now I don't even want to think about you much less be in your company. I have heard it often said that time is a great healer. This might be so for some people but my heart tells me I can never forgive your actions, your betrayal and your treachery. I owe that much to my mother!'

Carig sighed then stupidly asked the question

'How is Reva?

This angered Celeste to such an extent she stood up and pushed her father backwards to the ground, in rage she dropped on top of him with her knees, beating his face and upper body with her fists and arms as the anger built into a huge crescendo. Carig offered no defence to this manic onslaught. Finally she could hit no more, she was physically exhausted from the effort of the attack and mentally tortured after learning the terrible truth of her father's betrayal. She kicked him twice in the face whilst he lay prostrate on the floor.

Her father's face was a bloody mess; nevertheless he managed to stagger painfully to his feet before half collapsing again to the floor.

'I suppose you think I deserve that. Go then and leave me in peace but one day you may find you will need your father, and when that day comes, I will remember this' he pointed painfully to his face.

'I will never need anything else from you' she answered as she picked up her sword and made her way to the door.

She opened the door and went to step outside as Carig, realising he was about to lose her forever made one final effort to heal their rift, holding his hand out he cried 'Celeste please!!'

She didn't even look at him as she shut the door on his dwelling and on her own past.

Epilogue

It was late autumn again as Celeste finally crossed the river south of Bridgenorth and made her way back towards Valencia, she had stealthily crossed the border the night previously as the change of guard occurred, as it was there was only two of them since there was no longer an immediate threat to the north for Codencia, her flight with Malic and Bracen having been long forgotten. Throughout the week she followed the river Dyn retracing her footsteps until finally she reached a familiar sight. The cave in which she, Malic, Bracen and Cendibell had made their shelter.

Every bone in her body had ached to see Bracen as she bypassed Castletown the week previously but she knew that questions would be asked as to Malic's whereabouts and she did not want to risk putting Bracen in any kind of dilemma. She hoped one day she might see him again but today of all days she felt so lonely. After all her quest was over, and a failed quest it had been, she had lost everyone who was dear to her and could not yet return to her homeland to see her mother. Here in Valdencia was where she would have to make her home though she had no idea what to do next.

As she sat on the ground by her camp fire she heard a screech a long forgotten familiar sound, she looked up into the sky hopefully, there she saw three birds, surely falcons, it was a mother with her two young offspring. She stood up as the falcon dropped out of the sky to where she now stood, her two youngsters flying in her wake.

'Keri!' she said with tears welling in her eyes.

Printed in Great Britain
by Amazon.co.uk, Ltd.,
Marston Gate.